BEYOND
THE
PAGES

REIGN ATKINS

First Paperback Edition

Paperback ISBN: 978-0-6452831-7-4

eBook ISBN: 978-0-6452831-6-7

Dual Daggers Publishing,

South Australia, Australia

dualdaggerspublishing.com

Perception is power, so believe in yourself.

PROLOGUE

Two medical beds in a small makeshift clinic. And on those beds are the bodies of two young girls, roughly seven years of age. Their features are similar with mousy blonde hair, pointed chins and noses that point up at the tip. Their faces and bodies – lined with scars.

They could pass as identical twins, were it not for a few subtle differences. While their eyes are closed, they are not dead. That much is evident by the soft rise and falls of their chests and the stable beeping emanating from the heart monitors beside the beds. One of the girls – the one in the bed closest to the door – opens her eyes. A whirl of green with a dose of grey and brown.

She takes in her surroundings and confusion sinks in. While her hands are free, the rest of her body is strapped to the bed. She looks to her right – to the bed with the other girl and realization sinks in.

"Deets! Deets, wake up!"

Deets wakes up with a violent gasp, as if she has just sucked in her very first gulp of air. She turns to the girl who called her name. "W-What happened? I remember playing hide and seek and I couldn't find you."

"I was behind the couch. I must've… I must've fallen asleep… I think."

That's all the first girl can remember. She tries to recall something else. But it hurts to think. And suddenly, she feels dizzy and there's a pounding to her head and a warm substance dripping from her nose. She wipes at her face and groans at the blood. "Deets. I think I'm… I don't feel so…"

Her body convulses, violently. The beeping of the monitor becomes erratic.

Frightened, Deets yells out to whoever can hear. "SOMEBODY! ANYBODY! HELP MY SISTER! THERE'S SOMETHING WRONG WITH HER!"

1

ADELAIDE, SA – ERICA

'*The warmth of the Maranthinian sun cut through a crack in the boarded-up window. A true Maranthina Summer. Cody would've loved to stay in the shelter of their temporary base, but he couldn't fight the gut-feeling that something wasn't...*'

Subconsciously, Erica Blackburn fidgeted with the blue stone hanging from her silver chain necklace as she stared at the words on her screen. Had the Australian heat really affected her thinking capabilities that much?

She had already mentioned in an earlier chapter that it was Winter in Maranthina.

Not Summer, like it was in Adelaide.

That being said, her characters couldn't even feel the heat, thanks to their thermo-wiring systems. Two contradictions like that would certainly anger her readers, and she really didn't need that type of pressure.

Erica took a sip from her ice-cold water bottle and tried to think. But her brain refused to process. The first draft of her manuscript, *Rebirth* was to be sent to her agent at the end of the month, but she was only seven chapters in. There was no way she would make the deadline. Especially because in the past two hours that Erica had been sitting at her desk, she had checked her emails four times and completed a ten-minute quiz entitled: *Are you a procrastinator?* (She was).

She had also made two cups of coffee, drank one and then gotten distracted by social media... *again!*

The paragraph she had just completed was not only a complete contradiction to her manuscript, but it had also been reworded *four times!*

Erica stretched her neck, reached her arms high above her head, then rubbed at the long, faint scar in the palm of her left-hand, as her eyes drifted to a large black spider creeping towards her on the desk.

It captured her full attention. Her fear.

Fucking Australian spiders!

So big.

So *creepy!*

She tried to remember if it was one of the venomous spiders as it just continued to come at her.

Would it jump at her?

Bite her?

Would it kill her before she could call 000 for help? Erica could just imagine the news reports. *'Adelaide author killed by spider... Body found weeks later rotting and decomposed.'*

Of course, her mind could invent a story for her death – it just wouldn't cooperate when it came to her novel.

To her relief, the spider crept on by, leaving her alone… A battle for later.

As if able to register her need for an unearned break, her phone lit up from beside her.

ONE NEW MESSAGE FROM CHLOE.

The message brought Erica's attention to the fact that she was late for her lunch date with her best friend and number 1# fan, Chloe Ashcroft.

"Oh, crap!"

She leaped from her chair, grabbed her purse, and headed towards the front door of her small two-bedroom house, which was overly priced and nestled in the outskirts of Adelaide's CBD.

While her Maranthina book series made enough to afford half the rent, she still needed to put in long hours as a coffee waitress at *Frank's Coffee Bar*. The same place she was headed that afternoon with Chloe. And the same place where her overly attractive ex-boyfriend also worked. As she brought her hand to the doorknob her eyes fluttered to the mirror on the wall.

Her light brown hair sat in a messy bun on top of her head with strands cascading everywhere. Her grey-green eyes had dark rings around them. She looked so tired she could probably land a role as an undead in the next zombie-apocalypse show and they wouldn't even need stage make up. Maybe she shouldn't have stayed up all night playing video games. Even if it was her rostered day off.

Then again, Science Fiction games were an important form of research for the Science-Fiction writer, that she was.

Well, at least she thought she was.

In the last novel, Maranthina Institute of Technology had kidnapped Megan and Deets. Now, it was up to Cody to figure out that the girls were missing and form a plan to save them.

The problem was that Cody was no leader.

He was just a Coder with so many faults and glitches, that any escape plan led by him would be damn near impossible to carry out. His hacking abilities took him mentally into the virtual world of servers and networks, leaving him vulnerable to external attacks to his physical body... Like astral projection.

As an extra ability, he could decipher the creator of any text. Unfortunately, that gift had been rendered useless because books died out an exceptionally long time ago in Maranthina.

Megan had always been the badass leader of the group, and the love of Cody's life. She was an augmented Maranthinian with abilities that bordered on ultimate synthetic status. Then, there was Megan's fraternal twin, Deets. While Deets's abilities made her the ultimate Huntress, she was nowhere near as powerful as Megan.

While the girls looked similar in physical appearance, they were still fraternal twins.

Megan had grown her hair out past her shoulders and was opposed to further alterations of her body, which was the exact opposite of Deets.

Half of Deets's head was shaved and her body was lined with a beautiful array of tattoos from her neck to her toes. It was her way of covering the scars that both girls had endured throughout their life.

Then, there was Seth and Adam.

Seth possessed a powerful wrist screen which could only be compared to having a highly advanced computer built into one's body. It could do anything from reading the stats of another Maranthinian or console, to opening portals for fast travel... within reason, of course. He couldn't open portals inside MIOT because of their high security systems.

Adam was a first-generation prototype of MIOT's *Adam and Eve* project. Men and women built with the capabilities of procreating with any gender of the population. Ultimately, they were flesh and bone with similar upgrades to regular Maranthinians, but with highly capable self-defence skills.

They even possessed free will.

…Unlike *Victors* and *Vixens*.

Adams and Eves felt emotions like love, hate and sadness, but were built purely to expand the population since the great technological war took the lives of so many.

To Erica, her characters were more than just works of fiction. They were her friends. She cried when they cried. Smiled when they smiled. She would even find items or events in her everyday life and wonder just how her characters might react to them.

But now her writer's block was impeding her ability to connect with them.

Maybe lunch was a good idea.

Maybe it would give her some time to recompose her thoughts.

Her phone rang from in her purse, bringing her back to reality. She checked the ID and answered immediately. "Alright, Chloe. I know I'm running late. I must've spaced or something. Give me half an hour tops and I'll meet you there."

"That's great. But it's not why I'm calling."

"It's not?" Erica stood in the entranceway, holding the door open and looking out into her small, front yard as Chloe continued.

"Ah… Nick just started his shift. He's here. Now."

At the name, Erica froze. She hadn't seen Nick Cooper since their breakup three weeks ago. Prior to that, they had been together for two years before he dumped her on social media in front of his ten thousand followers.

And it had sucked, big time!

The problem was that Erica was still struggling to come to terms with their break-up. The guy was just too damn good looking. So good looking, he had even been mistaken for a Hemsworth, not once but *twice*.

What made matters worse was that he and Erica had purposely arranged their work shifts so they wouldn't need to work on the same day.

Today was Saturday.

They were both rostered to have the day off.

"Erica? Are you okay? We can always go somewhere…"

"…No, that's fine. Stay there, Chloe. I've got this." With a deep breath, Erica left, locking the door behind her.

###

MARANTHINA – CODY

"Shit. Shit. Shit. Shit." Cody rushed through the marble white corridors of the MIOT Testing Department as fast as he could with Adam and Seth on his tail. His plan to break into the high-tech Datsian facility through the air vents, had been a little noisier than anticipated, and now they were forced to run for their lives, with three scientists right behind them.

If only he had thought ahead and programmed his synthetic suit to take the form of a lab coat instead of black jeans and a blue *Electro* T-shirt.

At least, they had succeeded in breaking through the high-fences and fields without breaching any security alarms. In fact, it could potentially go down as one of the best breaches in Maranthinian history.

...Provided they made it out alive, of course.

Cody was now halfway into his twenty-third upgrade and as he raced through the MIOT facility he wondered if he'd see his twenty-fourth.

If any of them would.

That very thought forced him to turn to his pale lanky best friend, with red-brown hair and green eyes.

"Seth, please tell me you've located them.

But the guy was struggling to run and focus on his wrist screen at the same time. "I... I can't. They're jacking into my system."

Despite having been best friends for the past fifteen years since their time at what Cody liked to call, The Orphanage of Mishaps, Seth and Cody couldn't be more different if they tried. In comparison to Seth's pale skin, green eyes and red-brown hair, Cody's skin was brown. His eyes looked almost black and his dark hair, was short around the side and a little longer at the top. In fact, there was an annoying lock of hair that continued to fall into his eye.

While Cody's attire was set to a band T-Shirt, Seth's attire portrayed the latest in Maranthinian men's fashion. A green jacket and a grey set of overalls over a black T-Shirt.

Cody focused his attention on the scientists in white lab coats. There were three men in total. Adam, whose skin was much darker than Cody's and who was built like a tank, did his best to fight them off. But even with his skills, he was just no match.

One of the scientists had a wrist screen of his own, which was likely far more advanced than Seth's.

Whatever the guy did sent an agonising pulse into Adam, forcing him to buckle over, clutching his head in pain.

"Shit!" Cody swore again.

They had to do something.

No.

Cody had to do something.

He raced over to the access panel on the wall as the other two scientists grabbed Adam. Cody knew it had been a reckless decision bringing him. He had been created by MIOT, after all. It only made sense that they would have a failsafe in place.

Regardless, Cody smacked his left hand into the access panel's palm sensor. It was just one of many linked to the Testing Department's electrical system.

"What are you doing?" Seth barked.

"Get Adam and run," Cody ordered. "I'll get them off our asses."

Seth hesitated, but then cautiously stepped towards the scientists who had Adam captive.

They eyed him, ready to attack.

Cody mentally focused on the biometric scanner with his palm in place. Instantly, his eyes flashed from dark to rainbow as his mind was taken into the virtual world of MIOT's electrical servers.

It was a maze of darkness with a path of neon beams, which he needed to run through to achieve his goal. As usual, the electrical transfer was excruciatingly painful.

Just another harsh reminder that he had been built with some serious faults. But the pain he endured was better than the possible alternative.

The alternative of being recycled for spare parts.

Which was why they needed to rescue Megan and Deets and get the *pit* out of there, as fast as possible.

He rode out the painful surge of electrical mind-transfer until he felt nothing more than the subtle vibrations in his head. In his mind, he ran until he came to the pixelated version of the scientist with the wrist screen. The scientist looked like nothing more than flickering lights in the form of a moving man with a wrist screen.

Cody observed him, searching for a weakness or at least a way to exploit the man's hold on Adam. Red, green, and blue letters and numbers flickered in the air, hovering above him.

Cody's objective was simple; recite the correct pattern to disrupt the guy's electrical system.

'0-3-G-1-5-H-6...' Cody spoke out loud, but the scientist saw him and pushed a button on his wrist screen. The very action sent an excruciating throb straight to Cody's head.

'*ARRGGGHHH!*'

18

It was the scientist's virus protection fighting back. Or maybe, Cody had gotten the sequence wrong. Nonetheless, he tried again. '0-3-G-1-5...' Another fierce headache.

So, he *had* gotten the pattern wrong.

The numbers and letters shifted around again... and then, Cody *felt* it. He wasn't sure how, but it was as if something... or *somebody*... was telling him the real combination. And so, Cody voiced the combination that she had spoken to him. '0-3-A-9-V-7-B-J'.

The minute he said it, a red light appeared on the scientist's wrist screen, and the neon world disappeared around him and Cody's eyes flashed back to deep brown. The virtual world was replaced by the reality of MIOT's Testing Department and the scientists.

As usual, only a few seconds had passed.

Had the pattern worked?

As if to answer his question, sparks flew from the scientist's wrist screen. In seconds, the scientist's arm burst into flame, and he dropped to the floor to put it out. With his abilities now unhindered, Adam knocked the other two scientists back.

"Okay, go!' Cody ordered of his friends. Seth helped Adam to his feet and the two ran past Cody towards the door ahead. "Are you coming?" Adam called.

Cody looked towards the other two scientists who were assessing their unconscious friend.

"I'll be there in a minute. Just go!" Cody called back, and so Adam and Seth heeded his word and made a break for the door.

With his hand still at the panel, Cody's eyes flashed rainbow again. This time, he needed to jack into the cerebral wiring of the other two scientists. Once Cody was back in the virtual world, he raced through the neon maze until he found them – also surrounded by coloured letters and numbers. And again, he heard the same feminine voice telling him the patterns.

"Umm... 6-F-5-0-0-L-P."

The first scientist went down, instantly. Cody smiled. There was most certainly somebody helping him.

"H-9-M-4-S-8-D."

The second scientist went down, just as easily as the first and again, the dark virtual world disappeared.

Judging by the reaction of the final two scientists who dropped to the floor, he had just sent a surge to their cerebral wiring systems. That surge would render their thinking capabilities utterly useless until they slept it off.

With the last of Cody's mental strength, he focused on the control panel again, this time envisioning a map of the facility. He saw it in that virtual world of darkness.

Two red dots lit up in separate places of the map. One in the main laboratory. Another in the holding bay.

The locations of Megan and Deets.

Cody broke the connection and took off down the corridor, leaving through the same exit that Seth and Adam had.

###

ADELAIDE, SA – ERICA

Erica tapped her fingers on the heavy, wooden table as if she were performing a drum solo. And while she was supposed to be engaging in conversation with Chloe, her eyes remained fixated on Nick serving customers at the counter.

She and Chloe were seated in a window booth inside *Frank's Coffee Bar*. A café filled with wooden interior, large fake pot plants and the smell of burnt ham and cheese croissants.

"Hello? Earth to Erica..." Chloe said, snapping her fingers in front of her face. "*Oh no!* MIOT just killed another colony!"

"Wait, what?" Erica gasped, her attention back to her friend.

"Sorry. It's just the only way to get your attention. Speaking of, did you have any luck pushing past that writer's block? Or are we still stuck on the scene where Cody just learned they were missing?"

"I'm... a *little* further."

"Yeah? How far?"

Unable to hide her disappointment, Erica buried her face in her hands. "Only one page. How can I even call myself a writer?"

"Come on, it's not *that* bad."

"Not that bad? Are you kidding? It has to be in by the end of the month, and I can't even figure out how the hell Cody is going to save her. He might be a cute Coder, but he's no hero."

"So, why write it that way? Don't you usually leave the heroics up to Megan?"

Good question.

When Erica wrote her last book, she hadn't exactly thought about how she would start the next. The whole 'Megan and Deets being abducted' aspect was simply for the thrill of adventure.

Erica shrugged and focused her attention back onto Nick. His blue eyes rested on her for the briefest of moments, as if just realising she was there, before turning back to his customer.

"You could always blame it on your break-up. Tell your agent you need some personal time."

But Erica didn't hear Chloe. In fact, she was mentally strategizing just how the ever-confident Megan would handle herself in this type of situation.

Megan was a confident and fearless leader. One that never shied away from a battle. In the past, she had singlehandedly taken on countless MIOT soldiers.

And in a situation like this, Megan would take a breath, smile, and tell Nick... well, *Cody*... because Cody was Megan's boyfriend, just what was on her mind. Megan was the ideal version of herself that Erica longed to be... but always fell short of.

Well, if Megan was brave enough to do it, then Erica could too. She shot up from her chair and headed to the counter. Nick barely batted an eyelash at her arrival.

"I thought you weren't working today," Erica said.

"I need the money. What do you want?"

"I just want to talk. When we broke up, you said I didn't give you enough time and attention. So, here I am. Giving you all the attention in the world."

"It's too late, Erica."

"No, it's not. Please, just… just talk to me."

He shook his head and looked to the customer behind her, so Erica turned back too.

"Are you ordering or not?" The sixty-something year old man asked with sheer irritation.

"No, she was just leaving," Nick said, before adding in a low whisper. "Now, leave before I call Frank and tell him you're causing trouble."

Erica refused to break eye-contact with him.

"You can't be…"

"Uh, uh, uh!" Nick raised his hand, to silence her in front of the customer. Erica turned back to the man who was growing impatient, waiting for his coffee, and sighed. Defeated, she slumped back to the booth where Chloe was still waiting.

But Erica wasn't done…

Not by a long shot.

###

MARANTHINA – CODY

In the main, white-marbled laboratory, Cody, Seth, and Adam stared up at Megan strapped to the rubber bed, which had been raised upwards, directly facing the main entrance. Megan's eyes were currently closed, and judging by the lack of response, she had been placed into hibernation mode.

"We need to get her down," Adam said, clicking buttons at the control panel.

But Cody was hesitant.

Hesitant because the absence of workers sent a chilling sensation up his intuitive system. "Something's wrong. It feels like a trap. Like they've done something to her. I just… I just can't tell what."

Noting his concern, Seth pressed a few buttons on his wrist screen. "I'm jacking into Megan's cerebral network to wake her up. She'll know more than we do."

The moment Seth's screen beeped, Megan's eyes opened. "Cody, Seth, Adam," she gasped. "You guys found me. Where's Deets?"

Relief flushed through Cody's entire body, but he still couldn't fight that strange feeling. "Deets is being kept in the holding bay. What did they do to you? Are you hurt? How do we get you…?"

"…There's no time! We need to save my sister before they torture her like they did me. Adam, hit the release button, quick." In seconds, she was free. Cody moved to comfort her, but she brushed him away.

"Not now! We need to go!"

As if on cue, the surveillance alarms blared through the facility's speakers. "Intruders detected in the Main Laboratory of the Testing Department," the AI said. "This department will self-destruct in exactly three minutes. Please evacuate the Testing Department, immediately."

"Oh, shit!" Cody said.

"Do we have a way out?" Adam asked.

"Follow me!" Megan led them to the smaller side exit. "Cody, get the door!"

He slammed his left hand against the door's biometric scanner and the door opened, revealing another hallway, with at least twenty-something doors and a sign marked 'exit' at the other end.

At the same time, the main laboratory's larger door opened, allowing in an entire team of scientists.

"Take the third door on the right," Megan demanded. "That's the holding bay. Then leave through the exit at the end."

Again, the AI spoke up. "The Testing Department will self-destruct in two minutes and thirty seconds."

Megan turned back to the scientists with a determined look. She flexed her neck and squared her shoulders. Cody knew that look.

He *hated* that look.

"You're not staying here," he told her.

"Don't argue, Cody. Just get out of here. After what those sons of bitches did to me, I won't let them get away with it."

"Don't try anything stupid, girl!" one of the scientists said. To that remark, Megan let loose a bolt of red electricity from her right hand. It hit the scientist who had spoken, sizzling, and killing him, instantly. The other scientists hesitated.

"If we go, we go together," Cody said, knowing that Adam and Seth had already left in search of Deets.

"Just go! Now!" she demanded.

The scientists inched closer, fearing what she might do next. But those fears were not misplaced. She released two more red lightning bolts which struck down three more scientists, at once.

Arguing with her was pointless.

"Alright," Cody said. "Just make sure you're out in…"

"…Two minutes," the AI voice spoke up, as if to illustrate his point.

"I will. Now go!"

He wanted to kiss her goodbye.

He should have done just that.

But instead, Cody just left.

Left her to fend off an entire team of scientists after only just waking up from whatever torment she had previously endured.

Left her despite the horrible feeling he continued to get in his stomach. And again, that voice was in his head, telling him that it was the beginning of the end...

Whatever that meant.

Cody raced down the hallway just as the door to the main laboratory slammed shut behind him, trapping Megan inside. And as that damn AI speaker continued to remind him that his fate was running short, he ran even further until he reached the holding bay, which looked a lot like a high-tech hospital ward.

There were about a dozen beds filled with unconscious patients, who barely looked old enough for their twenty-fifth annual upgrades. Fortunately, Adam had already set to work freeing them.

To Cody's relief, Deets was already conscious and speaking with Seth by a bench filled with wires, devices, and chips. In her hand was a small green chip, about the size of a marble.

"We need to get out of here. Now!" Cody said.

"Yeah, we know," Deets shot back, handing Seth the chip. "Where's my sister?"

"She promised she'll meet us out there."

"One minute to self-destruct," said the AI speaker.

"I don't know if any of you are aware of our current situation," Adam interjected. "But we should get the pit out of here. Right now."

And so, they escorted the other patients out of the holding bay, through the corridor, and towards the final door, just as the AI announced that they had: "forty seconds until self-destruct."

They had made it to the exit.

Cody slammed his hand on the access panel, his eyes flashed rainbow and the door opened. But when his eyes flashed back to dark, he didn't see Megan anywhere.

Outside, the fields stretched on, until they were finally caged off by a large chain fence.

"Go, go, go!" Adam ordered. But his demand was needless. With their very lives at stake, they stampeded out the building praying they wouldn't be caught in the blast. As Cody made it out into the bright sun, he glanced behind. He needed Megan to make it out safely too. Even if it meant risking his own life in the process.

That was until that same feminine voice told him to run. Begged that he make it.

And that was all it took. He heeded the woman's words even though with every step he took, he knew he had just left Megan to die. But he just couldn't stop running. His feet hit the dirt, one after the other, hard.

He needed to make it.

He needed to *survive.*

It wasn't until he heard the large BOOM and felt the heat on the back of his neck that he turned to see the entire Testing Department go up in a billow of smoke and flame.

"Megan, no!" Deets cried as she tried to run back into the fiery mass. Adam restrained her, refusing to let go. Metal debris fell to the ground.

While everybody else shielded their eyes, Cody attempted to run back into the cataclysm. But it was as if there was an invisible force preventing him from going further.

'No, you can't die, Cody,' the voice said. *'It's only the beginning.'*

And so, he had no choice but to crumble to his knees and give into his grief. And while Cody and Deets grieved, Seth's attention remained on the multidimensional travel chip that Deets had given him. If she was right, it was a technologically powerful tool that could potentially change their universe forever.

…Provided it worked, of course.

ADELAIDE, SA – ERICA

Long after Chloe had left *Frank's Coffee Bar*, Erica waited outside on Rundle Mall, for the chance to speak with Nick. Sure, it was anything but female empowerment. She knew that. But at the same time, letting go of the past two years was just too hard to do.

After *three hours* of waiting, Nick finally left the café and walked right passed her, glued to his phone.

"Nick, wait," she called.

He turned to her. "Seriously, Erica? What do you want?"

"We can't just leave things the way we did. So, please just hear me out. Okay?"

He considered her request, sent a text on his phone then turned his attention back to her. "Fine. Talk."

"Okay, so... When we broke up, you said you still wanted to be friends, but..."

"...Hold on a sec." He chuckled as something on his phone caught his attention, sent off another text then motioned for her to go on, despite the fact he was barely listening. "Alright, go."

"As I was saying..."

"...Look, I get that you're still in love with me. Let's face it, who wouldn't be? But you lost your chance. I should've been your *only* priority, not that..."

"...Not my only priority. I mean, I still need to..."

"...Don't interrupt! I seriously could've had anybody, but I picked you and you abused that right. You just had to start this whole writing thing and..."

"...It wasn't just a *thing*. It was my dream *and* I actually succeeded with it. With each new book, I make enough to..."

"...Don't be so stupid, Erica! My point is that when I needed you, you weren't there."

She knew he was referring to the time he wanted her to cancel a guest talk at a local bookstore just to show her face in one of his live streams. But in her defence, she had made over five-thousand dollars, worth of sales that day. "I'm sorry I had an author talk when I should've been there to support your live stream."

"Not good enough. In this relationship, Erica, I'm the man. My career is far more important than yours."

The guy was an infuriating douchebag, but Erica saw herself as being in the wrong.

She should've been a better girlfriend. Should've...

"Naww, don't do that whole lip-biting thing. It's not very flattering."

Erica hadn't even realised she was doing it. Still, she stopped while Nick continued. "That being said, we did make a cute couple. Not to mention, your following base is pretty huge. I'll tell you what… If you can send some of those followers my way, I might consider going on another date with you. But you need to stop writing those silly stories and focus on us. Deal?"

Erica considered his proposal.

Stop writing about Maranthina?

Was that even possible?

"I… ahh…" Before she could get a word out, Nick raised his hand to cut her off, as his eyes went back to his phone. "Shit. I have to go. I'll text you later." He disappeared into the crowd of shoppers on Rundle Mall.

Erica, on the other hand, was left with the gut-wrenching notion of having to quit writing just to get another shot with Nick Cooper. It was a horribly daunting thought. Maranthina was, in a strange way, a part of her. Her characters too. However, the serious writer's block she had been enduring, did make the idea a little easier to consider.

###

ADELAIDE, SA – SETH

The chaos of traffic spread throughout the city under the harsh forty-three-degree Celsius weather. A crowd of shoppers poured out onto North Terrace from the Adelaide Railway Station, ready to shop, work and, otherwise, take in the sights.

Amongst that crowd, and looking very out of place, was Seth, and judging by a few dirty looks from around him, his Maranthinian style was a fashion disaster in Adelaide. But Seth had no time to change. Nor did he want to cause any more of a scene than he already had.

He rushed to cross the main road, quickly.

Big mistake.

An oncoming car stopped – abruptly – mere centimetres away, practically knocking him over. The angry driver beeped and called something out. But Seth had no time to listen or even to apologize.

Instead, he picked up his pace and rushed through the streets, pushing buttons on his wrist screen. It currently displayed a map of Adelaide. And on that map, two red dots appeared. One indicating his current location on North Terrace, the other indicating a location just outside the city. Surely, it wouldn't be that much of a walk. The last thing he wanted to do was bring up a portal in a technologically unevolved city.

It could cause an uproar.

Maybe even a war.

A war just like Maranthina had seen five hundred years ago when MIOT ceased control of the government with its innovative technology and manipulation of GX572.

Thanks to that war, rebellions revolted against science and two-thirds of the population had been destroyed. Of course, MIOT hadn't been remorseful, they had the means to create more people...

People they could control. But that was the price paid when corrupt politicians partnered with unethical scientists.

Whilst Seth had assumed his walk from the city to his destination wouldn't have been that long, the journey took an hour and twelve minutes to complete.

Now, Seth was standing at the knee-high fence of a small red brick house. The front yard was bare, but his wrist screen displayed movement inside.

The individual he was about to meet had always been nothing more than a myth, sometimes even the subject of conspiracy theorists.

What would he say?

How would she react?

Would she be mad he was there?

Seth hoped not, because nobody back home knew where he had gone. If they did, Cody would've found some way to stop him.

Adam too.

While Deets knew that Seth had taken the chip, she didn't know that he would actually use it, nor that it would actually work.

It had been six months since the explosion of the Datsian facility. Six months since... Megan's death.

And in those six months MIOT had grown angrier and desperate for revenge. Seth, Cody, and Adam had spent their time seeking refuge, running from one place after another. Deets had gone off the grid, occasionally sending encrypted messages to let them know she was safe. But none of them were truly safe.

Freeing himself from his thoughts, Seth stepped into the yard of the one person whom he knew could help.

After that step, he took another, and another. And with every step, his nerves washed over him like a tidal wave, until he found himself standing directly at her door. He breathed in, then out, and after another hesitation, Seth knocked on the door.

In felt unnatural.

Nobody in Maranthina knocked on doors. In fact, physical contact with foreign surfaces unless you were connecting your personal credentials was generally frowned upon. It was also unhygienic... Which was why palm prints had inbuilt sterilization systems.

But Seth wasn't in Maranthina anymore.

There was a click and the door opened, leaving him staring in stunned silence at the woman before him. She didn't look much like a creator.

He checked his wrist screen.

Her stats said:

Erica Blackburn. Author. Adelaide, South Australia.

Yep, that was her... *Apparently.*

But this woman was the absolute last thing he had expected. She was short... roughly five feet tall and approximately twenty-three upgrades in age. Her hair sat in a messy bun on top of her head with some of her hair falling past her face. Though despite appearances, Seth was in the presence of greatness, which meant he needed to act accordingly.

"Who are you?" Erica asked.

"Excuse me for a minute," he said.

Seth read the information pertaining to 'meeting royalty' under the 'customs' icon of his wrist screen. When he was done, he bowed his head as low as he could before her. "Your highness, I humbly ask of your assistance. I have come from…"

"…Woah, wait! Your accent? Are you from America?"

"…Ah, no. I'm…"

"…Please, don't tell me you're from Canada. I don't normally get those wrong."

Seth shook his head. "What's a *Canada*?"

"You're joking, right?" Seth shook his head and waited for her to go on. "Never mind. Just tell me who you are and why you're here."

Seth was tempted to run a search on how to get himself out of his current awkward situation, but he knew this was a once in a lifetime opportunity. He needed to improvise, quickly. According to all the vids and public theorists, there had never been a single person to step out of the Maranthina universe.

And for that reason, Seth couldn't help but feel a sense of pride. Though, that feeling quickly diminished as he remembered that Erica was probing him with her stare. "So..." Seth started. "Please don't *bug* out but... I'm from Maranthina and we need your help. I can see by your face that you're confused. You see, Maranthina is a world that... well, I really don't need to give you a full explanation because you..."

"...I'm sorry, what?"

Her hand was raised. He didn't understand the gesture. In seconds, her confusion was switched to something that closely resembled a mixture of amusement and realization. "Oh, you're a fan. And judging by your fashion-sense... You're cosplaying as Seth, am I right?"

Fan?

Cosplaying?

What in the pit did a processor have to do with 'cosplaying'?

Furthermore, what was *cosplaying?*

At least, she got his name right.

"Yes, I'm Seth. But you need to understand. Maranthina is in danger. Since the destruction of MIOT's Testing Facility in Datsian, Cody, Adam, Deets and I…"

"…Hold on a second. That never happened. MIOT never exploded. Did my agent send you?"

"Agent? No. The multidimensional travel chip sent me. And yes, Datsian's Testing facility blew up when we tried to save…" Seth's voice trailed off. He thought of Megan. They had been friends since the orphanage. She was by far the bravest, most capable of them all.

For a moment, Erica looked ready to say something, but then changed her mind with a sigh. "Why don't you come inside and start from the beginning?"

###

ADELAIDE, SA – ERICA

After having borne witness to one hell of an insane explanation in her lounge room, Erica bit the dry skin from her bottom lip until it bled. What *Seth* had just revealed would've made for an extremely fascinating arc in *Rebirth*. Except for the fact that she hadn't written any of it.

Her writer's block seemed impossible to push through. Not to mention, it was only a few days ago that she had promised Nick she would stop writing her book series and focus on their relationship.

Even if the sombre look in her cosplaying fan's eyes made her want to forget that promise altogether. In fact, this *Seth* seemed so invested in her book series that it bordered on insanity. He was *exactly* how she envisioned Seth to look and to top it off, his accent was perfect.

"I'm sorry for everything you're going through," she finally said. "But I don't really know what you expect me to do. I haven't exactly written that far into the novel and it's like every time I try, I get this insurmountable wave of writer's block."

Disappointment clouded his eyes. "There's got to be something. What was the last novel you published?"

Erica stood from her armchair and motioned for him to follow her to her office, where he marvelled at the book collection entitled, *'The Maranthina Chronicles.'*

There were nine books in total, starting from their years in the orphanage. Erica picked up the ninth book, opened to the final page and handed it to Seth. "Right here is where Megan and Deets were taken. And over the past few months I've been struggling to get through the first few chapters of the tenth book. Cody has only just learned that the girls are missing, while MIOT continues to put the girls through hell."

"What's *hell*?"

"It's… It's like my world's version of the *Pit*."

In Maranthina, *The Pit* was a hole deep enough to reach Maranthina's core, which was filled with white acid, fire and a compound known as GX572. That very compound could be likened to the acid in a battery and had been harnessed in a way that recharged the electrical energy of augmented Maranthinians. While grated coverings were normally placed over pits in public areas to allow for safe regeneration, it was common knowledge that most MIOT facilities were built over uncovered pits.

"Well, you need to do something," Seth said. "I just... I want to be able to return home with Adam and not need to watch over my shoulder every second."

Erica did her best to keep a straight face.

He really did believe her stories.

She took a pen from the desk and scribbled on the back page. *'Fortunately, Cody, Adam and the awesome Seth combined their skills and came up with a brilliant plan and it worked. Megan and Deets were saved. As a parting gift for MIOT, Cody jacked into the terminal at the exit and released a virus, shutting down the power of the entire*

Datsian facility, so that other abducted patients were able to escape too. The End.'

With a smile, she handed him the novel. "Look, I even signed it. You can keep that copy if you like."

Seth read the words with a newfound hope.

To show his gratitude, he placed his wrist screen on the inside of her forearm. A Maranthinian gesture of friendship. If she had possessed a wrist screen of her own, his details would've immediately been uploaded to hers. "Thank you," he said.

Erica was slightly taken aback by the gesture but returned it in the same fashion.

"You're very welcome, *Seth*."

Suddenly, there was a knock at the front door, which caught both their attention. "Oh crap. That'll be Nick. He'll freak if he sees you here. Quick, out the win…"

"…It's okay," Seth said. "You understand the secrets of Maranthina. Let me show you another." He raised his hand and opened a shimmery silver portal before them.

"Oh, my god!" Erica freaked. "What the hell is that thing?"

"I call it an MTP, or multidimensional travel portal. As the first Maranthinian to create one, I get to name it. Better than a typical portal, don't you think?"

"A… A multi… Umm… How…?"

There was another knock at the door as Seth stepped one foot into the portal. "You should probably get that."

"Yeah, I… I should probably get that."

Once the portal closed behind Seth, leaving Erica staring at absolutely nothing at all, there was another knock at the door. This time, louder.

Pulled from her trance by the incessant knocking, Erica rushed to open the front door, to find Nick standing before her.

"Hey, why aren't you ready?" he asked.

"Ready? Ready for what?"

Thanks to Seth, she had forgotten all about her lunch date with Nick. But in that moment how she was dressed was the least of her concerns.

She was struggling with her own grasp on reality.

Had she just hallucinated the entire meeting with Seth? Because there was absolutely no way, that the book series she had been writing for years, was real.

3

MARANTHINA – CODY

In a house surrounded by junkyards, which must've been abandoned long before the great war, as indicated by its lack of advanced technology, Cody studied the lines on his left palm. To anybody else, they looked like nothing more than the regular creases one would normally see in an unaugmented Maranthinian. However, for an augmented individual each line had a cable resting just under the skin's surface.

Cody's current focus was on the line one would call 'the heart line'. His had a break in it, indicating a break in the actual cable.

That was his own doing, of course.

Two weeks after Megan's death he had swallowed a pit-load of alcohol, cut open his palm and snipped the wire to render his emotions inactive... *again*.

It would only be a matter of time until it regenerated, giving him time away from that ugly heart-broken feeling. Cody only wished he could return home.

But they couldn't... yet.

Instead, they had to make do with the graffiti covered hovel, filled with smashed glass, cracked walls, and broken furniture. Cody had taken the place by the window. Whereas Adam had fallen asleep on the filthy grey couch.

In MIOT's bid to find them, soldiers had stormed Datsian City, interrogating and even killing civilians. Cody, Seth, and Adam barely escaped with their lives.

Their desperation had been so deep, they even hid out with Jynx, which led to Cody swearing against ever doing that again.

Surely, it would take a while for MIOT's spider network to find them, he hoped.

"It's not like Seth to go off the grid like this," Adam said, interrupting Cody's thoughts.

It had been two days since Seth had last checked in via mindlink, and they were both growing increasingly concerned. Yet, it was up to Cody to maintain composure.

"Maybe he went to check on Deets and…"

BOOM!

The ground quaked, sounding the alert and forcing Cody to stop midsentence. Adam shot up from the couch and made his way to the window.

"Where do you think it is?"

There were no control panels for Cody to link into, so whatever answer he gave would be nothing more than speculation. "A few miles, maybe."

"We need to get out of here."

"And go where?" Cody's tone was drenched with cynicism. "It's like they have us bugged or something. And it's not like we have Seth's…"

On the mention of Seth's name, a portal appeared, and the man himself burst into the room.

"You guys, I'm back. Has everything changed yet?"

"What in the pit are you talking about?" Cody asked. "Of course, nothing has changed. Where were you, and what is…? What's that?"

Cody pointed to the book, which Seth immediately hid behind his back.

"It's nothing. Don't worry about it."

Cody snatched it up and read the title. '*The Chronicles of Maranthina – Book 9# Gone.*' With Seth trying to swipe it back, Cody flicked through the pages and read. "What…? How is this possible? Books don't even exist anymore."

He turned back to the author's name on the front. "Erica Blackburn? Seriously, Seth! Where were you and how do you have this?"

"I... Ahh..."

The very scene reminded Cody of the time he busted Seth in the Orphanage archives, downloading stories about creationist theories. Knowing his friend would only try to improvise an excuse, Cody placed his left palm over the book's text and focused.

While it wasn't a control panel, the words could still be deciphered and give him an insight into the person who had written them.

And then he saw *her*.

A woman with brown hair and green eyes who was roughly their age. She sat at a screen watching words appear in the form of sentences. Sentences that included Cody's name and the names of his friends. She stared down at her fingers typing on the keyboard, bit her bottom lip and reflected on the sentence that she had just typed. '*Megan could tell that Seth was keeping something...*' she read out loud.

And it was at that moment that Cody knew...

It had been *her* voice.

She was the one who had saved him.

She was the one who had stopped him from going into that fire...

She was the one who let Megan die.

But how?

Cody allowed the vision to fade from his mind and focused on Seth. "Where were you? And who in the pit was that woman?"

"I can explain!" Seth said quickly.

"You better make it quick," Adam said. "You promised you wouldn't lie to me, again!"

Another loud BOOM shattered the grounds, forcing them to temporarily forget their problem.

"Oh shit!" Cody rushed over to the window to determine the location of MIOT's newest and largest invention.

"How far?" Adam asked.

Cody stared up at the fifty-foot-tall robotic spider that was standing right outside the window. Its visual scanners were focused on the very house they were in.

"They found us! Seth, portal, now!" Cody demanded.

"On it!" Seth opened one in the middle of the room. "Get in. I'm taking us to the one place they can't follow."

Adam ran through.

But Cody hesitated. "Where?"

"Just go! I'll explain when we get there."

Cody obeyed, just as a red laser shot through the ceiling, forcing the roof to crumble on impact. Fortunately, they both escaped into the portal, on time.

###

ADELAIDE, SA – ERICA

"I told my followers we were gonna see how things go," Nick said, his voice carrying over Erica's bewildered thoughts. They were sitting opposite one another at a street café enjoying gourmet burgers, in the very sheer bustle of Adelaide. "Blinkingbabe245 left a comment saying it wasn't worth it, but there were a quite a few comments in favour of us."

Lost in quiet contemplation, Erica thumbed her blue-stoned necklace. She had concluded that she hadn't, in fact, met a man who called himself Seth. Nor had he left through a magical portal back to the world of Maranthina.

Her only explanation for the event was that her writer's block had become so bad, she was beginning to hallucinate. Which was why her lunch date with Nick needed to go well. It was not only the perfect break from writing, but the sanity check her mental stability required.

"Were you even listening?" Nick asked.

"Uh, yeah. You were talking about your followers."

Again.

"Good. Anyway, I can't believe my follower count is actually sitting on ten thousand, eight hundred and fifty-two. This calls for a selfie. You want in?"

She didn't.

Nonetheless, Nick repositioned himself in his seat to get a selfie of them together. As Erica's blank expression turned to his screen, she noticed a group of guys approaching from behind. Once Nick had finished taking the picture and set to work on his post, Erica took in the identities of the guys that were headed their way.

To her alarm, Seth had followed her...

What was worse, was that he had brought friends.

"Hashtag together again. Hashtag perfect couple. Hashtag..."

"...Oh, god no!" Erica buried her face in her arms.

"What is it?" Nick's confusion was broken by Seth's immediate interruption.

"Erica, your plan didn't work. We really need you to come with us."

Erica shook her head in her arms, trying to fight off her own hallucination. "No, no, no. Not here. Not…"

"…Who are these people?" Nick asked.

Wait, how could he see them?

They weren't even real!

Maybe she wasn't hallucinating, after all.

Erica lifted her head and sure enough, Nick was staring right at Seth and his two friends. Which had to mean they weren't hallucinations, after all.

But crazy stalker fans…

And she had invited one into her house.

Yikes!

"Don't worry about them," Erica said. "They're just creepy stalker fans who take my stories a little too seriously."

"You can't be serious!" the guy who must've been cosplaying as Cody scoffed. "Have you any idea what you've put us through?"

"Hey man," Nick said, getting to his feet to oppose the guy. "Just back off, alright. I get you came all this way to meet us, but you could at least have the decency to let us eat our lunch in peace."

Cody looked Nick up and down with furrowed brows. "And who are you supposed to be?"

"Nick Cooper? Adelaide Influencer. I have fans from all over the world."

Cody shrugged, then turned his attention back to Erica. "We're literally running for our lives. Maranthina needs your help."

"Sorry mate," Nick chuckled. "But Erica won't be writing anymore. She's decided to focus her attention on more important things. So, if you don't mind..." he gestured for Cody and the others to leave. But while Adam and Seth went to obey, Cody punched down at the table. "No. I'm not leaving without her!"

"Excuse me?" Erica blurted, getting to her feet.

"You heard me, Miss Blackburn," Cody said, crossing his arms across his chest.

Just as the guy who introduced himself as Seth really fit the part, this man was the ideal Cody. His eyes looked far blacker than brown. He must've been wearing contacts or something.

Which meant that standing a foot away was the tall, dark, and handsome Adam. They were suited to the roles, perfectly.

Thanks to a crowd of people who had stopped to stare, Erica knew she needed to diffuse the situation, immediately.

"Cody, is it?"

"That's right."

"Here's the thing. I already tried to help Seth. Unfortunately, there's not much else I can do except tell you that the Maranthina book series is nothing more than fiction. It's all fake. Don't get me wrong. I love the cosplay. You guys are perfect. But I'm done writing. So, you need to just leave me alone or I'll call the police. Okay?"

"Fine. Call the police. And I'll tell them all about the people you've killed."

Erica's mouth gaped wide open. From her peripheral view she could see Nick filming the entire scene on his phone.

So much for him being helpful.

"What are you talking about?" she snarled. "I haven't killed anybody!"

"Are you sure about that? Let's start with the great war which destroyed two-thirds of the Maranthina population. Then, if we want to look at my personal life. We have Seth's parents and a whole lot of random deaths. Not to mention, all those lives lost when MIOT destroyed the orphanage. All those lives in the explosion six months ago. And let's not forget, Megan."

"You're fucking *insane!* What part of *'they're not real people'* don't you understand?"

Cody inched so close that he was merely a breath away, he lowered his tone. "How can you say that? Megan was the love of my life. And you... you killed her. You should've let me go in there. I could've saved her."

As fake as Cody was, the pain in his eyes was real.

The emotion… was *pure*.

He had truly lost somebody and evidently, he clung to the characters in her book series as a form of coping mechanism.

"I'm sorry for your loss," she said. And she meant it. "But I hope you find the help you need to deal with that loss. I'm flattered my book series was able to do that for you. But Nick's right. I can't keep writing anymore. I'm done." To break the uncomfortable tension, she turned to Nick. "Please put the phone away."

Nick turned the camera back onto himself. "That my friends, is my girlfriend. Now I'll talk to you all soon. I have a lunch to be had."

Erica took in Cody's silence. She pitied him, but there was no helping him. Then his very next words chilled her to the bone. "I should've known the creator would be a cold-hearted superficial psychopath."

Before Erica could argue, Seth intervened. "I'm so sorry. Please, don't mind him. We'll go. Won't we, *Cody*?"

And with that, Cody murmured something under his breath then reluctantly followed his friend down the street. Seemingly nervous, Adam approached Erica.

"Please, excuse them. They have no sense of decency when it comes to their emotions. Fortunately, I was built differently, and it really is an honour to meet you." He placed his inner forearm over hers, just as Seth had done previously.

"Thanks. Adam, right?"

"That's correct. I mean it, this is truly an honour. Despite the chaos, there is a lot of beauty in Maranthina... even if MIOT is determined to wipe it out. I just wanted to thank you for that." He removed his arm and smiled.

"Adam? Are you coming?" Seth called from down the street.

"Just a second." Without another word, Adam left Erica in a larger state of confusion than before.

###

ADELAIDE, SA – ERICA

After a highly eventful day, Erica ensured that all her windows and doors were locked, before retiring to bed earlier than usual. She really didn't want to stay awake contemplating theories behind multidimensional travel and the possibility of fiction becoming fact.

Nor did she want to face Cody again.

She hated how incredibly confident, handsome and... *Totally fictional* he was.

Though, as much as she tried to push those exhausting thoughts to the back of her mind, they were the first visuals that her dreams conjured up.

An ironic form of punishment.

Erica managed to sleep for at least a few hours, before waking up to a large shimmery, silver light which filled her room. As Adam barged into her room from the brightly lit portal, Erica screamed in horror.

"Get out of my house before I call the cops!" She shouted, while reaching for her phone on the nightstand.

"Try as you might but you'll find you have no phone service or Wi-Fi," Seth said.

"Wait, you hacked my...?"

Cody raised his left hand as he sat beside her on the bed. "Guilty. It was even easier than I thought. Your world really does need a few upgrades."

"Is that so?"

As the portal closed, rendering the room in total darkness, Adam switched on the light at the wall.

"Very much so," Cody continued. "But like I said before, we're not going anywhere unless you come with us."

"Go *where*, exactly?"

"Maranthina. Where else?"

Of course, they wanted her to go to Maranthina.

At that point about a million thoughts raced through her head. The portal. The hacked Wi-Fi. Her characters... well, the people *posing* as her characters. The fact that Cody was sitting on her bed... in her bedroom... She was just lucky she had fallen asleep in her clothes as opposed to sleeping naked like she normally did.

All of it!

She had to be dreaming, or even nuts.

Regardless, there was no way she could deal with any of it at two-thirty in the morning, without a strong coffee. So, doing her best to ignore her late-night visitors, Erica climbed out of bed, headed for the kitchen.

"Seriously? You can't just ignore us," Cody said, following after her. "We've nowhere left to go. At least, here we're not being chased by giant spiders."

Wait, giant spiders?

But there were no giant spiders in Maranthina. And if there were, she hadn't created them. She hated spiders with every fibre of her being. So why would she add them into her stories?

Erica pulled her favourite blue coffee mug from the cupboard, and noticed the knife block on the bench.

She grabbed for the sharpest knife and pointed it at her guests. "See this knife? I'm not afraid to use it."

Cody smirked so much so a dimple rose into his left cheek. "You're not gonna stab us."

"I will if I have to. I know self-defence."

Again, Seth intervened. "Come on, Erica. We're not here to hurt you. We just need your help."

"What am I supposed to do? It's not like I have any powers. I'm just an author."

"That's correct," Adam said. "You *are* an author. And not just any author, but *the* author. You created our world. It was through your will that things happened. Right now, that's the power we need to help us. So please… just help us."

Adam truly had a way with words. She had seen to that when she had created him. Erica lowered the knife. "I already tried, Adam. I wrote in the copy that I gave Seth."

"Yes, but you didn't publish it. Maybe that's the problem. Maybe…"

"...I didn't write the explosion on MIOT's Testing Facility, either. Nor did I write Megan's death." Erica looked back at Cody. "I never would've killed Megan, at all... Unless of course, I had a way to bring her back."

Cody avoided her eye.

But Seth carried on her train of thought. "Do you think maybe it's possible that Maranthina is evolving beyond your comprehension?"

Erica shrugged. "Possibly."

There was silence. A silence that indicated the fear of destruction that could arise if Erica was no longer in control. Her mind went back to the thought of her relationship with Nick.

He was her life.

Her reality.

Their relationship had ended because she had spent more time devoted to her fictional world as opposed to him. She turned back to her coffee cup and proceeded to pour her very much needed caffeine beverage.

"I'm very sorry, you guys. But I don't think I can help."

"I'm sorry, but I won't take no for an answer," Cody argued. "Not when it comes to my home."

A groan emerged from her lips, but she said nothing until after she had her coffee and was sitting in her armchair in the loungeroom. "So... Start from the beginning," she finally said. "Leave nothing out."

And they told her everything.

From two-thirty-seven in the morning until just after four am, Erica heard all about MIOT's recent change of leadership, to the giant spiders and even the traumatic raids in Datsian City.

Two more coffees later, Erica had finally conceded to the belief that they were actually talking about Maranthina. "I just can't believe it," she said. "And that you guys are sitting in my house. It still feels like some messed-up dream."

"It's not a dream," Adam said, from the couch next to Cody. "If you like, Seth can run a diagnostic check to ensure…"

"Ow!" Erica jolted thanks to the electric shock Cody had sent through her arm with his bare hand.

"See? Not dreaming," Cody said. "Now, can we get back to the matter at hand?"

"Did I really create you to be this much of an asshole?"

"No, you didn't," Seth replied. "Cody clipped his heart wire. He's been a real unpredictable dick ever since. I just can't wait until it regenerates."

"And I can't wait until we can eventually not live our lives in constant danger," Cody argued.

"Hey Erica?" Adam spoke up. "Can we read the rest of your books? I'm curious to know what other differences might've occurred without your intervention."

It was a good place to start. And the only option they had. But Erica was beyond exhausted.

"It's worth a shot. But I'm just too tired to think. I'll get you the books then I'm going to crash for the night."

"Crash?" Seth asked. "That sounds dangerous."

"Oh… it means sleep. I'm going to go back to sleep."

After handing them the books, Erica went back to bed, leaving the others to immerse themselves into their world, through her eyes.

4

ADELAIDE, SA – ERICA

As her eyes took in the egg-white ceiling, Erica felt as if the encounters with her Maranthinian characters were nothing more than a messed-up dream.

A dream that had left her more exhausted than she had been, before falling asleep. The blinding sunlight, which peered in through her curtain, was a certain reminder that it was Monday. She had work in the afternoon.

Surely, there was nothing stopping her from burying her head under her pillow and getting a little more sleep.

Then there it was…

A raucous of laughter coming from the kitchen.

And it was accompanied by the tantalizing smell of hot pancakes. "Oh, shit!"

Erica ripped herself out of bed and followed her senses to the kitchen, where she found Seth and Adam studying her novels at the dining table, and Cody happily cooking pancakes over the stovetop…

…And he was *shirtless!*

Like a moth to a flame, Erica couldn't help but notice that the guy had a perfectly defined, tanned body. In fact, she struggled to pull her eyes away, until she noticed Adam smirking at her.

She needed to stop ogling Cody.

It was wrong on so many levels.

But *DAMN!*

To Adam's amused smile, Erica joined he and Seth at the table and feigned a scoff. "Why is he shirtless?"

"There was a hot oil spill," Adam said. "Fortunately, thanks to our thermo-wiring systems nobody was really hurt."

Hot oil spill?

Was he teasing her?

Because all she could picture was hot oil dripping down Cody's muscular chest. Crimson filled her cheeks and judging by the look on Adam's face, he knew what she was thinking. Erica stared down at the pages on the table and attempted to change the subject.

"Find anything interesting?"

"You could say that," Seth said. "It's just amazing how you can get into our heads the way you do. It's almost as if you can read our minds."

"Amazing," Cody interjected, approaching them with a plate of pancakes covered in whipped cream and strawberries. "...and very creepy. There were a few seriously intimate scenes that painted some of us in an *interestingly...* descriptive light. Did you really need to use *that* much detail?"

He offered her the pancakes and Erica felt the blush of humiliation fill her cheeks for the second time that morning.

How could she have forgotten those damn sex scenes?

"I'm an author," she said quickly. "It's my job. What's with the pancakes?"

"Breakfast is a very important meal for both augmented and non-augmented people and you'll need your energy for today."

"I didn't know you knew my work schedule."

"What work schedule? I was talking about you coming with us to Maranthina."

Erica shook her head but dipped her finger into the whipped cream for a taste anyway. "Sure. Like that'll happen. I mean, because Maranthina is *totally* real and all that."

"This again?" Cody scoffed. "Just face it, whether you like it or not, Maranthina *is* real. And if my fifteen percent wiring system mixed in with my eighty-five percent flesh means anything, it's that I'm real too."

Before her scepticism could rear its ugly head again, Seth's arm unleashed a series of beeps. He pushed a button on his wrist screen and a hologram of Deets popped up. She was sitting in a cross-legged meditative position.

"It's about time you answered," she said. "What in the pit is going on and why can't I trace any of you in the network?"

"Because we're no longer in the Maranthina system," Cody said casually.

"You're not? Then where are you and who is…?" Deets gasped as she took in Erica's presence. And as Deets analysed Erica, Erica took in Deets's features and the purple synthetic bodysuit she was wearing.

"By the pit!" Deets cursed. "But I thought she was just a myth. How is…? How did you find her?"

"It was the chip," Seth said. "It worked."

"It... it did? You can't be serious... But then, of course, you're serious. How else would you guys be with *her?*"

Surprised to be pulled into the conversation so soon, Erica gave a quick wave. "Hi, err... Deets?"

Deets got to her feet and glared at Erica. "Let me get this straight. You decided to put us all through the pit, kill my sister and then just say 'hi'? You have some nerve, miss..."

"...We don't think she's responsible!" Adam cut in. "We might've found proof."

"What?" Erica and Deets asked in unison.

Adam held up book number six and continued. "Here, it says MIOT were working on some type of loophole theory. That everything that's happened has already happened before... Just... differently."

"I remember that press conference," Deets said. "Didn't something funny happen to that jerk-face politician?"

Seth laughed. "Yeah, the guy landed face-first into a pile of muddler-shit."

"Muddler? Wait, they're real?" Erica gasped.

"Man, she's dumb," Deets said. "Are you sure that's her?"

"Yep, it's her," Cody nodded. "And she doesn't seem as powerful as all those creationist theories led Seth to believe."

"Lay off, you two," Seth snarled. "I'm betting neither of you would last a day in her shoes."

"Point taken," Cody replied, turning back to Adam. "Did that chapter say anything more about the loophole theory?"

"No, it didn't," Erica cut in. "Because I didn't elaborate. That very theory was inspired by a movie I watched about a guy who had to keep reliving his day to learn the error of his ways."

There were blank stares all around, which led her to press on. "Let's just move on. I never elaborated with the loophole theory because Cody had…"

"…Been injured in that attack," Cody interrupted. "It took me three weeks to heal from that one."

"My theory," Adam continued. "Is that perhaps MIOT crosschecked the loophole theory with those creationist theories…"

"…But those were just fabled stories," Cody said.

"If they were just stories," Seth argued. "How are we here with Erica now?"

Again, Cody went to argue, but Adam overrode him. "…As I was saying… Maybe MIOT think there is some merit to the creationist stories after all, and believe that this is another revised story."

"So, technically by us being here, we might've just led them to Erica," Seth said. "We might've just landed her in danger. I'm so sorry, Erica. This is all my…"

"…HEY!" Deets yelled. "It doesn't matter whose fault it is. What matters is that if they've created one chip, they would have the means to create another and that it's our job to do something about it. That includes the almighty Erica too."

"I'm sorry, but I can't." Erica said, taking another bite of her pancake, which tasted surprisingly good. "I have a shift this afternoon and…"

KNOCK. KNOCK. KNOCK.

Perfect timing!

"…Somebody at the door, right now."

Without giving them the chance to respond, Erica dashed to the front door, glad to be temporarily away from the impossibly complicated scenario being had in her kitchen.

How could she even begin to help?

She didn't have electric, reading or coding powers like Maranthinians. She could barely brew a decent cup of coffee. She was the last person in the world… *worlds*, that could help.

Erica opened the door and barely noticed Nick standing in the entranceway, until he greeted her.

"Hey, are you ready to go?"

"Go where?"

"Out for breakfast? Did you forget?"

Yes, she had.

"Oh, umm. No? I just… I had a late night. Was up playing video games and I…"

"…Ah, Erica?" Cody's voice broke in as he joined her. And he was *still shirtless.*

"Seth might've found something."

"Wait," Nick began. "Aren't you the guy from yesterday? Why are you here? And why are you shirtless? Why is he shirtless?"

Why was he shirtless again?

Oh, right… something about hot oil.

…Hot oil dripping down his…

"There was hot oil. It spilled…" Erica stammered. "…All over his shirt while he made pancakes."

Did she really sound as pathetic as she thought she did? Oh, God!

"Are you saying he spent the night?" Nick asked.

She couldn't tell what was worse. The truth about Maranthina being real… or that Nick believed that she and Cody had spent the night *sleeping* together. But just when she felt the moment couldn't get any worse...

"Oh, I remember you," Cody said. "You're that Cooper guy, right?"

"*Nick* Cooper," Nick corrected.

"Whatever. Truth is, Erica and I spent one amazing night together. She didn't go to sleep until, what was it? Four in the morning?" Cody brought his arm around her waist.

"What are you doing?" she snarled.

"Man, she's a feisty one, isn't she?"

"Erica, what's going on here?" Nick asked. "Please tell me that he's just pulling my leg."

"Don't worry, Nick. Nothing happened. Cody, go inside. I'll be there in a minute."

"Sure thing, *feisty*!"

"Don't you *ever* call me that again."

He obeyed with a wink, leaving Erica to deal with Nick in private. To avoid being overheard, she stepped out into the yard, ready to begin her explanation.

"So, here's the truth. Maranthina actually exists. That guy you just met. He's Cody. He's a character. So are the rest of them."

"There's more in there?"

"Yes. And they need my help."

"Your help?"

His tone was vacant. She knew it well. "I know you don't believe me, Nick. But it's true. Maranthina is *real*."

Nick combed his hands violently through his hair, before letting her have it. "Maranthina is fictional, Erica. It's bullshit. That's what it is."

"I know it sounds crazy. Trust me, it took me all night for it to sink in. But they've shown me their tech, their portals. Christ, even muddlers are real."

"You're crazy! Do you know that? Fucking insane! But whether it's real or not is not what's important here. What's important is that you promised you would quit writing. Hell, even my followers are more loyal than you."

"Oh, screw you, Nick! You only have those followers because I asked my readers to follow you."

Nick's eyes went wide. "That's not... That's not true."

"It is. I asked them to follow you because I believed in your goal. I seriously wish you would've believed in mine."

"Grow up, Erica!"

"That's exactly what I'm doing. Growing up to realise that I can do so much better than a superficial narcissist, like you! You know what? We're done."

"Oh no, you don't! Only I get to say when..."

"...DONE!" she yelled over him. "I'm done!"

With nothing left to say, Erica stormed inside, slamming the door behind her. She entered the loungeroom, to find Seth pacing, Adam sitting on the couch looking highly defeated, and Cody leaning against the wall with his arms crossed.

The tension was evident.

"What?" she asked.

"That was harsh," Cody said. "You destroyed his dream. See? Feisty."

"Shut up, Cody."

He nodded to Seth and Adam, indicating that the current problem was far more pressing than Erica's complicated love life.

"Beret City was just attacked," Seth said.

"Beret City? Really?"

Beret City was a real gem of a city and the place where Adam grew up. Thanks to what he was, he was the only one in the group, who had been raised in a loving home as opposed to the orphanage.

"MIOT went there thinking Adam's parents were hiding us," Seth replied. "They didn't make it out alive. Deets just gave us the news."

Stricken with emotion, Erica joined Adam on the couch and pulled him into her arms. "I'm so sorry, Adam. We'll avenge them. I promise."

"Wait, did I hear that right?" Seth asked. "Did you just say 'we' as in that *you* will be helping us?"

Erica locked eyes with Cody, then turned back to Seth. "Yes. We need to find a way to stop the bloodshed."

"But you were right," he argued. "It's too dangerous. You don't have any…"

"…You already said they might be on my trail. If so, then there's a high chance they won't stop with Maranthina. They'll come here. So yes, I'll go with you. But if I hear one more arrogant comment out of Cody, I swear to God, I'll feed him to those spiders, you guys were talking about. Is that clear?"

"You heard her," Seth replied, sounding a little more optimistic.

Cody shrugged. "Alright, fine."

MARANTHINA – ERICA

From the moment Erica stepped outside the silver, shimmery portal, two feelings surged within her core.

The first was how interdimensional travel made her feel sick to her stomach.

It could only be compared to spinning in circles extremely fast on a ride at the *Royal Adelaide Show*. Yet, she hadn't been spinning. Just standing very still in a hurricane of silver energy.

Her second feeling was just how beautiful Maranthina truly was. How could she have created such a remarkable world?

Upon stepping out of the portal, her eyes darted to the world around her. "Wow, it's beautiful," she gasped.

They were standing behind Deets on a beautiful grassy cliff overlooking the Datsian crystal lake and the district's MIOT facility.

While the building was nestled on the other side of the lake, they could still see the large, automated drones repairing the damages. Erica turned her eyes to the forest behind them… The Bucklands forest. A forest so dense it could take years to venture through without proper navigational tools.

Getting to her feet, Deets gestured to Erica in mock disbelief. "That's her? She's a little *short*, don't you think?"

"That's what I thought too," Seth said. "I really expected her to be taller."

"I get that your author abilities didn't work on the book," Adam said, taking reign of the conversation. "But do you think they could work while you're here physically?"

"Like using the force or something?" Erica asked.

"I don't mean physical force but if you try to meditate and use mental willpower."

Clearly, he didn't get the reference.

"I guess I can try," she said.

"You do know how to meditate, don't you?" Deets asked.

"Of course, I studied yoga for three years."

As Erica sat at the edge of the cliff, closed her eyes, and focused on the elements, she heard Cody ask the others, "What's yoga?"

She certainly had a lot to teach them.

Unfortunately, the more Erica focused, the less things happened. There were crickets chirping, birds tweeting, and she could feel the others all staring at her, hopeful. There was just too much pressure.

After a few moments, Cody sat beside her and stated the obvious. "I'm sorry to burst your bubble, feisty, but nothing's happening."

"Nah, you think?" Erica asked, opening her eyes.

"Hey guys," Seth spoke up. "Shh…" He motioned to Deets, who was visually scanning the forest with her hunting vision.

Her eyes had turned neon green.

"What do you see?" Adam asked, as Cody assisted Erica to her feet.

"Infrared is giving me two… No, make that, three spiders," Deets said. "One North, two east through Bucklands. They're spreading out. I think MIOT knows we're here."

"Well, you did choose the only cliff that's in direct view of their facility," Seth replied.

"It's the only way to get good intel. So, portal, now!"

Seth obeyed, but as soon as he brought the portal up, it instantly tried to shut itself down.

"I think they're jacking my signal!"

With all attention focused on the portal, Erica's eyes darted to something that sent shivers through her very core. A fifty-foot grey, metallic spider with long legs and eight shiny cameras for eyes.

She screamed.

That very scream caught the attention of not only the others, but also the spider.

"Great, now you've just alerted them to our presence," Cody groaned.

"They already knew we were here," Deets argued. "Seth, hurry up with that portal."

"I'm... I'm trying!" Seth said. Finally, his portal stood wide open. "Alright, go through, it won't hold for long."

Adam ran through first. Then Deets.

But thanks to her fear, Erica couldn't move. The spider scurried quickly in their direction. "Oh, God! Look at all those legs," she groaned. "What do you think they need them for?"

"Cody, get her in there," Seth cried, visibly exhausted. "I can't hold out for long."

Hesitant, Cody stared down at his unbroken heartline. It had regenerated. Which meant, that his emotions had returned at the worst possible time.

But he needed to act fast.

He took a breath. Ready…

But at the same time, not ready.

"Seth, you go through. I've got this. Just be ready to seal it shut the minute we come through."

"Got it." Seth clambered through the portal, leaving it open behind him. Cody placed his hand on Erica's shoulder, igniting a spark of white light on impact.

"I know you're scared. That's a pretty creepy thing. The problem is, if we don't move, we die. Do you understand?"

She turned to him. "Ah, yeah. Right." Her voice was strained, as were her movements. "I've just never seen a spider that big… and I live in Australia, so that's saying something."

Urging them along, the spider released a red laser from its mouth-like opening and unleashed a blood curdling noise which sounded very much like a metallic whale.

"Shit," Cody cursed. "Go, go, go!"

Erica bolted towards the portal, just missing the laser – only for the gateway to close right before her eyes.

"It's shut," she said, this time being the one to state the obvious.

"Nah, you think? Shit. Shit. Shit." As Cody attempted to think of their next course of action, Erica refused to stick around a moment longer. She ran right into the forest. "Where are you going?" Cody called.

"I'm not waiting around for those things to find us."

And so, Cody rushed into the forest after her.

They kept running into the forest aimlessly, listening out for the haunting metallic roars that surrounded them.

"Deets said there were three," Erica puffed to Cody. "Do you remember their locations?"

"I think it was one North, two East? Maybe."

"Then we go West," Erica said, turning a hard left.

They ran and ran until they could hear the loud metallic clanging and haunting roars of three robotic spiders on their trail.

"We'll never outrun them," Cody said. "Not through this forest. They've got extreme-hunting skills."

"Just keep running!"

And they did, until a rock shifted in the dirt, right under Cody's shoe. His left ankle twisted, forcing him to stumble instantly. As he clambered to sit, he unleashed a painful groan.

"I think I've sprained my ankle."

Erica turned back to see the three large spiders in the distance. They were closer than she had previously anticipated, and they were closing in fast. Still, she tried to help him stand.

"Don't worry about me. My ankle will regenerate if you give me a moment. Just keep going!"

"We don't have time for you to play the hero. Let me help." She supported him to his feet and together they staggered into an assisted run. The spiders were so much closer now. But there were also enough trees to shield their view. They hobbled quickly until they spotted a thick trunk to seek shelter behind.

"You need to heal yourself," Erica demanded.

"And how do you expect me to do that? I can't just *will* it to happen."

"Yes, you can. Because if my author powers are good for something, it's creating little loopholes to help my characters. So, just breathe and focus. Try to heal your ankle."

He grimaced as he balanced his weight onto his sprained ankle. "And you couldn't just use your powers to get those spiders off our backs?"

"What do you think I was doing back on the cliff with my fears? I was praying with every fibre of my being that they didn't exist."

"Alright, fine! Come on, heal. Come on, do it. Argghhh! It's not... I don't think it's working."

Erica considered their options. "Just keep trying. I'll get them off your trail." And as Erica had hoped, it took a moment for him to comprehend what she had just said. She ran out from behind the tree, grabbed a large branch and moved into the open space.

"What do you think you're doing?" Cody called.

But she wasn't listening.

She spotted the spiders and called out to them, waving the branch in the air.

"Hey, I'm over here! Come and get me, you eight-legged robotic fre... Oh, shit!"

Her plan worked... *Unfortunately.*

The robotic beasts picked up speed as they scurried after her. The sound of metal against metal carried throughout the air. With her plan in motion, Erica ran.

All around her, branches broke off trees, letting in beams of light and glimpses of silver metal as the synthetic creatures chased after her.

It was gut-pounding.

Terrifying.

But strangely enough, it made her feel more alive than she had felt in an exceptionally long time. She was running for her life in her own Science-Fiction world and surprisingly loving it.

The experience was exhilarating.

Until she fell.

Her face and body hit the dirt, yet she clambered to her feet just in time to see a bright red laser loom overhead. Of course, that was how she would die.

"Erica!" Cody's voice ripped through her daze as he pulled her out of the laser's direction. He was still limping, but he had managed to catch up in time.

"Don't you ever do something so stupid like that, again, do you understand me, Megan?"

He called her Megan.

But she wasn't Megan.

"I'm not... I'm not Megan," Erica said, stunned. Cody froze, realizing his own mistake, when suddenly a large spider-silk net was thrusted over them, unleashing a grey mist into the air, making them just a little tired.

Under the weight of the net, they dropped to the floor. Unconscious.

###

"I don't understand. It should be working," Seth exclaimed as he struggled to open another portal in a room that Deets was highly unfamiliar with.

There was a flat screen television mounted on the white wall, a grey armchair, a glass coffee table, and a three-seater couch.

Yet, with Erica and Cody force to flee from the robotic spiders and Seth's portal technology not working, determining where they were was the least of Deets's concerns.

"This is what happens when you leave a man to do a woman's job," she grumbled, grabbing his wrist, and pushing the portal button on his screen, hard.

"Ow! That hurt!"

"And how much do you think MIOT will hurt the others if they catch them?"

"If they haven't already caught them," Adam said softly, drawing their focus. While it was a crippling thought, Deets wasn't used to hearing Adam surrender to her pessimistic way off thinking.

He had always been the optimist.

The *dad* of the group, so to speak. Deets and Adam slumped together on the couch and after a while, Seth gave up trying and joined them.

"So, what do we do?" Seth asked. Adam shrugged.

They both looked to Deets.

"Oh, you can't be serious," she scoffed. "I'm not Megan. I don't have all the answers. If it were up to me, I'd still be by myself hiding from those beasts. But now I'm…" Deets looked around. "Where are we?"

"Erica's home," Seth said.

Deets glanced over at the flat screen television. She had never seen a place so void of advanced technology. It didn't even have a self-cleaning service. "Damn, the tech here is so prim."

She pointed her hand at the screen sending a green bolt of lightning into it, switching it on. A gaming console, which was connected to television also turned on. As did the controller resting on the arm of the chair.

"What is this?" she asked, raising the controller.

"Put it down," Adam scolded. "We shouldn't be touching her stuff."

But Deets had already started up a game where the heroine was based inside a spaceship with alien companions. That was until a knock at the door startled them all.

"I hope it's not that Nick guy," Adam said. "I really didn't like the way he treated her."

"'Only one way to find out." Deets raced to the door, while the others went to oppose her.

"You can't go out there," Seth said. "They could call the authorities."

"I'd like to see them try."

Again, Deets attempted to make it to the door, but was pulled back by Seth. In one swift moment, Deets connected her elbow with his face, knocking him out instantly.

He fell to the floor unconscious.

"What the pit? I can't believe you just knocked out Seth!" Adam cried.

"Get out of my way or I'll do the same to you. And relax, he'll recharge in a matter of no time. Besides, I won't blow our cover. I like it here."

The moment Adam moved out of the way, Deets opened the door to see Chloe standing on the step, looking highly confused.

"Is Erica here?" Chloe asked.

For the first time in an awfully long time, Deets felt something that took over her entire circuitry system. She practically struggled to muster out her words.

"Erica? Oh, ahh… she's… Erica went out. She told me to mind the place."

"And who are you?"

Deets held her wrist face up, the gesture for friendship. "The name's Deets. And you are?"

With a brush of the inside of her own wrist, Chloe returned the gesture. "Chloe. Can you get Erica to call me when she gets home? Please?"

"Of course."

Deets watched as Chloe left, then closed the door and turned to Adam. Her usually strong-willed persona had been replaced by something else entirely. A feeling that made the circuits in her stomach buzz. She felt light-headed… nauseous even. "Adam? I think there's something wrong with me." She fell into the armchair with Adam fussing over her.

"Something wrong? Like what?"

"I feel… I feel… Like, I want to see her again."

"Who?"

"What do you mean *who?* Chloe!"

"Oh, there's nothing wrong with you. You're just in love."

"In love? No way. I don't fall in love. I…" She knew he was right. But there was no such thing as 'love-at-first-sight'. And even if there was, Deets was wired differently. Built differently.

She shrugged the thought away and got to her feet.

"Where are you going?" Adam asked.

Where wasn't she going? She was going to raid Erica's private possessions to get a sense of the world they were in… And a sense of who Chloe really was.

But as she took a step in the direction of Erica's office, the world around her changed and her point of view shifted, as if she had just fallen onto her back.

Now, instead of standing in Erica's living room, she was strapped to a medical bed in a small, makeshift laboratory. Deets had seen that place before.

She knew it, personally.

This scene had to have been locked deep within her memory core. But was it a memory?

A dream?

A vision?

She couldn't be sure. Deets looked down at her body, arms, and legs. They had shrunk to that of a small child.

Deets struggled to break free from the straps that had her bound, but her attempts were futile.

She screamed out loud for anybody to hear.

And her voice…

It felt freeing.

As if she had never used it before.

Riveted by such a liberating feeling, she screamed again. But this scream was filled with the innocent laughter of a child. She was alive.

Deets's noise must have alerted security because the door opened and in walked a small pale-faced girl with light brown hair. The little girl stood on her tiptoes with a sweet smile at Deets.

"Hi!" she said.

"Who are you?"

Deets should've been afraid of the situation she was in, but what harm could a little girl do?

"I'm your sister," the little girl said. "And we're going to be the best of friends."

Sister?

But she didn't look like Megan.

In fact, the girl looked a little like…

6

MARANTHINA – ERICA

Erica opened her eyes to the realization that she was strapped to a cold, hard surface in the recently repaired MIOT Testing Facility. To her left, about a foot away, Cody laid strapped to a white slab of his own. But from what Erica could gather, they were very much alone.

The last thing Erica remembered was the large spider throwing a white net over them. Had the net been lined with a sleeping agent of some sort?

It did sound like something she would write for a quick transition into the next chapter.

"Cody? Cody, wake up."

He groaned a response before opening his eyes, as the sheer realization of their situation sunk in.

"Erica, we need to get out of here."

"Trust me, I'm working on it. Judging by every story I've ever written or read, we have only a few minutes until someone comes in to…"

Her comment was cut short by the main doors to the laboratory opening. She peered over to the three white-coated scientists who entered the laboratory.

The first two were men. That much was certain.

But judging by the heels, Erica assumed the third was female.

"Whatever happens," Cody whispered. "You're our priority. You need to find a way to make it back to the others."

"Seriously, Cody? I think you've been playing the hero for far too long. If anything, I'm the secret weapon." Or so Erica had hoped.

Before he could argue, they were joined by the two male scientists. One was roughly in his fifties with grey eyes and a mole on his left cheek. The other seemingly in his forties had dark skin, dark hair, light stubble, and thick black glasses.

The third scientist worked over at the desk on the far side of the laboratory with her back turned.

One of Erica's fatal flaws when writing, was that she never gave too much detail on the scientists or individuals in crowds. But there she was, seeing the MIOT scientists with her very own eyes. And clearly, they were very real people with highly distinguishable features.

"We ran assessments not long after they were brought here," the scientist who looked to be in his fifties said, forcing Erica to wonder just how long she had been asleep.

"What did you find?" the other asked.

"The male is a level twenty-three Coder. His tracking signal was disabled immediately on capture in case his buddies come looking. His recharge address is 454 Neonite apartments in Datsian City and his repairs were made from salvaged parts. Must've been a back-alley job. However, his regeneration cables could be put to better use. Not to mention, he's had some interesting repairs made on his server interruption systems."

Uh oh!

That very assessment meant they were considering Cody for the recycling process and whatever was left would be discarded. Erica glanced over at Cody, who seemed far too calm for her liking.

She needed a plan.

And fast.

The scientists focused their attention on Erica.

"What can you tell me about her?" the slightly younger scientist asked, seemingly of higher rank. The older scientist leered down at Erica, making her feel very vulnerable.

"This one is a real marvel. No tracking chips and no signs of augmentation, whatsoever."

"Did you check for wearables?"

"Zero. The girl is entirely clean of tech. Not even a thermo-wiring system."

Their expressions said it all.

Erica was like nothing they had ever seen before.

"Good to know," the female scientist said as she finally joined them at the testing area.

"Megan!" Cody gasped the moment he identified the third scientist.

"Surprised, Cody?" Megan said with a smile.

"Well, I didn't predict that plot twist," Erica joked.

Megan smiled a little deeper, as if she was the only one present to understand Erica's remark. "Erica, at last we meet."

"You need to get us out of here," Cody pleaded. "Erica shouldn't even be here."

"Cody's right," Erica said. "I'm not even from here."

With that comment alone, Erica had broken one big rule in writing.

Never give the villains more information than needed.

"On the contrary," Megan replied. "Thanks to our connection, I was the one who brought you here."

"Connection?"

For a moment, Megan glanced up at the far wall in thought, before turning back to Erica. "To put it in a way that you will understand, when you wrote your stories, you saw Maranthina through my eyes. But when MIOT captured me, I was fitted with a powerful upgrade, which reversed our connection and showed me through your eyes."

"So, like… an author connection?"

"That's one way of putting it."

To Megan's explanation, Erica was equally astounded and highly entertained, while she should've been terrified. All she could think of was how cliché Megan sounded at that point.

Her sly tone.

Her cold mannerisms.

Megan had been the perfect protagonist but now, she was the perfect villain. She was also giving up so much exposition Erica knew she needed to listen intently.

"So, you know I'm the author?"

Megan smiled a knowing smile, which forced Erica to give into her whirlwind of questions.

"How the hell is any of this possible? How does your world even exist? It's supposed to be fictional!"

"Three vastly different questions. But you're not ready to even begin to comprehend the full complexity of the situation."

Erica tried to comprehend.

She thought about every Science-Fiction movie she had ever seen. Every video game she had ever played.

Every book she had ever read.

Every world simulation theory and every multiverse theory she had ever studied.

Unfortunately, Megan was right.

Erica was quite literally dealing with possibilities outside her own comprehension. In fact, she presumed even the scientists of her own world would struggle to comprehend it too. "This has got to be a dream. Some very twisted…"

While Erica didn't notice the nod Megan gave to the older scientist, she did feel the excruciating pain as her entire body was electrocuted through the straps that had her bound.

ZZZZZZZZZZZZZ.

"ARRGGGGHHHHH!" Erica screamed.

"LEAVE HER ALONE!" Cody yelled.

Megan sent another nod to the scientist, and he immediately pushed the button again, ending Erica's torment. But her body still winced in pain.

"Do you still think your dreaming?" Megan asked.

Erica didn't. There was no way that pain could have been imagined.

Still, Megan continued. "Every minor detail about your life, Nick, Chloe… Even your fear of spiders… they've all been implanted into my mind. Why do you think it was so easy to get you here?"

"You planted the chip for Seth to find, didn't you?" Cody asked.

"Yes, I did. Even Deets had no idea it was a ploy."

"What are you going to do to me?" Erica asked.

"Just a few tests. Don't worry. You're no use to me dead."

Tests? What type of tests would a fictional character want to deliver on their author?

"What did they do to you?" Cody asked.

Such a typical question, but it drew Megan's attention enough for her to leave Erica's side. Megan ran her hand along Cody's cheek and smiled in mock affection.

"MIOT gave me a second chance. They gave me knowledge, power, and control. They gave me a purpose better than ever before."

"And because of that you became their puppet? You're not the woman I fell in love with."

Megan cupped Cody's cheeks in her hands and forced a kiss against his lips. "Our love was only just an arc in a story. It was never real. What a pity the others won't be able to come for you. I have my own plans for them."

"Leave them alone, Megan!" Cody snarled. "Don't you dare hurt them!"

Megan looked to the other scientists. "Hold off on the recycling process. These two might still be of use."

After her villainess scene, Megan left, and the doors sealed shut behind her.

"Damn," Cody finally said. "I can't believe Megan…"

"…Could succumb to the dark side?" Erica finished. "Yep. Not even I saw that one coming."

"Dark side?"

Before she could even begin to explain the reference, Erica was met with an idea. "That's it!"

"What's it?"

Erica focused on the scientists. "Excuse me?"

"What are you doing?" Cody asked.

With their attention, Erica spoke in an almost hypnotic tone. "You guys really want to set us free."

The scientists laughed.

And so did Cody.

But Erica was being held hostage in her very own Science-Fiction world, so she refused to give up. She focused harder. So much so, her head hurt.

"You *will* unshackle us and let us go free."

"Very funny, Erica. Your sense of humour really is…"

CLICK. CLICK.

The scientists had pushed the buttons to unfasten their straps. They were free.

"I've always wanted to do that," Erica said as she and Cody hurried to their feet.

"*How* did you do that?"

"I'll explain later." Using the same tone as before, Erica turned back to the scientists. "You will now hand us your lab coats and take our places on the beds."

Again, they obeyed.

"How do we strap them in?" Erica asked, once the scientists were laying on the slabs.

"Like this."

Cody slammed his palm against each control panel, strapping both men in place.

"We need to contact the others. Let them know where we are."

"I already tried to mindlink them," Cody said. "No luck."

For the briefest of moments, Erica smiled to herself at the thought that mindlinks were actually real. While it still had a few bugs, the mindlink was a way to telepathically communicate amongst other Maranthinians. Like one would with a simple voice call on a phone.

"In that case, we need to get to the Communications Department," Erica decided.

"Do you know where it is? I'm a little foggy with the layout."

"Of course, I do. I'm the author."

As Erica went to leave, Cody held her back.

"Hey, Erica?"

"Yeah?"

"While I'm still a little hesitant to believe that you created us, I need to ask…"

Was he being serious? After everything, he still doubted her authenticity. "…Just spit it out."

"Did you guide me on our last mission here? The one where… Well, during the explosion?"

"Cody, I already told you. I never wrote that part."

"Yeah, but… I remember your voice. I remember you, *somehow*."

Erica looked to the scientists on the medical slabs, each in a trance-like state. There was no time for explanations.

"Cody, I swear to God, that I have no clue what on earth you're going on about. But now, we need to go before those scientists over there become unhypnotized. Okay?"

He released her. "Alright. Fine. Let's go."

ㄱ

ADELAIDE, SA – DEETS

"Are you sure it was nothing?" Adam interrogated as Deets sat confused in Erica's armchair.

"Positive. Now, just let it go. Okay?"

"Let it go? How can I just let it go? The last time you had a vision we…"

"…Lost my sister? Trust me, I know, Adam. I'm just saying, I don't think this vision means anything. It was just a memory. Nothing more."

Adam rested his hands at his hips and pulled a face. He didn't want to let it go. It was an eye contact showdown, but he knew he could not win against her. Deets's stare could take down a pack of ravenous muddlers. Instead, Adam looked to Seth still unconscious on the couch, while Deets shifted her focus to the window.

"We need to get out of here," she said. "I'm itching for a hunt."

"We're not leaving Seth. How hard did you hit him, anyway?"

"Not *that* hard."

On Adam's expression, she conceded. "Alright, fine. Maybe I was fitted with some cybernetic upgrades back at MIOT. I think they elevated my strength and visual senses while they were at it."

"Maybe?"

Deets shrugged.

Sure, MIOT had tested on her like everybody else, but she had undergone treatments after her rescue and there had been no signs of serious alterations.

Except for a twitching eye, a slight increase in visions... Oh, and the occasional vision of Erica.

Of course, she should've spoken to Dr Arack about the visions, but she had already experienced a lifetime of trauma at the hands of doctors. So, the temptation to do so, was next to none.

Adam lifted Seth's wrist to focus on the screen. But it simply showed his stable but sleeping vitals. He lowered Seth's wrist again. "Unfortunately, with him out like this, there's no way to check in with the others. You really should've thought your actions through."

Deets rolled her eyes.

The last thing she needed was another boring Adam lecture. She headed to the kitchen to find the breakfast mess just as the others had left it earlier.

But Deets wasn't in the mood for pancakes.

She raided the cupboards, fridge, and pantry until she was interrupted by the sound of Erica's phone ringing from the table. The lights and sound it made compelled her to check it out.

WORK CALLING.

Deets picked up the phone, just as she was joined by Adam. "What are you doing?" he asked.

"What is this thing?"

"I saw Erica use it earlier. I think it's how they make mindlinks."

Deets watched the flashing Caller ID with amazement. "I think… I think I should answer it."

"No, don't…"

"Hello?" Deets said, pushing the red button and accidentally ending the call. "Must've been the wrong button." Then the phone rang again.

"Pass it to me," Adam instructed, only for Deets to click the green icon and answer it immediately.

"Hello?"

At first, she could only hear a faint voice coming from the speaker. "Hold on, I can't hear you."

She pushed the speaker icon and the masculine voice of Erica's boss, Frank, spoke up. "Erica, why aren't you at work? Don't you know your shift started thirty minutes ago?"

"He thinks I'm Erica," Deets whispered to Adam as Frank continued talking.

"...Erica? If you don't walk through this door in the next hour, you're fired..."

Adam motioned for Deets to cut the connection, but the word 'fired' had Deets desperately improvising.

She imitated Erica's voice perfectly and said, "Sorry... sir. I'll be there. Please don't fire me."

It seemed while Maranthina had 'the pit' this world had its own form of torment. Something that involved fire. She pressed the red button and stared silently at Adam, just in time for Seth to walk in.

"Uh oh. What'd I miss?"

###

MARANTHINA – ERICA

"So far, so good," Erica said, as she and Cody crept along the corridors of the MIOT facility. Through her book series, she had always been able to envision the layout of the facility, perfectly.

But writing an escape scene and actually making an escape were two entirely different things. For one thing, there was a real fear of being caught.

Yet, she and Cody had ventured through three different corridors filled with workers and hadn't been spotted once. Even after a large door closed behind them a little louder than anticipated.

While Erica would've liked to put it down as sheer luck, she couldn't help but feel that there was something else at play.

Once they finally reached the Communications Department corridor, Cody approached the access panel beside the large, sealed entrance.

Beyond the door would be the Communications room where the communication team would be hard at work sending transmissions to other facilities via the holo consoles.

Erica and Cody's objective was simple. Sneak into the room and send an encrypted message to Seth. Unfortunately, getting him to open a portal in the middle of MIOT was not only risky but also next to impossible, thanks to the security restrictions on trespasser-augmentational abilities.

Thus, Erica and Cody's message would need to include a time and a location to meet up with Seth after they escaped the facility.

"How many do you think are in there?" Cody asked as he readied his hand to the biometric scanner.

"Since the Communication rooms generally have twelve consoles, I'm assuming there's that many in there… Give or take."

"Then we need to get them out of there."

Erica considered the biometric scanner. That very panel was linked to the room's security system. Security calls could even be made from that very panel and displayed in the room in case of emergency.

"Do you think you could distort my voice with that scanner?" she asked.

"Puleeese. That's level five coding abilities. Of course, I can. Wait, why?"

"Because I've got a plan."

"If you're thinking what I think you're thinking, it's a big risk. Megan has this way of speaking that…"

"…Relax. I based Megan on myself. We're good."

"Alright. But I should warn you I'll need to act as a bridge between the panel and you. And because you don't have any augmentations, while I can filter some of that energy through myself, you still might…"

"…Receive an electric shock?"

"To some degree, yeah."

Erica knew the risks. But their very escape depended on it. "I trust you, Cody. Just do it."

The minute Cody brought his left hand to the control panel, his eyes flashed a series of rainbow colours. He brought his other palm to Erica's hand and thin white bolts of electricity instantly zapped from another's fingertips.

Erica's first reaction was to pull away. "Oww!"

"I'm sorry. I'm trying to..." Before he could finish, Erica intertwined her fingers through his, igniting a surge of electricity to burn throughout her hand, despite Cody working hard minimize the impact.

Gradually, the pain eased.

Erica pushed the grey call button and spoke through the console. "This is Megan."

Just as they had planned, her voice came out identical to that of Megan. In fact, she hadn't expected their plan to work quite as well.

Still, she continued.

"I need to see you all in the... ah..."

She paused to consider the layout of the facility, before turning to Cody, who was still in his rainbow-eyed trance. He wouldn't be able to help while he was jacked into the system.

"Ah... In the infirmary," she improvised. "There's an outbreak on an augmentation virus which needs all hands-on deck."

A single masculine voice spoke back through the speaker, taking her by surprise.

"Isn't that a technical issue?"

Of course, it was a technical issue. Why would an augmentation virus require the aid of an entire team of communication specialists?

"Well..." Erica stammered. "We're dealing with a serious outbreak. So far, we've had five people come in with the same problem. So, you bet your ass we're going to have many more calling up about it. You're all going to need to know how to deal with those calls, so get in here and don't argue."

Erica nudged Cody, who instantly, removed his hand from the biometric scanner, and released hers.

"Impressive," he marvelled.

"Thanks. But we're not done yet. Act natural."

Suddenly, the door to the Communications room opened and a team of scientists poured from the room.

Erica leaned closer to Cody, posing as two scientists deep in conversation.

Cody, however, looked moderately unsure of himself. "Shouldn't we hide?"

"No. Just don't let them see your face."

As they waited, Erica couldn't help but feel the same excitement she had running through the Bucklands Forest. She had spent years planning and dreaming about Maranthina and now that she was there, it was as if she was truly home.

"Are you okay?" Cody asked, knocking her from her thoughts.

"Hm?"

"You just got this real far-off look in your eye."

"Are you two coming?" a foreign voice asked.

They looked up to see a dark-skinned female scientist with her hair in a ponytail.

Erica's entire body tensed up. "Ah... umm..."

"Just a minute," Cody said, as if he had done this countless times. "I had a theory about the QTX hacking system I wanted to discuss with my colleague."

"The QTX?" the female scientist asked. "Ugh! Don't waste your time with that one." She left quickly to join the other scientists.

The QTX hacking system had been a very buggy system which had caused many consumers and engineers so much trouble they scrubbed it, altogether. It was no wonder the scientist had left in such a hurry.

"Impressive," Erica smiled. "Why didn't I think of that?"

"Hey, I get ideas. I've just been waiting for my moment to shine."

Erica turned behind her, the science team had disappeared down the corridor and the Communications room door was seconds away from closing. Erica and Cody darted under the large door, into the large Communications room just in time.

Inside, there were twelve podium consoles all in rows of three, and at the front of the room there was a large blank screen. To Erica's surprise, two scientists remained standing at the consoles in the front row, with clearly no intention of leaving.

One looked to be a male of Asian descent, possibly in his late thirties. The other was a tanned skin female, roughly the same age. "I'd rather go to the pit than meet with the new CEO," the female said.

"Agreed. Did you hear how she made chief?"

While Cody jacked into the middle console in the backrow, Erica hid behind it, her attention on the conversation being had by the scientists.

"Not exactly. I heard it had something to do with the explosion," the female scientist said.

"She betrayed her friends by giving up their secrets. Then when the evacuation protocols were set off, she faked her death. Something about striking a deal with the man upstairs."

"What kind of deal?"

"Not sure. According to Briggs, it was all kept classified."

Upon hearing the news, Erica couldn't help but feel a pang of sympathy for Cody. His love for Megan had been undeniable since they had first met in the orphanage. It had been one of those stories where he had loved her from afar for so long until an argument forced him to spill his emotions.

Now, he was left with nothing more than the brutal fact that what he felt was only just an arc in a story.

Erica stood at full height and placed her hand on Cody's shoulder.

"I'm sorry," she whispered.

"It's not your fault," he said.

"It kinda is. I…"

"…Hey!" the female scientist called out to them. "Why have I never seen you around here?"

Erica looked to Cody, who was still sending his message to Seth. She needed to give him a little more time.

"Ah… We're new. We were sent to fill in for the team who were sent to the Infirmary."

"That so?" the female scientist asked, raising a portable scanner. "Well, this is a classified station. You should check in just to be safe."

"We did at the door."

The scientist checked her scanner screen. "Oh, really? Because your ID isn't coming up. Here, do it again."

The scientist held out the scanner for Erica.

Uh oh.

Just as Erica was about to use her 'author abilities' again, Cody announced, "I did it."

"You did?" Erica and the scientist asked in unison.

"Yeah. So, no need to use the portable scanner. In fact, we can go now. Right now." He sent a look at Erica confirming that the message had indeed been sent.

"Yeah, let's go," Erica agreed, as she and Cody backed towards the door, slowly.

"Not so fast." The female scientist scanned Erica and was surprised by the reading. "What do you mean, 'no chip found?" She scanned Cody just as he hit the open-door button and the facility's sirens started blaring.

"Intruder alert detected in the Communications Department," the security's AI spoke through the speakers. "Can all available security personnel report to the Communications Department?"

"You've done it now," the male scientist said.

Just as the large door opened from the bottom up, Erica crawled under the gap. "Cody, hurry!"

Once they had made it into the corridor, Erica and Cody darted towards the large metal door at the other end of the hallway, only to have it open in front of them, allowing in six AIA soldiers dressed in black.

The AIA were an army programmed for war and combat situations. And since the explosion at MIOT, they had been posted to the facility for added security measures. To make it worse, they were carrying big guns. "Oh shit." Cody swore. "It looks like they upgraded security."

Erica turned back in the direction that they had come, only to find more AIA soldiers closing in from behind. "We need an escape plan," Erica said.

"Try your abilities."

"You *will* let us go free," Erica commanded of the soldiers, but they simply raised their guns.

"I *command* you to let us go free!" Erica said, even louder this time. The male AIA soldier who seemed to be in charge, brought his finger to his ear, then nodded to a soldier behind Erica.

Still, with desperate fear, she tried to command them through her tone. "You *will* lower your weapons and…"

BANG!

Something knocked her across the head, and everything went black.

MARANTHINA – ERICA

Darkness.

It was the first thing Erica saw when she opened her eyes. In fact, it was so dark she couldn't tell whether her eyes were opened or closed. A soft, fabric brushed against her face as she clambered to her knees, and she could and attempted to move her neck. A sharp pain at the back of her head forced her to writhe.

Erica wanted to feel for the wound, but her wrists were bound behind her by a cold, metal restraint.

"Cody? Can you hear me?"

To her surprise, she heard him muffle a response.

"Erica? Where are you?"

"I'm over here."

But she had no idea where 'here' was.

The light breeze against her arms and the feel of dirt to her knees told her she was outside.

She attempted to stand and was relieved to find that her legs had been left unbound.

"Talk to me so I can figure out where you are."

"Uh... I think... I think we're outside. They must've let us go."

Using his voice as a beacon, Erica staggered towards him. "Cody, keep talk..."

Her foot kicked something, and she toppled over a large mound. "Oww!" they both groaned.

"Well, I think I found you," she chuckled.

"That much is obvious. You're on my leg."

As Erica shook what was now discovered to be a thick black sack, from her head she saw that Cody had just done the same.

They were sitting in the middle of a deserted wheat field with nothing else in sight. "Where are we?" she asked, clambering to stand again.

"It looks like we're in the Datsian outskirts. Dammit! It'll take forever to get to the city from here."

"Forever? Like… An hour or two?"

He stared at her. Hard.

"Without Seth, a day or so. We need to get to my apartment. Thanks to this change of plans, I'll need to send him another message via my holo."

A day or so?

Erica could barely walk an hour without stopping for a break. To make matters worse, she needed the toilet desperately, and her hands were quite literally tied behind her back.

Speaking of bound hands…

"Does it look like there's a way to get these things off?" she asked.

Cody analysed her restraint. "There might be, but doing so will include us having to meet with the one person I despise more than MIOT."

"Who?"

Cody scrunched up his face in disgust.

"We need to see Jynx."

Jynx was… an intriguing person. Charismatically good looking and one hell of a rogue-like character.

He was also a Reader, which meant he could visually scan any augmented individual and analyse absolutely everything about them. And while he worked as a freelance henchman if the price was right, his loyalty was not something that could easily be bought.

Of course, he would have some contraption to get them out of their binds.

The question was, what would it cost?

"Do you know where he's holed up?"

"Yeah. Right outside the city. Still, I don't get it. Why would they just dump us out here? Despite leaving us bound, it's like they just let us escape."

"It must be part of Megan's plan because it's one hell of a Deus Ex Machina move."

"A what?"

"I mean, it's like whoever is writing the story is helping us out. So that means we need to determine just how they're doing it and stop them."

Cody considered her theory. Judging by the look on his face, he couldn't be more confused if he tried. Still, he shrugged off the thought. "Why don't we just work out how to get to Dastian City, okay? We'll work out the rest, later."

"Do you know our way back?" Erica asked, doing her best to push the thought of her tiny bladder out of her mind.

Cody scanned their surroundings. "I'm guessing we head North?"

"You're guessing? You can't be serious!"

"Hey, Seth's the one with the mapping system, not me." Without another word, Cody took off in the direction he believed was North.

Again, Erica was met by the fact that she needed to find a toilet. It made her wonder just what her characters did in that situation. Sure, there were bathroom facilities in every building, but she rarely added scenes where they were used.

As they walked through the wheatfields she decided to take the leap. "Hey, Cody?"

"Yeah?"

"So... You guys do get toilet breaks, right?"

"Toilet breaks?"

"I'm talking about digesting bodily waste and fluids."

It took him a moment to register. "I know what you're referring to, but why do you ask?"

The answer was humiliating. But the thought of her experiencing an accident in front of him humiliated her all the more. "I... er... I need to go to the toilet... *Badly*."

What she didn't say was that it would be impossible to pull down her pants and maintain balance with her hands tied behind her back.

A range of expressions flushed across his face before he was met with a crimson blush of realization.

"Oh, uhh…"

His humiliation simply mirrored her own.

"Seriously, I really need your help," she said.

Finally, he nodded.

"Yeah, I can help. Under two conditions."

"If the first, is you keep your eyes shut, I'm all for it."

"Okay, so make that three conditions."

"Out with it, Cody."

"I was going to say we don't breathe a word of this to anybody and…"

"…Well, that's a given. What's the other?"

"You help me go, in return?"

"Deal. Now, just help me."

As Cody turned around to lend Erica the assistance of his bound hands, Erica couldn't remember the last time she had ever been so humiliated in all her life.

###

ADELAIDE, SA – DEETS

Deets sat at a booth with Adam and Seth in *Franks Coffee Bar* with no idea as to what Erica did as a job nor how to do it herself. Despite that limitation, she refused to let it destroy her plans.

"I've pulled up the image data for Erica's identity," Seth said, showing her his wrist screen. "Are you ready?"

"How can I be? I don't even know how to do her job."

"You pour the coffee and take the money. How hard can it be?"

Deets exchanged looks with Adam, who knew exactly what she was getting at.

"Seth," he began. "We don't know how this technology works. Nor do we know the value of their currency. Deets is in way over her head."

"Well, she should've thought about that before she took the mindlink on that device." Seth stopped to take in Deets's pissed off persona, then sighed in defeat. "Alright, fine. If worse comes to worse, just cough."

"Cough?" Deets asked.

"Yeah. And do it a lot. My research indicates that this world recently suffered a global health disaster which sets everybody on edge at the mere sign of a cough."

Deets nodded in approval.

"So, I'll ask you again… Are you ready?"

In response, Deets laid her forearm out on the table, with her wrist displaying a small, round silver chip in the centre of her flower tattoo. "Jack me up, Seth."

Seth pressed his wrist screen across her wrist chip and in seconds, the tattoos on her arm began to disappear, starting with the flower surrounding her wrist chip. It wasn't long until Deets had been replaced by Erica's identity entirely.

"Wow," Adam gasped. "You did it."

"He did?" the clone of Erica asked, looking down at her arms. While her face looked exactly like Erica, her clothes hadn't changed at all. Seth scanned her with his wrist screen again and checked the stats.

"While it did work, it'll only last an hour and you really need to try and stick to using Erica's voice. Do you understand?"

Barely listening, Deets got to her feet. Her eyes were focused solely on the girl who had just entered the café.

Chloe.

Deets rushed to greet her.

"She didn't hear me, did she?" Seth asked Adam.

Adam shook his head. "No, I don't even think she was listening."

"Erica?" Chloe gasped in surprise at Deets. "Where have you been and what are you wearing?"

Deets stared down at her purple, synthetic bodysuit, thinking she should've changed into Erica's clothes before leaving the house. Or at least downloaded a style that might've been a little more appropriate.

"Ah… this? It's just something new I was trying on."

"Something new? Shouldn't you be wearing a uniform?" But Chloe didn't leave her enough time to improvise. "Listen, I stopped by your house earlier and there was somebody there. She said her name was Deets."

"Oh. Uh… yeah! That was… that was Deets. She's my… my sister."

"But you don't have a sister."

Dammit, she saw right through that one.

"Did I say 'sister'? No, I meant cousin."

"Erica, what's going on? I thought Deets was the name of one of your characters. Was that some cosplaying girl? Because the resemblance was uncanny."

"Yes! Cosplaying girl. That's exactly who she was. So, what did you think of her?" Before Deets could get her answer, Erica's boss – Frank – interjected.

"Oi, Erica? Are you working or not?"

"I think Frank is calling you," Chloe said.

"Who?" Deets followed Chloe's gaze to Erica's fifty-something year old boss, who had a shaved head and blue eyes. Then she remembered.

"Oh, right. Frank. Erica's… I mean, *my* boss. I'll see you soon, okay?"

Without another word Deets disappeared behind the counter to start her first shift of covering for Erica.

9

MARANTHINA – ERICA

"Well, that was an experience that I never want to relive," Erica said, finally breaking the ten-minute long silence as she and Cody travelled through the wheat fields. Thanks to their bound hands, their toileting *experience* had certainly been one hell of an embarrassing debacle.

"Can we just... not talk about it? Ever again?" Cody asked, crimson filling his cheeks.

"Sure. But, if it's any consolation, you weren't built as imperfect as you originally thought."

An honest statement… even if it was a compliment.

"Ah… thanks?"

"You're welcome."

Erica kept walking until her eyes caught sight of the mountainous landscape on the horizon.

"Look over there."

"By the pit…" Cody stammered. "I was right. On the other side of those mountains is Datsian City."

"Great. Then we can get these shackles off, meet with the others and go home."

"It's not that simple, Erica."

"Why not?"

"Because those mountains are only one third of the way. They're just the sign we needed to confirm that we're on the right track. Besides, the sun's going down. We'll need to find shelter."

"But I'm good to keep walking throughout the night. I just want to go home."

In that moment, all Erica could think about was her crawling into her pyjamas and binging on television.

Yet without Seth's portal technology, she knew she was a long way off.

By the time the sun had set, they had reached the lush mountain range, which would've been much prettier in the daylight. The thick trees and steep ground made it nearly impossible to determine just where they were headed in the dark. They followed what must've originally been a rocky footpath a century ago, as hinted by the smooth stone that peaked through the vegetation.

There was a cool breeze in the air and the chirp of crickets sung in the grass around them. Overcome by hunger, Erica's stomach gurgled catching Cody's attention. "Did you hear that?" he asked.

"It was my stomach," Erica said. "We haven't eaten since..."

But Cody stopped and turned his head in the direction behind her. "No, listen."

At first, there was nothing but silence.

But then, she heard it. The crackling of leaves underfoot and an incessant beeping noise.

BEEP. BEEP. BEEP. BEEP. "...Is comin' from dis way," a distant voice said.

Cody's eyes went wide.

"Outskirters," he mouthed, silently.

Outskirters were groups of criminals that lived outside the city walls. They spent their time scrounging for parts to sell in the Underground Markets, and sometimes even resorted to murder.

The very mention of the word sent a shiver up Erica's spine. She brought her attention to her neck... to the necklace Nick had given her as a birthday present one year ago. It was made of cheap metal, but it could still be used as a perfect distraction.

"Do we have a way out of here?" she whispered.

Cody scanned the ground in front of them. The footpath they had been following, forked to the right then disappeared into a large crack in the stone.

It looked large enough for a medium-sized animal to burrow through. Where it led after that, was a mystery.

"Through there… I think."

It was their only option, and the footsteps were getting closer. As was the beeping.

BEEP. BEEP. BEEP. BEEP. BEEP. BEEP.

"Cody, do you see my necklace?"

Her voice faltered.

"What about it"

"I need you to rip it off me, and then throw it onto the ground as a distraction, so we can run."

"Are you sure? You won't get it back."

"It's either that or be killed and used for parts. I don't know about you, but I'm kinda in favour of self-preservation."

"Alright, bend down. I'll try to pull it off." He shuffled to turn, as Erica knelt low so that her neck was level with his hands.

The beeping grew louder and was now accompanied by footsteps crunching dry leaves.

"Hurry," she whispered, as Cody's fingers found the chain.

"Ma scanna's pickin' up sumfn big!" a rough voice called out. It was followed by a raucous laughter.

As Erica's focus was drawn to the noises coming closer, she was pulled back to reality by the sudden, sharp pain to the back of her neck, as Cody slipped the necklace free. "Sorry, if that hurt."

"It's fine. On three, drop the necklace and run. We'll try to slip through that burrow over there."

"Okay."

 Erica's legs shook as she got back to full height.

"One..."

BEEP. BEEP. BEEP. BEEP.

She turned her gaze towards the trees, where she could see a flashlight flicker in the distant darkness.

"...Two..."

Her voice was even lower this time. She merely prayed Cody could still hear her.

"There's definly somef'n big o'r 'ere," the voice said.

"Three."

The moment she said it, Cody dropped the necklace with a light jingle, and they sprinted along the overgrown path as quietly as possible.

Once they reached the crack in the rocks, Erica hesitated. The hole looked big enough to have been made by somebody... or *something*.

Her fears quickly subsided as she heard the voices of the Outskirters getting closer. She shuffled to her stomach, wiggled into the hole – feet first, and slithered backwards, reaching for the bottom of the cave behind her. But there was no bottom.

Uh oh!

Her fears elevated as she spotted the flashlight flickering in the distance.

"Come on, Erica," Cody said. "Hurry."

After taking a deep breath for courage, Erica dropped into the hole and landed on her backside, hard.

"Oww!"

Cody quickly crawled through after her, but fortunately, his height allowed him to land on his feet.

From her position on the rocky ground, Erica could see that they were in a six-foot high cave. The crack in the rocky wall was roughly five and a half foot high. No wonder she hadn't been able to touch the ground.

She deduced that the cave must've been used for a shelter in the great war, five-hundred years ago.

A scurry of footsteps from the ground above, forced her to clamber to sit below the wall's entrance beside Cody, just as a flicker of white light reflected on the rocky wall in front of them. Her breath hitched in her throat as particles of dirt and stone rained from above.

They peered up to see a gauntly, shaved head with a flashlight for an eye scanning the inside of their hideout. He was accompanied by the smell of rotting flesh.

There was no doubt about it, the man was an Outskirter.

A scream threatened to escape from Erica's mouth, so she bit down on her bottom lip and exchanged glances with Cody. His dark eyes were wide, but his mouth was sealed.

"Jakie, what're you doing o'er 'ere?" another voice called from outside. *Jakie* turned his head to peer behind him.

"I fink I seen sufing scurry in here."

"It was prob'y a rat. Bring 'at light 'ere... I fink I found sufing."

Erica could feel her breath desperate to return, but she wouldn't release it, yet. She'd rather pass out in silence than allow herself to be caught by an Outskirter.

She peered upwards again just in time to see *Jakie's* gangly hand reach down from above. As a reaction, she shifted her head to the right, smacking it into the rocky wall beside her. There was an instant throb, but she resisted cursing.

"Hey, Jakie! Get yer ass o'er here b'fore I rip 'at light frm yer socket!"

To Erica's relief and with a grumble of words, Jakie left their hideout and headed back to his companion, taking the light with him.

"Are you alright?" Cody whispered.

"Yeah. I just... I can't see anything."

"That's okay. I can see a little."

Of course, he could.

He was a goddam Maranthinian. All Maranthinians were given adequate night vision for their fifth-year upgrade. While his night vision wasn't as good as Deets, it was still far better than Erica's night vision by a long shot.

"What do you see?" Erica asked as they both clambered to stand.

"Ah... this cave it's... there's a larger chamber a few paces in front of us. I can't see any other entrances. We should be able to shelter here for the night."

That revelation brought sheer relief. Erica was hungry, exhausted and her arms had grown so numb, she wouldn't even know if they dropped off.

"Great," she whispered. "Lead the way."

Cody grabbed the fabric of her shirt and directed her deeper into the pitch-black cave. Despite having him guiding her, and her eyes constantly playing tricks on her amidst the darkness, Erica relied on her other senses.

There was a thick stench of cold rock, dirt, and dust. Her foot kicked a pebble across the floor, forcing it to smack into another.

"Are you sure there's nobody else in here?" she asked.

Cody stopped walking, forcing her to stop too.

"Positive. Just some bugs. There's enough room for us to sleep right here." He released her and moved a few steps away.

"Here?"

"Yes."

"I wish we could start a fire. It's so cold," she shivered.

"You're *cold*?"

"I'm freezing, Cody. We weren't all built with a thermo-wiring system."

"I wish I knew what that felt like." he said, as he shuffled around in the dark.

"Maybe we could rub some of these rocks together to…"

A light sparked against a stick, forcing her to stop speaking. Another spark gave her the quick realization that Cody was seated on the ground, trying to start a fire using his own electrical charge. After his third attempt, a flame appeared.

He dropped the stick into a pile of small burnt-out branches. "It's a primitive method, but it totally works."

As Erica slumped to warm herself in front of the flame, she looked around at the cramped, rocky interior and laughed at his comment. "Primitive? That method is nowhere near primitive. But judging by the way these rocks have already been lined into a fire pit, somebody else must've been here before us. You don't think they'll come back, do you?"

"Doubt it. It looks like it's been untouched since the war. Are you a little warmer now?"

A shiver raced up her spine as the flame removed the chill from her body. "A little. Thank you."

He nodded, but his dark eyes remained fixed on the flame, highlighting a world of emotions written across his face. A blend of misery and confusion.

"I'm sorry she betrayed you," Erica said.

He shrugged and adopted a smile that failed to rise into his cheeks. "It's not your fault."

"Yes, it is. I should've seen the clues... I should've found some way to stop Megan turning into a badass villain."

"I'm not upset because you couldn't stop her. I feel *conflicted* because after everything we've been through and even now that my heart wire has regenerated... I feel absolutely nothing towards her."

A surprising twist of events.

Was he lying?

Cody loved Megan. That type of love didn't just die out with the snip of a wire or a change of words on paper. Erica had poured everything she had into their relationship.

"You can't be serious! You'd have to be feeling something. You and Megan have loved each other since the moment you first met. She was your soulmate, whether I believe in that word or not."

"You don't believe in soulmates?"

"No. It's just a matter of personality traits, compatibility points and chemistry that... you know what? It doesn't matter."

Cody considered her words, took a breath, and then locked his eyes directly on her. His gaze was almost as warm as the flame itself.

"Okay. Sure, I feel betrayed... but at the same time... It's like I feel free. Like I've been unlocked from the confines of a role, that I've been playing for far too long."

"From your character arc?" She couldn't determine whether it was a question, or a statement to herself, but Cody answered it, regardless.

"I don't believe you controlled our actions… but yes, that's exactly how I feel. Free from Megan. Free to live and love how I choose."

In that moment, Erica regretted every choice she had ever made in every single one of her stories. She had forced her characters to behave in ways that seemed fitting to the plot. She had forced them into relationships for the sake of a compelling story…

A story that she had been telling through the eyes of Megan. But at the time, all those choices felt right.

She wondered about Seth and Adam. How did they feel about the roles they had played? She had always shipped them together. Almost as much as she had shipped Cody and Megan. Her thoughts were interrupted by Cody speaking up again, concerning himself with her wellbeing.

"What about you? Today's been rough. We took you from your world only to… Well, you get the point."

Yes, she did get the point.

They had taken her from her safe and happy life and threw her into the chaos, that she had subjected them to their whole lives.

"It's been a real eye-opener," she finally said. "But it has also been remarkably interesting. A real adventure."

A cool breeze swept in through the entrance behind her, sending a shiver up her spine and forcing the flame to flicker. The fire wouldn't be enough to keep her warm that night.

"You should get some sleep," Cody said. "We have another long walk tomorrow."

"Don't you need to recharge?" Erica asked. "You guys were awake all night."

Another shiver crept up her spine. The cold was really coming in fast. She cursed herself for dressing in shorts and a tank top for the Australian Summer.

"I do," Cody said. "But I need to think for a bit. I'll sleep when I'm ready."

He was hiding something. Erica knew his tells better than he did. But at the same time, she didn't care. Her body temperature was decreasing by the minute and her arms had become nothing more than dead weights attached to her.

She curled up into a ball on the hard, uncomfortable ground, as close to the flame as possible, and as her body gave the occasional cold shiver, she gradually drifted off to sleep.

IO

ADELAIDE, SA – SETH

At their table in the *Frank's Coffee Bar*, Seth compared the local time with that of Maranthina on his wrist screen. It was currently 2:15pm in Adelaide and 11:32pm in Datsian City.

Which meant that while it had only been almost two hours for him since he had left Erica and Cody in Maranthina, for them it had been at least twelve hours.

But that didn't explain why he hadn't yet heard from Cody. It wasn't like the guy to not send a transmission.

What worried Seth more, was that he couldn't locate his friend's tracker. That had never happened before.

Seth could only assume that Cody and Erica had been captured by MIOT, and because he couldn't open a portal directly into the facility, there was nothing more he could do.

"Are you alright?" Adam asked.

"I haven't heard from them," Seth said.

Adam took Seth's hand in his. "They'll reach out. Cody's resourceful. Besides, he's with Erica."

That wasn't as comforting as Seth would've liked to admit. She was powerless in the very world that she had created. Their actions had led her to a possible catastrophe, and Seth was riddled with guilt.

"How can you say that? You saw her face when she saw that spider. We couldn't even save Megan, and the moment MIOT realise who Erica is…"

"Shh… It's okay. I believe in her. You read those books too. She has more power than any of us know. If anything, she'll be the one to save us all. I don't doubt that for a second. And you shouldn't either."

"Wait, are you talking about Erica?" Chloe's voice broke in over their conversation. As Adam turned to her, Seth did his best to conceal his wrist screen.

But it was too late. Chloe had already seen.

"I knew it. You guys *are* from her books, aren't you?"

"I… I don't know what you're talking about," Seth said. "How could somebody come from a book?"

With a smug grin, Chloe sat in the booth across from them. "Something tells me it has something to do with that computer on your arm. Am I right, *Seth?*"

"How do you know about that?" Adam asked her.

Before Chloe could respond, Deets rushed over with her face buried in her arm, feigning a coughing fit. "You guys…" Cough. "…We need to…" Cough. Cough. "…Go…Home, right now."

Immediately, Seth and Adam got to their feet, just as they were joined by whom Seth could only gather was Erica's boss. "You need to leave, Erica. I can't have you infecting my customers."

Clearly, the balding man couldn't see that the face of *Erica* had transformed back into *Deets*.

But Chloe saw.

In fact, she got to her feet too and followed the others out of *Frank's Coffee Bar*.

"Wait! I know the truth," she called after them.

Seth, Deets and Adam exchanged glances. But while Deets and Adam kept running, Seth stopped and waited for Chloe to catch up.

"What do you mean you know the truth?"

"I've read Erica's books more times than I can count. I even read the rough drafts of the chapters that were never published. That's why I know you're from them. I just don't know how it's possible. How are you actually… *here?*"

On those words, Seth needed to hear more. "What do you mean never published?"

174

"When Erica first wrote her stories, she needed a sounding board. As her best friend, I was that sounding board. I read every single page. When the stories were published, they made her leave some stuff out, due to marketability. So, she rewrote them. If you like, I can help you find them."

Her words gave Seth hope. Maybe those pages were the missing link. "You would do that? You'd help us?"

Chloe glanced over at Deets and Adam who had just joined them, before turning back to Seth.

"I'll help... Under one condition."

Seth narrowed his eyes. He had absolutely nothing of value to offer. "What is it?"

"Tell me how this is possible. How is it that you guys are... *here?*"

Information. Now, that was something Seth could give. He only prayed that she could be trusted.

###

MARANTHINA – ERICA

Thanks to the stiff pain radiating up Erica's arms and back she didn't need to open her eyes to know that she was bound. But she couldn't quite remember why. Was it possible that she had passed out on the couch in the weirdest sleeping position ever?

No, that couldn't be it. Not this time.

She remembered falling asleep cold. But now, there was a considerable amount of heat coming from a solid object behind her. That very object was pressed against her so tight that she couldn't even move her arms. And from what she could gather, it curled around her from her upper back to her bent legs. Had she rolled up against the rocky wall?

Rocky wall?

Wait, that was it.

A cave. She was in a cave.

A cave in Maranthina.

But what was the thing behind her?

She felt around with her hands at what must've been a limb of some sort. Was it a beast?

A muddler, perhaps?

If it was, she couldn't make any sudden movements. Muddlers were fierce predators when provoked.

Erica opened her eyes to see that the fire must've died out during the night. The only light, as dim as it was, came from the sunlight pouring in through the cave's small entrance.

So far, so good.

The unknown creature didn't move. Slowly, she shuffled her body forward, giving herself a little space to sit without disrupting the thing behind her. And then, pushing up through her hands, Erica sat up.

The creature shuffled into her personal space, startling her. She turned her head only to find out that it wasn't a creature, after all.

It was Cody.

He was sleeping curled up on his side, in the same way she had been, with a lock of his dark hair falling across his face. Clearly feeling her gaze, his eyes drifted open. "Uhh… Morning. Is it morning?"

"Yeah, I think it's morning," Erica smirked. "So… Sleep well?"

"We slept in an uncomfortable cave with our arms bound, so…" It wasn't until he noticed the hint of amusement in the corner of her cheek, that he realised just what she was referring to. "Oh. You're talking about me sleeping beside you…" he anxiously struggled to sit, then clambered to his feet. "I assure you, that whole sleeping arrangement was purely because you were shivering, and my body constantly maintains heat. So, it was the obvious solution."

"Uh huh." Her smile had evolved into a widespread grin.

"I'm serious. You were shivering. You could've died."

"Alright. I believe you." But her smile didn't waiver. She was silently referring to the perfectly natural, though entirely involuntarily occurrence that happens to many men in the early hours of morning. And at that moment, he understood her expression entirely.

He glanced down at the very evident bulge in his dark blue pants and crimson filled his cheeks. "Oh... Ah... That's... That's a biology thing. It happens to men... here... in Maranthina. The warmth and the..."

He turned his whole body away and struggled to compose himself with his arms still bound.

Erica burst into laughter. "...Relax, Cody. It's not exclusive to Maranthinians. It happens to the guys in my world too. Anyway, the sun's out. So, let's get moving." As Erica headed towards the cave entrance, Cody breathed a sigh of relief and followed after her.

It wasn't long until they were trekking through the lush mountains, under the warm sun.

"I'm surprised there are so few trails through here," Erica said to distract herself from the gurgling, ravenous beast of her stomach. "This place would be perfect to go hiking."

"Why would somebody actively choose to go hiking through the mountains?" Cody asked.

"Same reasons they would in my world. For exercise and to consort with nature. Most people have cars, but they still go camping."

"You sound like Deets. She loves the wilderness."

"And you don't?"

Cody shrugged and stepped over a large rock. "I probably would, if we weren't always just trying to keep ourselves alive. But hey, maybe one day you'll write about me retiring by the Diamond Stream with not a care in the world."

Despite his sarcasm, Erica couldn't shake off the image he had conjured up. It was the perfect element of hope, even if the Diamond Stream was nothing more than a myth. Consisting of fresh, pure water, the stream was supposedly located in a large underground garden untouched by modern Maranthinian technology.

In fact, it was the same place Erica clung to in her mind when she needed to escape the harshness of reality. Just like the concept of the Garden of Eden.

While Erica had mentioned the Diamond Stream in her stories, she had never written about her characters actually seeing it. For it was just as much a myth to Maranthina, as the lost city of Atlantis, was to her world.

"Maybe one day I will," she said. "Maybe that's where you'll get your happy ever after. You'll build a house and live off the fresh fish and crops while watching the waterfall from your peaceful front yard. Oh, but that'll be after we stop MIOT for good. Because then, they'll never bother you again and you'll be free."

Cody's smile deepened as he truly considered the dream. "You really do paint a beautiful picture."

"That's because I've seen that place in my mind more times than I can count. It's my safe place."

"Your safe place?"

"What I mean, is that when I went through therapy, thanks to the PTSD of being a kid in the foster system…

and then when I used to meditate... the Diamond Stream was the place I'd see in my mind. The clear stream, the sounds of the waterfall splashing in the distance... The smell of roses... The sun..."

"...Peering through the top? Oh, and the shimmer of those sparkly diamonds in the rocks," Cody finished.

"Wow. I must've really held that place over you."

"Perhaps. Or maybe you only ever imagined it, because I believed in it first, and you were able to read my thoughts through your visions."

"Seriously? How can you doubt me after everything you've seen? You quite literally came to my world, read the novels, and saw me work my magic on those scientists. Face it, I'm your creator."

Cody stopped and turned back to her. "No, you're not. Deets and Megan get visions too. So, those books aren't exactly proof of anything."

"What about my control over the scientists?"

"Freaky... but probably just some advanced manipulation."

"What about the fact that even Megan admitted to reversing the author connection? And she's been made privy to…"

"…If you ask me, Megan was humouring you for her own benefit. There's a connection, yes. But I'm sorry but I don't exactly see how you could create us just by writing a damn story. I'm not Seth. I believe in fact, not fiction."

Erica scoffed.

"Look at the world we're in. Look at the abilities that you possess! To anybody from my world… all *this* is fiction. Science Fiction to be exact! So why can't you just believe in…"

"…believe in what? *You?* Erica, my own parents discarded me because I wasn't what they paid for, so I grew up in an orphanage where testing on kids whether the children survived or not, was acceptable because it was for the greater good. So, I'm sorry to burst your bubble but I stopped believing that there was a greater being protecting us a long time ago."

His words stunned her into silence. Their lives weren't so different. *They* weren't so different.

Erica didn't believe in a god, so why should he? Maybe because no matter what he went through, she *had* always been there with him… Every step of the way.

"Okay," Erica conceded. "Whether you see me as your creator or not… we'll agree to disagree. But I watched you go through all of that… and I never once lost faith in you. So, just believe in me for a second. That's all I'm asking."

"Believe in you?"

"Yeah. Magical abilities or not, I've got your back."

Cody considered her words just as her stomach growled again. He smirked. "Alright, almighty Erica, I believe you've got my back… and that if we don't find something to eat soon, that monster in your stomach will burst out and devour our enemies."

Erica laughed and they continued on their way just as she spotted the perfect element of hope. "Hey Cody, look!" She gestured with her nose. "It looks like the almighty Erica paved the way to our possible salvation."

Cody followed her gaze to the winding dirt road up ahead which led up and around the mountain.

"Good. But it's not celestial greatness good."

"You really are a pain in the ass," she said, rushing on ahead. "Now, let's go get these shackles off."

By the time the sun was sitting high in the sky, they had followed the dirt path all the way to the other side of the mountain. Their stomachs ached with hunger, their lips were parched, and it took all the will they possessed not to collapse onto the ground, with exhaustion. At the same time, they were met with a large sense of relief, as they stared down at the small farming town, just outside the giant gates of Datsian City. "There she is," Cody said with a hint of pride. "Datsian City. We should be there soon. Until then, we can rest up at Jynx's place for a break."

Erica scanned the small village of Datsian Valley, which was nestled right outside the gates. From their location, she could count fifteen farmhouses.

While nobody farmed by hand, thanks to the machines that tended to the crops and livestock, there was still far less technology in Datsian Valley than there was in the city.

As Erica took a step forward, Cody spoke up. "Just a warning... Please, don't reveal anything about yourself to Jynx. Alright?"

"Isn't he a Reader? Won't he be able to see that I don't have a wiring system?"

Cody considered the thought. "Yeah... but... He can't know that you're not from Maranthina. Or that... you think you're the creator."

"I don't *think* it, Cody. I..."

"...Whatever. Jynx tends to..."

"...play by his own rules? I know that too, I wrote him, remember? We'll need a story."

"Got something up your sleeve?"

While Erica couldn't think of anything, Cody adopted a look... and then a smile. "I've got it!"

"Got what?"

Without divulging anything further, he took off down the dirt path, headed towards Datsian Valley with Erica trailing behind.

It took approximately half an hour to reach the doorstep of Jynx's rundown, red-brick farmhouse. The screen of the door had been torn beyond repair, but the metal crisscross frame was still intact. It offered them a full view of the musty white walls and the wooden floors that lined the interior.

A filthy brown couch sat on the deck, beside a table with empty Recharge cans scattered on top. Noticing the empty beer cans, Erica couldn't help but smile.

She had always imagined *Recharge* tasting horribly bitter. Far more bitter than the beer in her own world. But *Recharge* was a beer perfectly designed to get the consumer to feel more pumped with energy, than a strong cup of coffee. It also got them drunk so much quicker… and sent their wires into an electrical frenzy.

Drawing her attention, Cody stood on his tiptoes, in a bid to reach the dirty grey hand panel, by the door. When that didn't work, he jumped in another attempt to reach it. With his focus on the panel, he didn't notice Erica until she knocked – loudly – with her hands still shackled behind her.

"What are you doing? There's no way that'll work."

In minutes, the door opened and for the very first time since meeting any of her characters, Erica was struck by stunned surprise to see Jynx standing before them.

For one thing, he was shirtless, which exposed his pale muscular torso and the intricate pattern of shiny metal, which ran from just under his eyes, down his body, and disappeared under the soft grey fabric of his pants. He was practically six foot tall, and his smile was that of a charming rogue. His eyes were green, and he bore light stubble to his face.

While the top of his head possessed short, dark waves, it was shaved around the back and sides.

The moment his eyes landed on Erica he unleashed a roguish smile into his left cheek. "Mmm. It's not every day I find stunning prototypes at my door. Who might you be?"

Erica couldn't speak. How could she have ever underestimated just how *hot* Jynx would be? "Ah…"

But then, Jynx hesitated. His eyes opened wide as if he recognised her from somewhere, then that recognition turned into confusion.

"Wait, we know each other. Don't we?"

"N-No. We don't."

"Yeah, we do. I just can't… I just can't figure out how… Your face… It's so familiar…"

"We need your help," Cody intervened.

"…Hello to you too, Cody. I should've guessed this beautiful woman would be a friend of yours. But I don't recall you ever bringing her here. So, it doesn't exactly answer my question of how she and I know each other."

"We don't know each other," Erica said.

"Yeah, so drop the act," Cody added.

"This isn't an act," Jynx replied. "I know I know her… I just can't remember how… which is odd, because I have a photographic memory when it comes to…" Cody's unwavering glare forced Jynx to get back to the matter at hand. "…Okay, never mind. What do you want?"

"Well, as you can see…" as Cody began, Jynx turned his attention back to Erica, determined to find out how the two supposedly knew each other.

He held her chin in his hand, examining her features, then raised her face to look her in the eyes. "I know your face, that's for sure. But that scar is new."

Erica bit down on her bottom lip, in a bid to maintain her composure. "I recognise that lip biting thing too… All too well. What's your name?"

Damn, he was hot.

His green eyes even had electrical sparks running through them.

They were almost hypnotic.

Almost.

What *was* her name again?

No, Cody had told her not to give up her identity.

"My name is…" she stammered.

"…She's my Vixen," Cody exclaimed, bringing her back to reality. Upon hearing those words, Jynx pulled his hand from Erica's face, while she glared at Cody, relentlessly.

"Your Vixen?! I'm not your…"

"…Yeah, my Vixen. And before you ask, she's a real feisty one. Dr Arack built her to help me deal with Megan's death."

Erica knew he was trying to downplay her identity. But the way he was going about it, was infuriating. Vixens and Victors were built like Adams and Eves with only one difference… Their purpose.

They were hot as hell, built like Adams and Eves, but with minimal wiring systems. However, while Adams and Eves were built with free will, Vixens and Victors were programmed to *love* their masters and mistresses only. Technically, they were glorified sexbots. The finished product of money, technology, and corrupt individuals.

Jynx raised an eyebrow and, again, looked her up and down. "She doesn't even look like she's had any augmentations. And was that an accent I caught? She sounds exotic. Not to mention, I really can't shake the feeling that I know her, intimately."

Cody sent Erica what she assumed was a silent apology, then continued his conversation with Jynx. "Maybe Dr Arack downloaded her image data from a vid or something. But no, you don't know her. She's a unique prototype. There's none like her."

"Such a pity. We could've had fun together."

Erica held her tongue. Damn, he was forward.

"So, are you going to help us or what?" Cody asked, drawing Jynx's undivided attention.

"Help you?"

"As I was saying before... we're kind of tied up."

Another smile flashed through Jynx's eyes. He turned back to Erica. "Sex game gone wrong?"

Erica burst into laughter, forcing Cody to stare in disbelief. She was horrible at playing along. Again, she bit down on her bottom lip, refusing to say a word.

"For your information," Cody said. "We were captured by MIOT. And before you ask. They apparently disconnected my chip, so now we need to get into the city and contact Seth to find us."

But as Cody talked, Jynx continued to observe Erica. His smile widened and it was at that point that she remembered his abilities.

He was a Reader.

Uh oh!

Was he scanning her for a wiring system? Did he know they were lying?

Jynx turned back to Cody. "Alright, I'll help. I'll get those restraints off you... and I'm assuming you'll need a little money to get back home. I'm thinking eight hundred credits."

Eight hundred credits?

Damn, that was a lot of money. It was the equivalent to ten thousand dollars in Erica's world.

"You'll do that?" Cody asked in disbelief. "What's the catch?"

"I'm sure we can work something out."

Either the Maranthina temperature had just dropped significantly, or the tension between Cody and Jynx was enough to give Erica hypothermia.

"No," Cody argued. "Tell me your conditions, here and now. I know better than to go in blind."

"I want your Vixen."

"No deal. She's not for sale."

"Not even for a night?"

The eye-contact showdown between them was unwavering. "Not even for a minute... Not that it would take you that long to get your charge on."

Ha! Cody just made a sex joke. Erica was impressed. But Jynx was absolutely unphased. He considered his next price.

"You help me with a job."

"A job?"

"I'm breaking into Bateria, and I need a Coder."

"Why can't you get that other guy? Casey? His upgrades are platinum."

"We had a falling out."

"What happened?"

Jynx sent a quick glance at Erica before changing his demeanour, entirely. "That's not important. So will you help me or not?"

"I told you I was out."

Jynx went to step back into his house, until Cody finally conceded. "Alright. I'll help. But we leave Er... ah... Vixen out of it. Do you understand?"

"Deal. Now, follow me, the both of you. Let's get those restraints off." Erica and Cody followed Jynx into his small farmhouse.

One thing Erica loved about the farmhouses in Maranthina was that they allowed their residents to be self-sufficient without having to lift a finger.

While Jynx had personally chosen not to acquire animals like many others did, his vegetable crops were all tended to, thanks to technology. In all her years of writing the Maranthina books, Erica had always found the thought of self-cleaning houses brilliant. Personally, she loved a clean house – but didn't like cleaning, in general.

The moment she stepped into Jynx's house her excitement hit its peak. All around her, the floors and benches initialised their self-foaming settings to clean themselves.

Once they had reached the kitchen, Erica was alerted to the sound of water splashing and immediately searched for a dishwasher. She couldn't see one. Instead, the sound was coming from the cupboards.

Plates, cups, and cooking utensils could be put away in the cupboards – still dirty – and would undergo the adequate cleaning and air-drying needed.

"Let me take a look at those restraints," Jynx said, after leading she and Cody into the middle of the kitchen, right by his spotless dining table and two dining chairs. Erica turned around and raised her arms as high as she could to give him a better look.

She felt the slight pull as Jynx raised the contraption and knelt almost level with her waist.

"Hmmm... It seems MIOT used the TLX 25 model."

"That won't be a problem, will it?" Erica asked, turning to face him as Jynx stood back at full height.

"It won't be easy. But I love a challenge."

The tease in his voice was enough to raise the frustration in Cody, again.

"Just get the key," he said.

"Fine, have it your way." Jynx bowed his head to Erica and left the room.

"The wiring on that guy is way off circuit!" Cody huffed.

"I can't believe he's an actual Reader."

"I thought you knew that."

"I did, I just didn't expect his powers to be so... strong?"

"You and every other woman… and occasional man who meets him. I just need you to be careful, okay?"

"Just chill, alright? Did you really need to tell him I was your…?"

"…I found it!" Jynx declared on entrance. He was holding what looked like a similar scanner to the one Erica had seen at the MIOT Facility.

"Are you sure that'll work" Cody asked. "It's the C2 model. These are…"

As Cody spoke, Jynx placed his hand on Erica's forearm to turn her around. "…Cody, Cody, Cody. And you call yourself a Supreme Coder. All I did was upgrade it with the 26.5 chip and what we have here, is the ultimate skeleton key."

There was a click, which escaped Erica's attention thanks to the distraction of Jynx's fingers trailing soft circles on her arm. His hand trailed up the back of her shoulder, and towards the back of her head.

He shifted her hair from the base of her head, sending shivers up her spine.

"Hmm… What do we have…?"

Automatically, Erica's elbow swung back and connected with his face. Then, before he could react, her fist collided with his groin, forcing him to crumble as her restraints fell from her wrists. "Owww!"

"I'm *so* sorry, Jynx. I flinched."

"Flinched? Pfft! That was deliberate!"

"Like I said," Cody added. "She's my Vixen. I made sure she was built feisty."

"But I was only observing the…"

"…I already told you," Cody said, stepping between them. "They disconnected our tracking chips. Unless you have a communicator tucked away back there, then we need to head to the city." Cody's stomach gurgled. "…And get a bite to eat."

"Fine. But you're both very welcome to eat here," Jynx said, getting to his feet. "And I promise, I won't make another move on your Vixen." He paused long enough to make them think he was being sincere… "Unless of course she secretly wants me to."

He was cunning.

Beyond cunning.

But as he scanned Cody's wrist restraint, Cody and Erica exchanged glances. Despite their hunger, neither of them wanted to stay.

"If you don't mind, I'd rather just eat at home," Cody replied, as his wrist restraint hit the floor. "In fact, my bed is also sounding very appealing." He stretched and flexed his arms happily, before holding out his forearm to Jynx. "Now, you promised me funds."

"You remember our deal?"

"I help you with a job. We keep her out of it."

"Correct. The job's tonight."

Cody froze. Clearly, he had screwed up. Tonight, they had plans on reconnecting with Seth and the others, and working out a way to stop MIOT.

"I can't do tonight."

"Sorry, Cody. You can't back out now. If you don't help me tonight, I get to choose my alternate prize."

Jynx's eyes lingered back onto Erica.

"Fine!" Cody said, raising his voice. "But you never said it was to…"

"…I didn't? My mistake." Jynx hovered his forearm over Cody's arm, which ignited in a minor display of silver sparks.

"Money's in there," Jynx said, pulling away. "You'll find I even added a little extra. Buy her something special for me."

He sent Erica a wink, forcing her to mentally debate whether she hated or loved the type of character he was.

Regardless, he was somebody she could totally write a spinoff series for. Maybe she would send him on an adventure, where he meets a kickass heroine, who puts him in his place.

"It's time for us to go," Cody finally announced. "We have some things to take care of."

"Of course! Until tonight," Jynx said, leading them to the door. As Cody stepped outside first, Jynx placed his hand on Erica's shoulder and whispered, "Until next time, *Vixen*."

At that point, she knew that something was amiss. Did he know their secret? His fingers trailed up to the back of her head, and she instantly felt the same sharp pain that she had felt earlier.

"Are you coming?" Cody asked from the open door. She sent another look at Jynx, then made her way outside.

"Man, it feels so good to have movement back in my arms," Cody said as the two left the farmhouse.

"Agreed," Erica replied, staring up at the giant metal gates in the distance. "How long do you think it'll take us to get to your apartment?"

"About three hours."

"Good, because I'm just dying for something to eat."

"Same." There was a hesitation before he added, "I'm sorry for insisting that you come here. I guess I thought you could help us stop MIOT. But... all I've done is put you in danger."

It was a typical character response. But Erica wasn't just another character. "It's alright. It's not like you forced me through the portal. I came on my own volition. For one thing, I wanted to see that this place actually existed with my own eyes. I guess we can't even blame Megan for that one, huh?"

Erica thought back to Megan revealing that she had reversed the connection. While it was certainly a cruel form of punishment to dump them in the middle of nowhere with their hands tied, it felt like there had to be more to Megan's scheme. Did she have something to do with Seth's portal malfunction?

Or worse, was Seth in on Megan's plan?

If that was the case, how would she ever get home?

"Are you okay?" Cody asked, breaking the silence.

"I'm fine. But I won't be going home until I find out just what it is that Megan wants."

"I don't think so. We're sending you back to your world, the minute we find Seth."

"But I'm the answer to stopping her."

"And that's why it's safer for you to not be here. What if she kills you?"

"If she wanted me dead, I'd be dead already."

"No, we're sending you back."

His stubbornness made her grin.

Then, that grin evolved into laughter.

"Dude, I'm the author. You're *my* fictional character. Therefore, I'm the one holding all the cards. Now, let's just drop it, okay?" And with that, Erica stormed in the direction of the metal gates.

"You *were* the author, Erica."

She stopped, turned to him, and waited for him to go on. "But you have as much control over Maranthina as I do… No wait. You have even *less* than I do. You're absolutely *powerless*."

Unfortunately, he was right. After nine books she was ultimately powerless to control anything in the world of Maranthina.

||

ADELAIDE, SA – DEETS

Pressing her back against the wall, Deets watched Chloe pace Erica's living room, struggling to grasp the true reality of the situation. "So, you all came in through a portal?"

"Yes," Deets said. "Seth's portal, in fact."

"God! How is any of this possible?"

Seth held up his wrist screen to show Chloe the lights and icons built into his forearm. He pointed out the icon labelled 'transport'.

"By pushing this button here, my screen will display a menu where I can input the..."

"...I don't think that's what she was referring to," Adam cut in. "What I believe Chloe is trying to say is that she doesn't understand how Maranthina exists at all. To her, we've all been a work of fiction, up until this point."

"That's right," Chloe said. "Erica is an author, not a god. She doesn't have magical abilities."

"That's where you come in," Seth said, still focusing on his wrist screen to locate Cody's tracking chip. "You know the real Erica. Can you show us these unpublished pages? Maybe they hold the secrets we need."

Chloe considered his request, forcing Deets to wonder if they could truly trust her. Sure, the girl was pretty. But Deets had been fooled by pretty faces before.

"Yes," Chloe finally said. "But you need to promise you won't tell Erica that I granted you access to her computer. There's a lot of stuff on there. If it got out, she'd probably kill me."

The thought of Erica killing anybody made Deets giggle. While Seth believed Erica was a god... their god, in fact... to Deets, Erica was something else. She just couldn't quite figure out what that something else was.

She thought back to the vision of the little girl. There was no way Erica could be that girl. She wasn't even Maranthinian. Deets placed her tattooed hand on Chloe's shoulder. "I won't let Erica hurt you. You have my word and protection as a Huntress."

After an awkward glance, Chloe led them into Erica's home office and started up the laptop.

The screen requested a password. She typed in one after the other. Both were unsuccessful. "Dammit. I thought that second one might've worked."

Deets gestured for Chloe to give up the seat. "Child's play, Chloe. Watch the Huntress at work."

The minute Deets was in the seat, she hovered her fingertips over the laptop's keys – right where Erica's fingerprints were bound to be – and closed her eyes.

At first, she felt a light tingling as the electrical sparks ran from the computer and into her fingertips, initiating the connection. "If I was the creator of Maranthina," Deets said. "…And Megan was my main character, even though Deets is far cooler and more powerful…"

"…What's she doing?" Chloe asked.

"Getting into the mind of Erica," Adam replied. "She possesses some…"

"…Shh!" Deets hushed, just in time for pictures to form in her mind. "I'm getting something." But they weren't the visions she had expected… not at first, anyway. She saw Erica, a teenager, sitting in a guest chair of a dull, grey office.

Her fingers tapping on the desk.

Anxious.

Erica's eyes raised to the woman sitting before her. Long, mousey blond hair tied back in a ponytail and thick glasses. The woman looked to be in her forties.

"Don't leave me in suspense," Erica said. "What'd they say? Do they want me?"

The woman stared down at her notes then back at Erica. Mild disappointment.

"Erica, they read what you wrote in your journal."

Erica's face fell. "Oh, uh…"

"…They suggested you see a therapist."

"I'll do that. I promise. But did they…?"

"…No. They would rather keep looking."

"For fuck's sake!"

"Erica, don't swear."

"Sorry. But I'm guessing they'd prefer a kid who isn't as fucked up as…"

"…What'd I say?"

"As *screwed* up as me. A recycled, piece of paper that's been scribbled on, scrunched up and…"

"...Quit being so dramatic. What did we say about resilience? Besides, you'll be sixteen in a few months and provided you do agree to see a counsellor, I'd like to put your name down for the youth housing program. What do you think?"

Erica's eyes went wide.

Before Deets could hear her response, the vision changed to an older Erica sitting at her computer, with a *Create New Password* message in front of her.

Deets focused on the buttons that Erica typed on her keyboard. After the first attempt and error message appeared. *Password must contain 1 uppercase, 1 number and a symbol.*

Erica groaned, rubbed at her face, and made her second attempt. This time, a new error message appeared. *Cannot reuse old password.*

Frustrated, Erica tapped her fingers on the desk willing herself to come up with a new password.

"What are you doing?" a voice from behind made her jump. She turned to see Nick standing in the doorway, phone in hand.

"I need to come up with a new..." Erica started.

"...Hold on," Nick said, his eyes on his phone. He turned back to Erica. "Neko414 wants to know when Cody will finally declare his love to Megan."

A sheepish smile spread across Erica's face as she thought to herself. "Ah... soon. And he's going to be so sweet about it too. Tell Neko..."

"...Yeah, okay," Nick interjected, typing his response, and leaving her in peace. Erica, on the other hand, smiled to herself. Indication of a secret she would never voice out loud. She typed in her new password only for the computer to read: *Password has successfully been changed.*

"I've got it!" Deets declared, as she typed in the twelve-digit password that she had watched Erica create. The computer logged in to reveal the desktop image of an attractive actor who could've easily portrayed Cody if Maranthina were ever to be adapted for film and television.

"What was the password?" Chloe asked.

"I'd rather not say… It could prove useful later."

Chloe exchanged glances with Adam and Seth before taking control of the laptop and beginning her file search. When she reached a folder entitled: *Deleted Scenes*, she opened it to reveal eighty-seven documents with different titles. She clicked the first one entitled, *The existence of Maranthina.*

They all leaned forward and read in wide-eyed wonder.

###

MARANTHINA – ERICA

Erica stared up at the dark steel gates – which must've stretched beyond two hundred feet tall. Horizontally, it spread on forever, reminding her of a reinforced Wall of China, despite never having ventured there.

Standing at the entrance were four heavily armed security guards, all possessing heavy augmentation. Planted on the gate behind them, was a biometric access panel.

Despite the high security, Datsian City was anything but a safe and secure city.

"Is there anything I should know before we go inside?" Erica asked.

"Like what?"

"You've already made it abundantly clear, that I don't know everything about Maranthina… and that I'm powerless to do much else than manipulate a couple of lowly scientists with minimal willpower. I just need to know what else might happen, before I willingly walk in through, what could potentially be, the gates of hell."

"I wasn't trying to be a jerk. I was just…"

"…And I don't need an explanation. Just, what else will I need to be prepared for? Are we going to get attacked? You aren't going to trap me in there and make the security guards throw away the key, are you?"

"Erica…"

"…Forget it. I'm just hangry."

"Hangry?"

"Let's just get in there, okay?"

"Alright, but they're going to ask you for identification if I don't…"

"…If you don't register me as your sexbot."

"…Vixen," he corrected.

"Same damn thing."

"Not to me, it isn't. For one thing, I…"

But Erica didn't wait for his explanation. She hurried towards the security guards just as they aimed their weapons onto her. She stopped abruptly, just as Cody caught up and placed his hand on the access panel.

"She's with me," he said.

Driven by fear, Erica focused on her feet. She never did believe in a god, but in that moment, she prayed that some higher being would keep her safe.

The green light on the panel scanned Cody's hand, transmitting messages to the wrist screens of each security guard. The Officer nearest them read the transmission out loud. "Level Twenty-three Coder. Serial number 357AC98284JC. Home Port: 454 Neonite apartments, Datsian City."

Cody nodded. "That's correct."

The Officer pushed a few buttons on his wrist screen.

"It says here, your tracking chip was deactivated. Is there a reason for this interference?"

Judging by his expression, the question threw Cody off track. There was an unspoken rule in Maranthina, which was that MIOT could do whatever they wanted with no disregard for the law. Therefore, Cody explaining that MIOT had deactivated his tracker could either force the security guards to report their appearance directly to MIOT or otherwise render them as suspicious.

Cody shrugged. "Vindictive ex-girlfriend. She had it deactivated and stranded me out in the middle of nowhere."

"Make sure you get it reactivated before leaving again," the Officer said, before turning his attention back to Erica. "And who is she?"

"I'm..." Erica's eyes, again, landed on the large guns.

They didn't have guns like that in Adelaide. They only recently banned replica toy guns just for looking like weaponry. Suffice to say, she was terrified.

"...She's my Vixen," Cody said, wrapping an arm around her. "My ex did a number on the both of us, and I need to take her to Dr Arack ASAP. Poor thing can't even speak properly."

Despite him lying through his teeth, Erica could only assume that the Security guards were Readers just like Jynx. Maybe even more advanced. Still, they studied her for what seemed like forever. She could've sworn they would've shot her down at any minute.

That was until the Security Officer pushed a button on his wrist screen, and the gate behind them opened upwards, revealing the massive city on the inside.

Erica was stricken with awe.

Datsian City was so beautiful, so crowded and so technologically advanced that she thought she was dreaming.

Grey, black, and white skyscrapers disappeared into the clouds at every turn. Not only were there long traffic jams on every four-laned road, but there were also just as many vehicles flying through the sky. There were street vendors on every corner and people *everywhere*.

Every single person in Dastian City, bore at the very least, three physical augmentations each.

Cody passed through the gates and into the Maranthinian metropolis with a deep-set smile of pride.

In her awe, Erica forgot she was still standing in the gateway. "Wow. So, this is Datsian City," she remarked.

With a smile, Cody grabbed her hand. "Come on, let's get you something to eat." He led her into the hustle and bustle of the main street, with neither of them noticing the loud echo of the gate closing behind.

Across the road was a street vendor selling what looked like burritos but smelled like something else entirely. Cody bought two, with the scan of his palm, and handed one to Erica which she bit into instantly.

"It's a burrito," she assumed. "Only it tastes funny."

"An Amaralla, actually. Made from Muddler meat, grains... and yes, cheese. Would you like something to drink?"

"God, yes!" she said with her mouth full of food.

Erica took another bite. Sure, it tasted a little different to a burrito, but it still tasted good.

Cody's smile deepened as he pulled her towards a drink merchant, where he purchased two *Sparks*. While the drink was bitter, he assured her that it was safe for her consumption.

Next, they entered a Maranthinian version of a clothing store, filled with rows and rows of wired onesies all in assorted colours and sizes.

As Cody led Erica to a rack filled with women's onesies, she asked, "What are we doing here?"

"I'm buying you your very first synthetic suit. Pick a colour, any colour."

"Blue."

He took a blue onesie off the rack and handed it to her. "Go and try this on in the change rooms."

"It looks too big, Cody. I'm a size…"

"…Relax, it'll adjust to your size. It's the only suit you'll ever need."

"The only suit, really? What about when it's in the wash?" She thought her comment was a witty one, until he showed her the silver bracelet covered in buttons and a small screen, attached to the right sleeve.

"This grey button here is for self-cleaning, while these two buttons here let you input the occasion and design of your choice."

Erica stared at the garment.

Yes, her characters had worn them in her stories… But there she was in a Maranthinian shop, about to possess one of her very own.

She peered over at a console by a fashion portrait. "Let me guess, that's where I buy my design?"

"You can, but my home console allows us to order designs from other apps. It's so much cheaper that way."

Erica took the blue onesie and disappeared into the change rooms. Once she had changed out of her old clothes and into the suit, she was deeply disappointed, by how it looked on her. Sure, it had shrunk to fit her body, but it wasn't very flattering, in the slightest.

The silver button bracelet looked bulky and there was a zip at the back. The pant legs barely made it to her ankles and the neckline felt way too tight.

Erica peered through the curtain until she spotted Cody waiting a few feet away. "Hey, Cody? It's not very flattering."

"Of course not, you need to input the data first. There should be a sample console in there with you."

A sample console?

She turned to the console behind her. There were no buttons. Just a screen.

How the hell did she work the damn thing?

She peered out at him again. "How do I use it?"

"You scan the bracelet."

"Yeah, but where?"

His mouth dropped.

Surprise – or maybe, mild embarrassment.

He looked around to ensure that nobody was watching and entered the changeroom, forcing the space between them to become limited. Cody grabbed Erica's bracelet cuff and scanned it at the front of the console and the pale white screen lit up, displaying a menu of categories ranging from *Everyday Wear* to *Sleepwear.*

"All you need to do is pick a category," Cody said, as he tapped *Everyday Wear.* The screen showed eight images of different clothing styles. Four ideally for women and four ideally for men. There were also up and down arrows on the right of the screen. "Then pick whatever option you want to wear."

"So, I can pick any?"

"That's right. But you only get one free design with the suit. Anymore will cost extra."

As soon as Erica spotted an outfit she liked, she clicked it and pressed confirm.

"Not yet." Cody started. "Wait until I've…"

But it was too late.

Erica's onesie flickered translucent, instantly revealing her black bra and underwear before generating the style chosen.

"… left first," Cody finished, trying to not make eye contact with either her body or the mirrors surrounding them.

Erica's cheeks blushed almost as red as the dress style that she had chosen. "You could've told me it would do that."

"I didn't think you would confirm it *that* quickly. Even Deets takes an hour minimum to decide what to wear. How was I to know you'd pick the first style you saw?"

"Well, I'm *sorry* if I take less than the universally acceptable time it takes women to choose a style. I guess I'm just not like other girls."

He lowered his eyes, ever so slightly. "I beg to differ."

"Woah, hey! My eyes are up here, Casanova!"

His eyes travelled upwards again.

"What's a Casanova?"

"It's a man who… You know what? It doesn't matter, so get out!"

"Okay, but this makes us even."

"How does you seeing me in my underwear make us even?" He grinned with a raise of his dark eyebrows.

Whether he was silently referring to the humiliation he experienced upon waking up behind her that morning, or the multiple hand-cuffed bathroom breaks, she couldn't tell. Regardless, his reaction made her laugh. "Oh no. We're totally not even. In fact, this means war."

"War, huh? Suit yourself. But at least it looks good on you."

There was something about being so close to him that altered the moment, reminding her of just how attractive Cody was. There was also a bashful side to him that she found overwhelmingly adorable.

Especially when he smiled.

However, the very situation itself was dangerous, because it made her believe that he was more than just a character in her fictional book series...

It made her see him as a real person with a real life and real emotions. She needed to stop.

Erica glanced down at the red dress that the onesie had taken the form of.

There was a plunging neckline and the hemline reached just above her knees.

It was simple. Elegant. Stunning.

A little too stunning for the Datsian City streets.

"I think this might be just a little over the top for Everyday Wear," she said.

"It's fine. You've seen what the other women are wearing, right?"

"I have and my point still stands. Now, get out so I can get changed."

"As long as you're sure you have that *highly* advanced console sorted out."

"I've got it, don't worry."

"Are you sure? I can certainly stand by and…"

"…Out, Cody!"

He laughed but left just the same, giving Erica her much needed space for quiet contemplation. As she scanned through different clothing styles, she couldn't help but consider her current predicament.

She had only been in Maranthina for two days and already, despite the dangers, it felt more like home than Adelaide ever did.

To make matters worse, by creating Cody, she had subconsciously designed the most perfect love interest imaginable. Especially when she compared him to Nick.

###

ADELAIDE, SA – SETH

From his seating position on the floor of Erica's office, Seth pressed his back against the wall and continued to scan for Cody's tracker via his wrist screen.

In his frustrations, he had already mentally tuned out the conversations of Adam, Deets and Chloe as the three of them read through Erica's unpublished chapters. For in Seth's mind, he was to blame for the disappearance of his friend and the creator of Maranthina and nobody could tell him otherwise.

He tried to remember what had possessed him to locate Erica and ask for her help, then remembered it was an act of sheer desperation. He knew his end was coming soon and he wanted to ensure that there would be a happy future for Adam, Cody and Deets.

From the moment the orphanage burned down, while it was a somewhat joyous occasion, life had only gone downhill from there. The skills Seth and his friends possessed were only ever good for freelance work. Whether those jobs be erasing corporate data, jacking into government databases or other more malicious and scandalous roles.

That was how he met Adam.

And got noticed by MIOT in the first place.

But it was never the life Seth had chosen for himself, and after the death of Megan, well, they needed a clean break. Which was why he had sought out the one person who could save them all.

The very person who had a hand in everything.

Their creator, Erica.

Again, Seth refreshed the signal tracker only to be met by the same frustrating message.

CODY NOT FOUND.

"Damn it!" he got to his feet. "I'm done waiting around. I'm going back to Maranthina."

"But you'll never get through MIOT security," Adam replied.

"I know. That's why I'm going to enlist help."

"From whom?" Deets asked. "I'm not sure if you're aware, but we have *nobody*. Dr Arack can't risk getting caught again. And I'd rather go to the pit than work with Jynx. I can't believe Megan actually twitched him. Bleh!"

"Wait, what?"

Deets's mouth dropped. "Umm… I said nothing."

"No, you said that Megan twitched Jynx."

"Did I? No. I didn't."

"Yes, you did," Chloe argued. "That was never in the books."

"Alright, fine. Yes, they jacked into each other. I guess I'd just hoped I could push it out of my head. Like it was all just some bad dream or something. But yeah, it happened."

"Woah, woah, woah. A bad dream? So, she didn't tell you?" Seth asked.

"Of course, not. It was that disgusting twin thing. Like it was me sleeping with him… and enjoying it. But then when I looked up and caught sight of my reflection in his ceiling mirror. I was Megan and Jynx was… Well, gross! Please, don't tell me you're going to work with him."

Seth shook his head. "No. But when was that? Was it a memory of when she was alive or…?"

"Pit if I know. I had the dream a week after her death. I wouldn't put it past her to cheat on Cody. You guys always did believe that I was the evil twin."

"In that case. We'll leave Jynx out of it. Dr Arack too. Do we know other Coders?"

Adam thought for a moment. "Well, there is Casey. And that woman… Damn, what was her name? The one with the eyes?"

"Nika?" Deets asked.

"That's the one."

"Perfect," Seth said. "We can use the console at Cody's apartment. See if we can maybe jack into the security terminals again and…"

"…What about me?" Chloe asked. "I wanna help."

"I'm sorry. But you'll need to stay here. Maranthina is too dangerous."

"Seth's right," Deets added. "We need you to keep reading through all this. My intuition is telling me the clues are here. *Somewhere*."

At least, they had a plan, Seth thought to himself. It was more than they had, five minutes ago. He just wasn't sure if it would work. But he couldn't just stand around and do nothing.

Seth held out his hand to open a portal in the middle of the room, pushed the portal button on his wrist screen and envisioned Cody's holo console.

He closed his eyes, took a breath and...

Nothing happened.

He tried again.

Still, nothing.

"What's wrong?" Adam asked.

"I... I'm not sure."

"Are you sure you're doing it right?" Deets asked.

"Of course, I am. Maybe, I'll try taking us to the Datsian City gates." Seth input the coordinates to the new destination into his wrist screen, pushed the portal button and, again, waited only to receive the same result.

"Uh oh," Deets said.

Seth tried two more destinations, but still couldn't open a portal. "I think we're in trouble," he finally said.

"Can you send any messages to Maranthina?" Adam asked. "Try sending something to our home console."

Seth sent a test message to *HOME CONSOLE*, but his wrist screen came up with a single error message.

CANNOT REACH HOME CONSOLE.

He showed the others.

"Oh, shit!" Deets said.

Though nobody spoke the unsettling truth out loud. The truth, that they were stuck in Erica's world.

12

MARANTHINA – ERICA

Following their shopping trip – where Erica settled on an emerald-green blouse and a pair of black tights – Cody led Erica to a fifty-two-storey apartment building west of the city.

The heart of Datsian City was filled with fountains homing exotic fish, upscale buildings with highly advanced architecture and clean streets with a supposedly non-existent crime-rate.

Unfortunately, that all changed when Erica and Cody travelled west where every smashed building and sidewalk was covered in graffiti and chaos.

In the time, it had taken them to arrive at the neonate apartment complex, they had already bore witness to three muggings and one gang-related electrocution.

Erica followed Cody into a caged elevator where he placed his palm on the panel to get it going. His apartment was on the thirty-third floor.

"You're quiet," he said, acknowledging her silence.

"I guess I'm just tired. It's been one hell of a day and my legs hurt."

Erica was surprised to find the elevator only took a few seconds for the doors to reopen, before Cody led her up a dimly lit hallway, to the ninth door on the left.

"One more palm panel," he joked, as his advanced home security system opened the door to allow them entrance into his neatly furnished – though very compact – apartment.

"Welcome home, *The Coding Master*," the feminine voice of his AI security said. "It has been five months, three weeks, and twenty-two hours since you last checked in. Thank you for your automatic rental payment of five-hundred credits. Your electricity has been restored. Would you like me to register your guest?"

"No, Della," Cody replied. "That won't be necessary."

"Acknowledged. Would you like me to set the mood for sensual lovemaking? May I recommend Cuatro Synthesis?"

Soft mood music began to play, and the lights dimmed, forcing Erica to giggle and Cody's face to turn bright red. "No, Della. Just shut off!"

"Would you like me to...?"

"...No, Della. Shut off... Shut off!"

"Acknowledged. Shutting off, *The Coding Master*."

"Advanced home security, my ass," Cody remarked. "Sometimes it's near impossible to get those things to shut up."

Erica laughed, merely glad that it wasn't her in his place. It was also cute to see him powerless to deal with his own home security system.

Once again, it made him... *real.*

Uh oh!

In a deliberate attempt to take her mind off her troublesome train of thoughts, Erica glanced around at her surroundings. The apartment had a U shape layout.

Just past the entrance way sat Cody's desk with a laptop, a holo console cube and two monitors. The desk chair looked like it had been made from expensive leather. Next, there were two large windows to the city outside. Facing the windows, were two grey-seater couches and a glass coffee table in between. A double bed without blankets was nestled in a cube-shaped cove opposite the couches. Parallel with the desk was a kitchen sink, oven, and fridge. Just past the kitchenette was another door, which Erica only assumed was where the bathroom was located.

"Nice place," she said.

"Thanks," Cody replied, taking the seat at his desk, as he switched on the holo console then gestured to the door on the other side of the apartment. "The bathroom is through there. Make yourself at home while I send a message to Seth."

"No worries."

"No, *what?*" Cody glanced at Erica, as she made her way to the window by the couches.

"It's just Australian slang. It means 'okay'."

"Huh. Well, no worries then." He turned back to his console and set to work.

From the large open windows, Erica took in the view of Datsian City, directing her focus to the cars that were literally flying past the windows.

"How do we know the cars won't smash into the window?" she asked.

"That's impossible," Cody said, looking up from the console. "Each car is designed with energy barrier technology, which automatically stops it from hitting other vehicles and objects. Just like the ones that don't fly."

"But what's stopping them from floating up into space? Why do they stay on route?"

Cody chuckled. "Didn't you create them, oh *wise creator*? You tell me."

Erica stopped, stunned. She should've known the answer to that one. She was the goddam author and it was a simple question of Maranthinian physics.

But why didn't she know it?

Cody joined her at the window before answering her question. "The cars are programmed with directional control and built-in fail safes in case of hacking or rogue viruses. So don't worry. We're safe."

A very comforting thought. Erica focused on a stylish silver car in the distance and subconsciously pressed her hand against the glass. To her surprise, the glass turned black, forcing her to retreat. "Oh, I… err… I think, I broke it."

"No, you just set up the television. Those buttons to the right there control it. So can Della."

Erica observed the buttons to the right of the screen, analysing what each one did, as Cody headed back to his desk. Suddenly, a soft persistent beeping emanated from the holo console.

"Shit!" Cody cursed, forcing Erica to make her way over.

"What's wrong?"

Cody pushed the button labelled *Holo*, then pressed Seth's name. The screen went blank.

"I can't reach Seth."

"Why not?"

"I'm not sure. Even if he has gone back to your world, I should still be able to reach him because his current location upgrades are through the roof."

"What about the emergency servers? Maybe there's an interference."

"I tried. I can send transmissions… He just doesn't seem to be receiving them."

"Wait, didn't Megan plant the chip for Seth to find? What if she did something to it?"

"Like plant a virus, or something?"

"Perhaps."

"While that's a possibility, his system would've automatically cleaned the chip the moment he installed it."

"But it could potentially explain that portal malfunction he was having earlier. Maybe Megan's plan all along was to separate us from the others. Trap them wherever they are, while we're trapped... here."

"That's..."

"...Exactly how I'd write it in a major plot twist."

"Erica..."

But she wasn't hearing him. Her mind was running a hundred miles a minute. "...I'm guessing she wanted to..."

"...ERICA!"

"Yeah?"

Cody sighed and lowered his tone. "Megan might be cunning and vindictive but despite all that, she saw Seth as a brother. Sometimes they were even closer than she and Deets. Insinuating that she would betray Seth that way is a little farfetched."

"Yeah, and the love story between you two could surpass a billion life-recycling times yet look how that turned out."

Cody lowered his gaze to the time on his console. "Whatever the situation is, I need you to stay here. Keep trying to reach Seth and the others. I'll register you with Della and grant you privilege to order food, access the television and even use the shower."

"I need privilege to use the TV and shower?"

"It's more about personalization. You'll figure it out. But I need to get ready to meet up with Jynx. Alright?"

Good on his word, Cody headed out not long after registering Erica with Della. After three more failed attempts to send messages to Seth, she decided to try her luck with the window TV screen, only to find that

Maranthinian television was nothing like she had ever imagined.

In her books, her characters never had time to watch television, for they were far too busy with their adventures. But now that she was living their reality and bored out of her mind, she had been thrust into the world of science-fiction soap operas and MIOT infomercials. Sure, they weren't real science-fiction soap operas... they were regular soap-operas.

But to Erica's perception of life, science-fiction soap operas were exactly what they were.

After the tenth MIOT product advertisement, she decided to go for a shower.

In the match-boxed sized bathroom, she was surprised to find that there was room for not only a toilet, sink and shower, but also a spa bath underneath the shower. Mirrored tiles lined the walls from floor to ceiling and, to Erica's surprise, there were no taps.

"Della? How do I turn on the water?" Erica asked.

"*Almighty Erica,* would you like to utilize the shower facility or the bathtub?" Erica chuckled at the registered name and considered the question.

"I'll have a bath. Thank you, Della."

At her request, a faucet emerged from the wall and immediately began filling the tub with water.

Erica undressed and climbed in, to find that the water was too hot.

"Della, can you please add some cold water?"

"Very well, please notify me when the water is of the right temperature and height."

Erica did just that, and even requested for the spa jets to be turned on, and it wasn't long until she was relaxing with the taps hidden back into the mirror-tiled wall.

As she lathered her hair with shampoo, she couldn't help but flinch at the pain to the back of her head. Remembering who or what had knocked her out at MIOT, was almost impossible, but the bruising still hurt to touch. She massaged it lightly until her thumb brushed against something small and hard sitting just under the base of her skin. It had four hard edges and was about the size of a small coin.

She separated her hair and positioned herself, to see the back of her head through the tiled mirrors, where she was met by sheer horror.

There was a small, rectangular object implanted just under her skin.

Was it a chip?

How had she not noticed it sooner?

Her mind instantly went to Jynx's earlier observations. Had he seen it? And if so, when was he going to tell her about it?

MIOT had to have done it after they had caught her the second time. But why would they disconnect Cody's chip, only to install one into her, instead?

"Farfetched, my ass!" she cursed. MIOT had clearly led Erica and Cody into a false sense of hope.

Those fears only led to Erica's next question.

If they had already planted a chip into her head, what else had they had done without her knowledge?

And with that thought, Erica's moment of relaxation was over. She hurried out of the tub and searched desperately for a towel, only to find that there were none. "Della? Where are the towels?"

"Have you finished with your bath, Almighty Erica?"

"Where are the goddam towels?"

"Cannot locate 'goddam towels' in the Maranthinian vocabulary. Have you finished your bath?"

"How can you not know what a towel is?"

"Almighty Erica, have you finished your bath?"

"Yes, I've finished my bath."

"Initializing drying sequence."

Before Erica could determine what 'initializing drying sequence' even meant, air vents emerged from the walls, instantly unleashing hot air, like an electric blow dryer. The heat was hotter than anything Erica had ever felt. "Oww, oww, oww! Okay, Della stop!"

But Della didn't stop. The vents were too loud for the AI to register her voice. Erica tried to open the door, but it wouldn't unlock.

"Open the door and stop the vents!" Erica said, even louder this time. Red burns began to appear all over her body. Erica crumbled to the floor.

"STOP THE VENTS, DELLA!" she yelled.

Finally, the vents stopped and disappeared back into the walls. Erica clambered to open the door. It was still locked. "Unlock the door, Della." There was a click and the door opened. Erica retrieved her blue onesie and bolted out of the bathroom into the arms of an incredibly surprised Cody.

"MIOT planted a chip in my head and your bathroom just tried to kill me," she yelled.

"And you're *naked*... wait, what did you just say?"

Upon realising what Cody had just said, Erica became very well aware of just how bad her situation had become.

Not only was Cody there to see her wearing absolutely nothing at all... But Jynx was there too.

And he saw *everything*!

After Cody had escorted Jynx out of his apartment so Erica could get dressed in private, the three sat on the couch explaining the complicated situation. In a normal Maranthinian world, Vixen's didn't usually complain about the chips implanted in their heads. So, the fact that Erica had done exactly that was a dead giveaway of the lie she and Cody had told Jynx earlier.

"Cut the crap, Cody. I'm a Reader, remember?" Jynx said. "Maybe if you had just been honest from the beginning, I would've told you I read the chip the instant I met her. Just as I could've also told you that there were no other wiring systems in her entire body... at the time."

"Wait, you scanned me?" Erica scoffed.

"Of course, I did. You're a fascinating prototype. When I look at Cody, I immediately see his internal coding network, his thermo-wiring system, his chips, motherboards… and all that other junk. You piqued my interest because of how familiar I found you."

It was an eerie thought.

"You haven't had any other upgrades that allow you to see flesh through clothes, by any chance, have you?"

"Sadly, no. But my photographic memory of you walking out of that bathroom earlier will certainly suffice."

Erica groaned.

"Has it ever occurred to you, that those sleazy pickup lines only make you appear less attractive each time?"

"Has it ever occurred to either of you that it would've been much easier if you had just been honest from the start? Like first of all, where are the others? And second, how have I never met anybody with your accent?"

Just as Erica attempted to come up with another quirky line, Cody shook his head in defeat.

"Her name is Erica," he said.

"Seriously, Cody?!"

"Well, he was bound to find out eventually. And let's face it, we might need his help."

"Alright, fine! Yes, I'm Erica and I have absolutely no augmentations... except for this damn chip in the back of my head, because I'm not even from here."

"Where are you from?" Jynx asked.

"An entirely separate universe."

Jynx didn't even seem surprised. Erica was about to explain further when his eyes turned pure white, and his face adopted a blank expression. He was receiving a mindlink. "Alright. I'll be there," he said after a moment of silence.

Once his eyes had returned to their original green, he addressed Erica and Cody quickly. "My apologies, it seems I'm needed elsewhere."

"What about Bateria?" Cody asked. "I thought you needed me to jack into their systems tonight."

"I do. But right now, you've got bigger problems. If you like, I can ask around. See if I can get some intel on the whereabouts of Seth and the others." Before Cody could reply, Jynx disappeared out the door.

"Do you trust him?" Erica asked.

"Not personally. Wherever he's gone, it must be big."

"MIOT?"

"Possibly."

"What are we going to do about this chip?"

Cody glanced at the door then shrugged. "I was thinking of taking you to see Dr Arack tomorrow. Until then, it's getting late. You're welcome to take the bed if you want."

Erica peered over at the bed. There were absolutely no blankets, and the cold was coming in fast. And thanks to the Maranthinian inbuilt thermo-wiring systems she doubted anybody owned a heater. "Do you think maybe you could lend me some clothes or something? You don't exactly own any blankets or *towels*."

"The only clothes I own are socks and underwear because our suits clean themselves, remember?"

Then he understood her point. "Oh… huh!"

Well, that made things awkward.

After having Cody see her naked, the last thing Erica wanted was to complicate things by sharing the bed with him for body heat.

"It's alright," she said, getting to her feet. "Maybe I can order a clothing style on that app."

"Sure. I'll help you."

After two hours of searching, Erica was disappointed to find that no matter what design she chose, the thickness of the material was just too thin to successfully battle the Maranthinian cold.

Thus, she was left with two choices.

The first was to invest in a full body augmentation of thermo-wiring. The other… was to swallow her pride and share the bed – and body heat – with Cody.

Despite her frustratingly complicated thoughts, she picked the latter and as the cold swept in through the windows, she couldn't help but guiltily feel at peace with that decision.

Cody's arm wrapped around her waist, careful not to land anywhere that might be misconstrued. His breathing was soft and relaxed, leading her to assume that he had fallen asleep relatively quickly, which gave her time to think.

There had to be some clues to Megan's plans.

A reason for the chip.

Was there a clue that Erica was missing?

Something...

"...Has anybody ever told you that you think too loud?" Cody asked, startling her. His voice was a mere groan, so he had to be either half asleep or talking in his sleep.

"Think too loud?" she asked, turning to him in the dim light. His eyes were closed but he still answered her.

"Just stop your thoughts and go to sleep. We'll discuss it in the morning."

He ran his fingers through her hair, forcing her eyes to close, lazily. But when Erica's eyes opened again, she was no longer in the bed.

Instead, she was on her back in a large bathtub, kicking and screaming as a pair of feminine arms held her down – forcing her beneath the surface of the water.

"No… no…!" Erica spluttered.

The water filling her lungs.

As hard as she struggled, she was too weak to overpower the mysterious woman. Erica brought her – *somewhat smaller* – hands to the woman's arms, gripping her tight.

Was this a memory of her youth?

Despite growing up in the system, Erica couldn't remember being forced underwater.

Not like this.

Maybe she had unlocked some memory which had been hidden by trauma.

As her lungs filled with water, Erica focused on her small hands, clasping the woman's arms tight, and feeling the static ignite from her palms.

Then she saw it.

Small white sparks of electricity flickering from her very own fingertips.

There was no way this could be a memory.

She wasn't Maranthinian.

Maybe it was her imagination.

A scene she needed to write.

Erica wasn't drowning.

No, she had to be dreaming.

But why did it feel so real?

The woman's hands gripping her shoulders – drowning her. Her lungs filling with water.

It all felt too painfully real.

Dream or not, Erica needed to free herself. She focused on the sparks emanating from her hands and closed her eyes, praying for the best outcome.

Until she heard a gut-wrenching scream as the woman fought for her life against a violent electrocution... The electrocution Erica was delivering to save her own life.

...And then, there was silence.

13

MARANTHINA – ERICA

For the briefest of moments, it was easy for Erica to forget that she wasn't in her own bed. She could feel the sunlight pouring in through a crack in the curtains. Her breathing was soft.

Relaxed.

Her eyes still closed.

There were no portals to Maranthina. People weren't built with electrical wiring systems and advanced technological augmentations. It was all a world of science fiction that she had created to make a few bucks.

Nick was right. She needed to stop writing.

ZZZZZ.

What was that noise?

ZZZZZ.

There it was again.

And then, she felt it. There was something digging into her back... and it was *vibrating*.

Was it her phone?

She thought back to the previous night. Had she gotten drunk and left a certain *item*, out of her bedside drawer?

She brought her attention to the weight of an arm pressed against her waist...

How much did she drink last night?

ZZZZZ.

She moved her hand to fish behind for the vibrating object and froze, the instant she made contact.

Realization hit...

…Uh oh!

Her eyes flashed open as she remembered the reality of her situation.

Portals were real. Maranthina was real… and there she was sleeping beside one of her main characters.

And that vibrating thing in her hand?

Well, that was the morning glory of a Maranthinian male with an electrical wiring system.

She sat up at the exact same time as Cody. Each of them as stunned as the other.

"What the hell?" she spat.

"What do you mean, *what the hell*? You're the one with your hand on it!"

She was?

Oh, right.

She was.

And it was still *vibrating*.

Erica ripped her hand away and jumped out of the bed. "Oh god, oh god, oh god! I can't believe I just… Why the hell was it vibrating?"

Cody remained on the bed, awkwardly focusing on living through the experience. "Because that's what it does when a guy reaches full recharge."

"Full recharge?"

It sounded so bad.

"You know? After a goodnight sleep or when he… Well… Never mind. I thought you knew all this."

She did know it.

Only she had never anticipated experiencing it, firsthand… Quite literally, in fact!

However, no matter how embarrassing it was, it could never pale in comparison to her running out of the bathroom naked, the night before. With that memory still fresh in her mind, and Cody sitting on the bed dealing with his own humiliation, Erica hightailed it to the bathroom, preferring to take her chances with the death-defying air vents.

As Erica sat on the toilet, looking around at the spaces in the walls where the air vents had emerged the night before, she vowed that she would find a store that sold fabrics just to make towels and blankets for herself.

Then, she scolded herself for not being more determined to find a way back to Adelaide.

That was her home, after all.

But what then?

If she returned to Adelaide with stories of actually having visited Maranthina, her world's doctors would consider her mentally unstable, lock her away and throw away the key.

Then again, all writers were crazy, to some extent.

They could create worlds and characters which felt far too real but were nothing more than figments of their imagination.

And if the writer did their job well enough, they could persuade readers to believe in those works of fiction too.

But there was a fine line between the mental instability of a writer and the purely insane.

Unfortunately for Erica, she felt as if she had surpassed that line altogether. Maybe these experiences were nothing more than hallucinations while she underwent shock therapy.

Did they even do that anymore?

Whatever the case, it would make for another brilliant story.

An intrusive knock on the other side of the door, stole her from her thoughts. "Yeah?" she called out.

"I was thinking of making breakfast before we see Dr Arack. Did you want anything?"

The mere mention of food made her stomach growl.

"I'll be out in a minute," she called back.

Erica finished on the toilet, washed her hands, and focused on her long-sleeved blue pyjamas in the tiled mirrors. Not an ideal choice to wear in the Maranthinian streets.

She pushed the self-cleaning button on the metal cuff and was instantly alerted to the soft vibrations all over her body as the suit did its job.

Thankfully, the suit didn't use excessive heat.

Once the cleaning process was over, a fresh floral scented mist was unleashed under her armpits.

A built-in anti-perspirant?

The nanotechnology of the suit was incredible!

With newfound excitement, Erica pushed the *Style Change* button and watched her reflection as the suit changed from one fashion to translucent fabric, to another style again. She found it mesmerising how each particle of fabric changed colour, shape, and size just by the touch of a button.

It reminded her of chameleon skin.

Erica settled on one of the outfits, an off-the-shoulder blue top, with faded grey jeans, before fixing her hair with her hands. As she combed through the back, she brushed against the chip, which she had almost forgotten about.

At least, it wasn't too noticeable.

Not that it mattered much in a world filled with augmented beings. But it was a reminder of the haunting dream she had experienced through the night.

She brushed off the thought and left the bathroom, in time to see a shirtless Cody stirring a bowl of batter, beside the stove. A strange sense of normalcy in a world filled with such advanced technology.

"You live in a world like this, yet you still cook like somebody from my world," Erica jested.

He turned to her but kept stirring with his wooden spoon and a smile.

"Why not? I find it enjoyable. Did you know the ancient Maranthinians used to cook like this?"

"Yes, I did." Erica joined him at the bench. "It also makes me wonder why you never opted for major augmentations like a wrist screen or a built-in communicator, which really would've come in handy these past few days."

Cody brushed a short lock of hair from his eye before tipping small amounts of batter into the frying pan. "I'm surprised *you* don't have an answer for that. You literally got into all our heads while writing our stories."

"It didn't suit your character. I guess I felt controlling your free will, to better suit the plot, felt pointless."

"Every choice I've made, whether it has been recorded in your books or not has been of my own accord," he explained as he flipped a pancake perfectly. "Sure, you believe you set up the events that made me fall in love with Megan. But you weren't responsible for my feelings. Nor are you responsible for her actions now."

She wasn't?

But that was the very job of a writer. To make her characters fully experience stories as people did life. Love, hate, happiness and anger were all parts of that.

"Why do you think that?" she asked.

Cody turned down the heat and gave her his undivided attention. "Let's say the theory of you being the almighty author is correct. Here, you are in a world that you created, and you only possess a minimal sense of control. Technically, you should be able to snap your fingers and have anything you wish. But you can't. You've proven that already."

"But that's what makes it a hero... or heroine's journey," Erica argued as he set to work serving the pancakes onto the plates. "The heroine finds herself in a crazy situation where all the odds are stacked against her. Then gradually, she learns to genuinely believe in herself and saves the day. Only when I've reached the pinnacle of my arc, will I be able to embrace my true author powers and get the ending I want or need."

"And which ending is that?"

That simple question left her stumped. Initially, she believed the ending would be for her to break through her writer's block, but now her arc had profoundly changed so much, in such a brief time.

Taking her silence as a queue, Cody pressed on with that matter. "Do you know what I think?"

"No. But you're gonna tell me."

"I don't think you're looking at this story correctly. Yes, you have some powers which prove you're tied to this world... You can see into our lives... our minds... But you can only see the things you're allowed to see. I think you're tied to us in a different way. And when you learn what way that is, only then will you understand what you're ending is supposed to be." He handed her a perfectly decorated plate filled with pancakes, fruit and cream and took his own to the couch.

"That theory just makes things more complicated than they have to be," she argued, following him.

But Cody merely shrugged a smile.

"I guess we'll see. Maybe Dr Arack will be able to give us some answers."

###

ADELAIDE, SA – DEETS

Thanks to the complicated Maranthina-Adelaide time difference, it was currently 11:15pm as Deets, Seth, Adam and Chloe found themselves strategizing in Erica's home office. "What do you think they're doing right now?" Chloe asked Deets who was poring over a stack of rough drafts they had printed out.

To be perfectly honest, Deets had no clue. But with the adorably friendly Chloe asking, she felt obliged to say something. Yet, before she could offer an attempt at an answer, Seth spoke up with his eyes still glued to his wrist screen. "I'm not sure. I just hope they got out of MIOT alive. If not…"

"…Don't talk like that," Adam said. "Maybe they did survive, and whatever is interfering with your portal system is the same thing preventing them from sending us transmissions."

"It's possible," Seth replied. "Or they could be dead."

Deets furrowed her brow at Seth. It wasn't like him to be so blunt. That was her job. Alas, Seth's comment brought out a side in Adam that was rarely seen.

"I can't talk to you when you get like this. You're starting to sound as pessimistic as Deets!"

That was it!

Deets couldn't bear to watch her friends fall apart. "To the Pit with both of you!" she exclaimed, getting to her feet. "I get it. We're stuck here. But we've been through tougher shit than this. Can't we just…?"

She stopped mid-sentence, as she was met by a violent vision, forcing her entire body to freeze into a standstill and her eyes to turn pure grey.

"Deets?" she could hear Adam say. "She's getting a vis…" But his voice died out as she dropped to her feet and screamed in pure agony at the pain in her head.

A series of images raced through her mind.

Chaos. Destruction. Death. Maranthina was dying.

And she saw it all.

She was standing at the mouth of an acid pit, alongside Adam and Cody in the dead of night.

Tears of anguish on all their faces.

But where was Seth?

Deets tried to ask her friends just what was going on. But the words just wouldn't come.

Then she saw it.

The silhouette of a woman. Her face was cloaked in shadow. Despite not being able to see her, Deets knew the woman almost as much as she knew herself.

She was one of them.

Was it Megan?

The woman hugged Adam.

It *had* to be Megan.

Then she approached Deets.

But Deets couldn't bring herself to look at her. Instead, she forced her gaze to the ground. She didn't want to break down and cry. Yet, the mysterious woman cupped her face and brushed away her tears with her thumbs, forcing Deets to look up.

No, that didn't make any sense.

Deets couldn't cry.

She had purposely gone through a procedure to prevent herself from crying, a long time ago.

Still, Deets looked up through tearstained eyes knowing that it was time to say goodbye. "Don't go," she begged, as the woman's face came into view.

But it wasn't Megan.

...It was *Erica*.

"I have to," Erica said.

"No, you don't. I was built to protect you. To make sure you live. I can do this. *Let* me do this."

But Erica was adamant. Far more adamant than Megan had ever been.

"No. This is my destiny. I love you."

Deets nodded. She had to let Erica go. She had no choice but to. Erica turned her focus to Cody.

"I'm not letting you throw your life away," he said with sheer conviction.

"I'd rather sacrifice myself than watch you all die," Erica replied.

Bravery suited her all too perfectly.

"Well, I'd rather die than live without you," Cody argued.

"You won't be alone forever. None of you will. I promise." Erica turned back to Adam. "Say hello to Seth for me."

Those words.

Again, *where was Seth?*

Erica stepped backwards and they all tried to reach for her… But it was as if there was an invisible forcefield preventing them from moving forward.

Erica gave one last smile, before allowing herself to fall backwards into the pit… Gone forever.

Deets wiped at her face to remove those damn tears. The moisture soaked into her inked hands. And then, reality sunk in, and she was no longer standing by the pit. She was in an entirely different world.

Erica's world.

With Adam, Seth, and Chloe.

But the pain from the vision felt far too real.

Deets stared at her hands.

They were dry.

No tears.

Just the trauma of a horrible hallucination. Then Seth's voice rang in as music to her ears.

"Deets? What did you see?"

14

MARANTHINA – ERICA

"How much can we tell him?" Erica asked, walking beside Cody through the rundown, though bustling streets of Datsian City. They were on their way to Dr Arack's clinic, and in her bid to fight off the overwhelming excitement.

Doctor Arack was a truly remarkable scientist with a heart of gold, responsible for building some of the most incredible augmentations known to Maranthina. Despite all his success, he had always managed to stay humble, even after having worked for MIOT.

Presently, he managed a rundown clinic where he assisted down-on-their-luck Maranthinians, who were unable to afford the expensive upgrades that MIOT often provided. Erica couldn't help but channel her excitement into an outpour of questions which Cody was obliged to respond to.

"You mean, how much can we *trust* him?" Cody asked, diverting Erica's attention from a lightning fight across the street.

"What I mean, is that you keep telling everybody this guy built me to be your sexbot. Do we need some false story to back that one up? If so, give me five minutes to come up with something remotely better."

"Better than being my Vixen? I don't see what your problem is, we've already slept together twice, I've seen you naked... and don't even get me started on the events of this morning."

Erica stopped to glare at his smiling face. "You might just be the worst character I've ever created."

"I thought the worst character you created was Jynx."

"I thought so too, but you just stripped him of that title."

"I think I'm okay with that." He walked on ahead, causing Erica to consider about a million ways to kill him off in her next book.

"We can tell him whatever we want," Cody finally said. "…But I should add, he's not exactly how you wrote him."

"What do you mean? And before you say it, I know he's been known to get his merch from unethical places like the Underground Markets. I can live with that."

"That's not what I was referring to. But it's good to know. What I mean is, he can be a little unstable."

Erica stopped. "Are you saying, he could potentially kill me with a simple chip removal?"

"No way! His work is brilliant. I just mean… Well, you'll see. Follow me." He led her down a dark alleyway, towards a filthy door located behind a large dumpster.

The location couldn't be more suspicious if it tried.

Oh, wait, yes it could.

The clinic had certainly seen better days. Its windows had been smashed, the chairs in the graffiti-covered room were broken beyond repair and the lighting was almost obsolete.

Cody approached the reception desk where a woman with bright red hair and almost as many tattoos as Deets, sat drinking a can of *Spark*.

"Name and ailment?" she said.

"I'm here on behalf of my friend. She's new." Cody said.

The woman looked at Erica, pushed a couple of buttons on her wrist screen and held it out to her. "Please scan your wrist and Dr Arack will see you shortly."

At the thought of being found out so easily, Erica's eyes grew wide. Sure, Cody used his left palm to connect with consoles, but his credentials chip was still located under the skin of his left wrist.

But Erica had nothing more than blood, bones, and veins under her skin.

She exchanged looks with Cody, and he immediately came to her defence.

"Can we just put her under my details?" he asked.

"Why? Is she here illegally?"

Cody's eyes practically bulged out of his head.

"No. Not illegally. Just…"

"…Cody!" The voice of a man looking to be in his sixties, with kind green eyes, an electrical visor and silver metal running from his balding head, down under his pale collared shirt, called from the doorway by the pot plant.

Cody turned to him with a large trusting smile etched into his cheeks. "Arack, you're looking like an antique since I saw you. What's it been? A month?"

"Ha! Very funny, boy. Keep that up and I might accidentally slip when delivering your twenty-second annual upgrade." Dr Arack said as he approached Cody and Erica at the desk. Cody's smile was quickly replaced with concern.

"You mean my twenty-fourth."

"Are you sure?"

"Yeah, you gave me my twenty-third seven months ago. Remember?"

But then, Dr Arack's confusion turned into a grand smile. "Got you! Two can play at that game."

Cody laughed. But Erica could tell he was deeply concerned. She had seen similar cases with elderly people dealing with Dementia.

It sent a pang to her gut, but she retained her smile even as Cody introduced her. "Dr Arack, I want you to meet my friend. Erica."

Dr Arack's kind eyes directed to her, and they were accompanied by that same friendly smile as he held out his forearm for her to connect with. Before Erica even knew what was happening, she found herself doing the same thing. Giving the traditional Maranthinian greeting.

"It's so good to finally meet you, Dr Arack!"

And she meant it.

"No, the pleasure is all mine, Araca."

"It's Erica," she corrected, adding emphasis to the E.

"My apologies. What did I say?"

"You said, *Araca*. But that's okay. Must've been the accent."

"Ara…" Dr Arack stared down at their wrists. His smile evolved into a look of confusion, urging Cody to intervene.

"That's actually partly why we're here, doc. Erica doesn't have her credentials in her wrist."

There was a long pause as Dr Arack stared at Erica.

It was awkward, though somewhat familiar to them *both*. "No, she doesn't. Does she?"

The doctor's voice sounded blank. As if he was trying to remember something but couldn't quite comprehend what that something was.

"I know she doesn't," he continued.

"You do?" Erica and Cody asked in unison.

"I just… have we met before?"

Feeling more uncomfortable than she had ever felt, Erica ripped her arm away as Cody took the reign of the conversation. "No, you don't know her. She... Can we just go to your office and talk in private? Please?"

Dr Arack agreed and escorted them to his makeshift office, which was in only a slightly better condition than the rest of the clinic.

"This is what I meant by unstable," Cody clarified as he and Erica followed close behind.

Unstable was *one* way of putting it.

As Dr Arack closed the door behind them, his bubbly personality quickly returned.

Amongst the mess of the office, Erica could make out a surgical bed, a desk, three chairs, and several cupboards filled with medicines, wires, and surgical equipment.

"So, what brings the two of you here?" Dr Arack asked, gesturing for Erica and Cody to sit with him at the desk. "Are we talking artificial inception, joint augmentations, weaponry... Stop me when I get it right... partner communication devices?"

Surprising even herself, Erica took the lead.

"I'm not from here."

"You're not?" Dr Arack asked. "You're from Beret, aren't you? I'm so glad you made it out alive."

Beret? Did he really think she was from Beret with the accent she had?

"Not from Beret…" Erica said.

This was why she loved writing. At least she could plan out how to say something first, instead of coming off as confusing or crazy.

Cody took Erica's hand in his. "Erica isn't from Maranthina at all. You see, during the explosion at MIOT, Seth found a multi-dimensional travel chip. It turns out that the chip worked… and Erica is from a different world."

Dr Arack stared at her. Then something clicked in his mind. "The multidimensional travel chip? Those sons of bitches stole my idea. Damn it!"

He punched down on his desk startling Erica… But not Cody, who hardly seemed surprised.

"You need to breathe, doc. That's not all they have done." The doctor looked back up at them through frustrated eyes, urging Cody to continue.

"The moment we brought Erica here, they kidnapped us and stuck a chip in her head. We need to get that chip out before she can return to her home."

While the frustration had drained from Dr Arack's eyes, the wheels still seemed to be turning in his head.

"So, you actually saw her world? What was it like?"

Cody chuckled. "Weird. Primitive."

"Hey!" Erica exclaimed, which made the doctor chuckle and Cody go on with his debriefing.

"There were no flying cars. Their networks were seriously slow, and buggy and they actually read books like the ancient Maranthinians used to. Also…"

"…Can we just get back to the chip in my head?" Erica interjected. "Stop dissing my world."

Dr Arack rubbed at his eyes as he struggled to comprehend just what he was hearing. "This isn't right. You can't be from another world. Other worlds don't exist. We tried... we tried it all. Everything was destroyed. They told me I was crazy. I lost everything for believing in those theories. How could they do this to me?"

Again, Erica felt uncomfortable. He was referring to the time MIOT had forced him to work for them before stripping him of everything. Still, she had a chip in her head that needed removal. She took her hand back from Cody and leaned towards the older man.

"I know it's hard to comprehend, Dr Arack. But it's the truth." She held out her forearm for him to scan. "I have absolutely no credentials, no thermo-wiring systems, and no augmentations. I can barely survive Cody's bathroom." Cody chuckled while Erica waited for the doctor to concede to the truth.

Finally, Dr Arack pulled down his visor, raised his wrist screen over her arm and scanned. Erica could feel the sparks – painlessly – zapping at her skin. When the doctor was done, he raised his visor and stared at her, impressed. "You're really not from here, are you?"

"Nope. I'm an Aussie. And it's so good to meet you, Dr Arack."

"That's not even the crazy part," Cody said. "Did you know, Erica actually wrote about Maranthina before finding out we were real? It's like she can see through our eyes."

"You don't say?" the doctor got to his feet and gestured for them to follow to the surgical bed.

"It's true," Erica said, taking her place on the bed. "I've been writing about this world for years. I used to dream about it so much that I knew I had to write about it. And those stories were so good I managed to get them published."

"Impressive," Dr Arack said as he put on a set of latex gloves. "I had a daughter who was obsessed with the possibility of other worlds."

"You did?" Cody asked. "You never told me that."

Dr Arack gathered his tools and sterilised what looked remarkably similar to an ear-piercing gun.

"I didn't?"

"Nope. Was she pretty?"

"Very. Smart too. You would've loved her."

Dr Arack brought the piercing-gun tool to Erica's right arm. "What is that thing?" she gasped.

"It will give you a dose of anaesthesia so I can remove the chip without having to put you to sleep."

"Okay."

She hated injections.

This wasn't any better. She glanced at Cody who was sitting beside her with a slight smile on his face.

"What?" she asked.

"Nothing. You're just... You just look so scared, right now."

"You find my fear amusing? You really are... OW!"

A sharp prick in her right upper arm forced her to flinch and for Cody to burst into laughter.

The guy was pure evil.

"You're a horrible person. You're the villain of my story. Do you know that?"

He shrugged again.

"Alright, Erica," Dr Arack said, cutting into their conversation. "I need you to lie face-down on the bed."

She obeyed and he set to work opening the skin at the back of her head. Thanks to the anaesthesia, all she could feel was a combination of pulling and prodding as he inspected the chip.

Despite the painless inspection, she couldn't help but feel entirely vulnerable.

"Is everything okay?" she asked as Cody joined Dr Arack to get a better look.

"Ah... Everything's fine," Cody said.

"You're lying. Now, tell me the truth."

There was silence as Dr Arack stitched her head back up and Cody returned to his seat, avoiding her eye.

"What is it, Cody?" she demanded.

Dr Arack discarded his tools then assisted her to a seated position. His concern mirrored that of Cody. "I'm sorry, Erica. I can't remove the chip," the doctor said.

"You can't? Or you won't?"

"Both."

"Both? What's that supposed to mean?"

Her anger was flaring out of fear. There was no way she could go back to Adelaide with a chip stuck in her head. She needed it out… Now!

"Erica… The chip. It was built by MIOT."

"I know that. That's why I want it out of my head. Tell him, Cody!"

Cody looked at a loss for words. "Erica. The chip has roots," he said.

"Roots?! What's that supposed to mean?"

"There's a network of roots stemming from the chip," Dr Arack continued. "And from what I can tell some lead into your brain, while others… I'm assuming lead to other parts of your body. Unfortunately, there's no telling what the chip does, just by looking at it."

"Network? What it…? What the *fuck!* That can't be right. Cut the roots and rip them out. I can't have some alien chip sending wires into my body. I'm not some *damn* Maranthinian!"

Cody coughed as if to be choking on nothing at all, but Dr Arack continued to address Erica's concern.

"Even if I wanted to… that chip has been designed to not be removed. It could potentially detonate."

"Detonate? Are you saying that it could blow up? In my head?"

"Yes."

There was nothing in the world… *worlds*… that could ever prepare her for that news.

"Shit!"

Erica's immediate visceral reaction poured from her mouth in the form of liquid fruit and pancakes.

15

MARANTHINA – ERICA

While it had taken exactly two hours and twenty-three minutes for Dr Arack to explain everything he knew about the chip, Erica had struggled tirelessly to register a single word spoken.

Normally when life went to hell, she would mentally escape into her Maranthinian stories, because at least there she had a little more control. But now that life was going to hell in Maranthina, finding control in her situation was damn near impossible.

"What do I do?" Erica finally asked as she and Cody found themselves sitting on the couch back at his apartment.

From Erica's recollection, Cody had listened intently to everything Dr Arack had said. It was because of that and the fact that he was mostly made up of wires and chips that she deemed him the best person to ask for advice.

But to her disappointment, he just shrugged. "I don't know what answer you want me to give, because what *I* would do, and what somebody from your world would do, are two entirely different things."

He had her there.

"Okay, so what would you do?"

"I'd wait to see what impact the chip has on my body then decide from there."

He was right.

That *was* vastly different to what she would do.

"What if it kills me?"

It was the very predicament she had subjected her characters to time and time again. The difference was that she could always find a way to bring her characters back if it killed them. This time, there was nobody who could bring her back.

Just as she allowed herself to suffer with those thoughts, Cody positioned himself to look her squarely in the eyes. "I doubt that MIOT wants you dead. The others and I... we can be used for recycled parts one hundred times over. You... Not so much."

"If they don't want to kill me, why would they put this ticking timebomb in my head?"

"It's Megan. I'm guessing she's playing the long game. Whatever that chip is programmed to do, I believe it's to keep you here."

In that moment, Erica was forced to remember the dream she experienced the night before. The one where she had possessed lightning abilities. She had killed the woman who had attempted to drown her. Was the dream some sort of prophecy? Like the type of prophecies Erica had subjected Megan and Deets to throughout her stories?

"I think, you might be right," she said.

"Huh? Are you feeling okay, or did you just agree with me?"

Erica started pacing. Her thoughts raced faster than she could process. "Last night, I had this dream. Like it was a memory that I don't remember having. Maybe it was from Megan's past. Or even Deets's past. I'm not sure."

"A dream? Like a vision?"

"Yes!" Erica said. "In it, I was a little girl, and I had these lightning powers. A woman tried to drown me... I couldn't see her face. Just maybe Megan is trying to tell her story through me... Or something..."

"...But that would mean..."

"...Megan's trying to be the author. It makes sense."

"Interesting theory... But why would she do that?"

"Revenge, for all the shit I put her through, perhaps?"

Cody gave a non-committal nod. "I can see it. But Megan was always one to go big or go home. There has to be more to it. Something bigger planned."

But Erica's thoughts were steamrolling in her head. "…as the author, Megan has the power to control an entire world, right at her fingertips. Not to mention, she's also working with MIOT… And MIOT has literally invented the technology to travel into my world."

"…Stolen. They stole their research from Arack."

"Still, they have it. They used it to get me here. I was their test… So was Seth and the others… But the question is, why?"

Erica's words came to an abrupt halt as she stopped pacing directly in front of Cody. He knew where she was going with her thoughts.

As did she.

But she spoke it anyway. "MIOT's going to destroy my world." With that realisation, Erica bolted to Cody's apartment door, until Cody stood in her way.

"Where are you going?"

"What does it look like? I'm going to stop them!"

Cody brought both his hands to her shoulders. "Erica... How can I put this lightly? Don't be so stupid!"

"Excuse me?"

He released her and took a breath. "I'm sorry but no other word comes to mind. You have seen through our eyes as we have gone up against MIOT repeatedly. You've seen Megan for what she is. You also have a chip doing Pit knows inside your brain. You have no electrical powers or major... as you call them... 'author powers', and here you are proposing to go up against MIOT by yourself? You'll get yourself killed! And if you really are the author, like you and Seth are so desperate to believe... than theoretically, you could potentially destroy both our world and yours!"

When he put it that way, it did sound a *little* stupid.

"What else can we do? I can't be the reason MIOT wipes out my home. I just won't allow it."

"I'm not saying you have to. I'm just saying there are better ways to go about it."

"Like how?"

"Ah, like... maybe we can keep trying to reach Seth and the..." As Cody tried to formulate a plan, Erica used that time to rush out his door, and down the hallway. She made it as far as the elevator, until she remembered she needed Cody's handprint to activate it.

"I'm not letting you throw your life away," he said, from behind her.

"This isn't your choice. Now, give me your hand so I can get on this damn thing."

He crossed his arms against his chest as she grabbed for his hand. They struggled, both as stubborn in their own convictions. Tempers equally rising.

"LET ME GO, CODY!"

"NO! I'm not losing you, *again*!"

Their stunned surprise provided Erica with the perfect opportunity to grab his palm and push it against the elevator panel.

"I'm not Megan. I just wish you would figure that out already."

The caged elevator opened before them, and Erica attempted to take a step. That was until the concern in Cody's softened tone drew her attention.

"Erica?" She felt a warm, thick substance oozing from her nostril and instinctively brought her hand to her face, to inspect the bright red smear of blood against her fingers. Then she felt the outpour as more blood trickled from her nose. It was quickly accompanied by an excruciating pain that radiated through every inch of her body.

"OWWWWW!" She screamed, dropping to her knees in front of the elevator. "My head... My body... It all hurts... What do I do? It hurts!"

Cody collapsed to the floor, holding her in his arms as she cried out as if her very insides were burning her alive. Whatever that chip was doing, it couldn't be good.

16

MARANTHINA – CODY

Watching Erica writhe in pain on his bed as the two waited for Dr Arack to arrive, had to have been one of the most excruciating moments of Cody's life.

But now, he was left sitting on the couch as the doctor administered pain relief and went over Erica's vitals. And as he watched Arack work his magic, Cody couldn't help but replay their earlier argument of Erica leaving. Most specifically the part where she had believed him to see her as Megan.

But Cody hadn't seen Erica as Megan.

He had seen her for who she was.

Erica.

But why had he used the word, *again?* Had he known and then lost Erica before?

Surely, that was impossible.

Wasn't it?

Cody glanced at the bed, where Erica was sleeping peacefully.

Finally.

After Dr Arack packed away his tools, he approached Cody with her stats visible on his wrist screen. "She's stable."

"You said that back at the clinic. Right after you told her what the chip was doing to her. But look at her. She is NOT okay." While it was rare for Cody to lose his temper with the man, who was the closest thing Cody had to a father, he just couldn't help it.

"That's because she *was* stable then. I can't control what is happening to her, but I can help her manage it."

"Do we, at least, know what it's doing yet?"

The doctor glanced at Erica then back to Cody before hesitating to respond. "It seems your theory on MIOT wanting to alter her DNA was right on the mark."

"What do you mean?"

"They seem to be injecting GX572 into her body."

Cody felt his entire body go cold, despite the effects of his thermo-wiring system. "But that could kill her!"

"You would think that. But, what's astonishing to see is that while it should be burning her from the inside out, it's altering her in a way I've never seen before. It's almost remarkable."

"Oh really? Because it certainly didn't look that way out in the hall." Again, Cody couldn't hold his anger. If that chip killed Erica, he would blame himself. He was the one who had convinced her to come to Maranthina, after all.

"I'm sorry, Cody. But I'm doing all I can. I've left some medicine and anaesthesia, along with my injector on the bench. You already know how to administer it, so give it to her, accordingly. I'll check in on her tomorrow morning."

"So, that's it? Just let the chip do its thing?"

"It's all we can do."

Of course, Dr Arack was right... *again.*

It had become routine that whenever MIOT injected anybody with anything, the individual had no choice but to simply treat the side effects and deal with the consequences. The government allowed it in the name of science. And when augmented mistakes were taken and recycled for spare parts there was nobody – not even the authorities – to stand in MIOT's way.

How else could the Maranthinian Institute of Technology continue to improve their innovations in augmentations?

In truth, every single person in Maranthina was wearing some recycled part from a dead person.

As the doctor reached the door he looked as if he had just been disturbed by his own thoughts.

"Hey, Cody?"

"Yeah?"

"You mentioned earlier that Erica liked to write about our world. Did she ever go into detail about what happened the night my daughter died?"

That was the very last question Cody had expected for him to ask.

"Ah… No. And she didn't seem to in the books either. Why do you ask?"

Dr Arack sent another look at Erica then brushed off the thought. "Never mind. I'll see you first thing tomorrow."

Once he was left alone with his thoughts, Cody trailed the floor until he was at Erica's bedside, where she was sleeping on her side, peacefully.

She looked eerily pale.

Everybody… especially Seth… saw her as the author and creator of Maranthina, thanks to her ability to see through their eyes and write stories about their lives.

And clearly, even Megan was determined to trade places with her.

But the more Cody got to know Erica, the more he saw her as a Maranthinian... with or without her abilities. She was strong and stubborn. That much was certain. But she was also entirely flawed and made mistakes just like him.

Cody shifted the medicines aside and sat on the bed, lifting her hand into his. She barely flinched.

He thought back to their argument and to the prospect of losing her *again*.

It didn't take a scientist to know he had very strong feelings for her. He had known it from the minute they first met.

Cody just couldn't comprehend as to why he felt the way he did. As if he had loved her through countless lifetimes. As if they were *soulmates*.

###

ADELAIDE, SA – DEETS

It was eight am when Deets decided to pull her ass out of Erica's bed and get in some breakfast. Thanks to her horrible vision the night before, the others had been adamant that she sleep as comfortably as possible.

She knew they were simply hoping she would receive another vision – preferably one telling them how to get back home.

And while that hadn't happened, Deets didn't mind being treated special for once, for it had always been Megan the others doted on like a queen.

After having used her own heat from the palm of her hands to cook up two slices of toast, Deets lathered on a chunk of vegemite and took her breakfast into the loungeroom. She had always prided herself on having the self-sufficient augmentations. It meant while her friends required access to communication networks and appliances, she could survive by using her huntress abilities alone, no matter her location.

Aside from the television on a low volume in the loungeroom, the house was silent. Following her vague vision debriefing the night before, Deets had gone directly to sleep to minimise the interrogation.

How could she tell her friends that it was Erica who had jumped into the pit, as opposed to Megan.

They barely knew the girl.

Thus, the entire vision had left her feeling confused and – though she would never admit it – eerily vulnerable.

With her vegemite on toast, Deets attempted to sit on the couch, only to be met by a bumpy mound beneath her. "What the...?" She jolted to see Adam and Seth asleep and shirtless on the couch. Well, they had been asleep, until Deets had sat on Adam's chest.

"Ergh, Deets!" he groaned. "What are you doing?"

"What does it look like? I wanted to sit." To garner a little support, Deets decided to play on his empathy. "I had another vision last night and I'm just trying to figure it out."

At those words, Adam immediately sat up, waking Seth in the process, and giving Deets some space to sit.

"I really hope you guys weren't... you know..." Deets continued.

Seth and Adam exchanged glances before Adam continued with the conversation. "Just sit down. What was the vision? Did you figure out a way to get us home?"

Deets sat beside them and took a bite of her toast. The vegemite was disgusting, so she handed it to Seth.

"Here, have this. It tastes like *Recharge*."

Seth took a bite. "Mmm. It's good."

"You were saying?" Adam probed.

"So, this vision..." Deets began. "...Was totally..." She stopped as the television garnered her attention and pointed in wide-eyed horror at the screen.

"What about the vision?" Seth asked.

"It was all a joke. Just look at the screen!"

"What do you mean, *a joke?*" Adam asked.

"SHUT UP AND LOOK!"

Adam and Seth obeyed, turning their attention to the live news report, where images of MIOT's giant spiders wreaking havoc in the cities, were being broadcasted.

"How do I turn this thing up?" Deets asked, with her finger still pointed at the television.

Seth used his wrist screen to turn up the volume. "...These giant metallic spiders have been spotted in cities worldwide wreaking havoc and collecting people for reasons unknown."

The footage showed the spiders in cities such as Adelaide, Los Angeles, New York, and Paris.

"It looks like MIOT broke through." Adam said.

"And we have no way of stopping them," Deets added. For the very first time in a long time, Deets was frightened to her core. Not only were they in perilous danger in their own world, but they had also brought that devastation to an entirely new and unevolved world. There was no telling what could happen next.

17

MARANTHINA – ERICA

Erica opened her eyes to the dim light of Cody's apartment, where she was curled up in the foetal position, unsure as to how she had gotten there.

The last thing she remembered was the sheer pain as if her body was burning from the inside out. But now, that pain had been replaced by a strong sensation of pins and needles. A welcomed alternative.

"Finally, you're awake," Cody said, lying beside her.

She turned to him and instantly remembered their argument. She had been determined to go up against MIOT despite the chip in her head.

Yet, he had been too worried about losing her.

Worried... As if she were Megan.

But she wasn't Megan.

She was the author responsible for everything that had happened in Maranthina. And now it was her turn to suffer as all her characters had done before.

Karma really was a bitch.

But she really wasn't in the mood to argue with him.

"Yeah, I am," she sighed. "It's kinda hard to believe after all that pain."

His dark eyes softened as he pursed his lips together.

There was something serious on his mind.

Something he was afraid to say.

"Dr Arack left you some medicine and the anaesthesia gun. He asked me to administer as needed."

"Medicine? So, he *does* know what's wrong with me?"

There was that look again.

He was hesitating.

Big time!

Finally, he conceded. "Erica... That chip has been injecting you with GX572."

Erica's mouth dropped.

GX572 was technically Maranthina's battery acid.

How the hell could they do such a thing?

"Are you okay?" he asked.

Erica closed her eyes to let the information sink in.

No, she wasn't okay.

Her entire body was flowing with acid. Only a few hours earlier, she had been suffering from excruciating pain, with blood pouring out of her nostrils.

But on the bright side... at least, she wasn't dead.

Finally, she opened her eyes.

"I'll be fine," she lied. But her tears betrayed her. She wiped them away, furiously. "I'll be fine," she said again, wishing her words had the power to make it so.

Cody pulled her into his arms. Erica tried to push him away, but he just wouldn't budge. He just continued to hold her as she gave into her grief.

"I knew we should've removed it," she said, half expecting him to remind her of the consequences.

Though, he remained silent.

His hand trailed circles against her back as she cried into his neck. Even beneath his dark blue shirt she could feel his solid chest.

He was just so human and insanely perfect.

It sucked how all the men in Erica's life could never compare to him. She had written him to be the perfect love interest. An incredible work of fiction.

But at the same time, he *was* real.

Far more real than she could ever think possible.

She was literally dealing with the same torment that MIOT had put her characters through countless times, and Cody was the one holding her. Supporting her through it. Almost as if they had been through it together, before.

And while they had – in a way – it had never been like this. Erica had led Megan, Cody, Seth, Adam and Deets through the hell of their lives... But she had also guided them through to the other side as their author.

Erica tilted her head up to take in the dark stubble on his chin. He was eighty-five percent man. Fifteen percent robotics and hardware. But there were scars to his tanned skin. Creases and blemishes too.

All the markings of a real person.

She pulled her head away from his chest, as Cody continued to watch her in the dim light.

Studying her.

His thick lips delivered a friendly smile into his left cheek, before he sucked his bottom lip between his teeth. A gesture he often made when nervous. Though that nervous gesture made her forget about her own grief. Her tears had stopped.

If only temporarily.

There was nothing more than the electrifying tension between them, as Cody's fingers continued to trace circles at her back. His touch sending her soul into a nervous state of her own…

Until he stopped.

That subtle lack of movement was enough to elevate the chemistry to the next level. Their lips met in the space between, following the rush of adrenaline flowing through their veins.

Cody's hand swept from her back to just under her chin, as he repositioned himself and pulled her closer.

There was a strength in him she had underestimated until now, accompanied by his surging need. Erica's hands slid from his shoulders to his dark hair, while her tongue slipped into his mouth.

The more she gave, the more she became increasingly aware of the reality of their situation. He was only there because she had created him within her imagination, and while the logic behind it made no sense whatsoever, there were still rules. Rules that dictated they couldn't be together.

No matter how much they both wanted it. And because of those rules, Erica went against her own desires and pulled away. "Cody, we can't do this," she said, breathless.

His eyes drifted open.

"It's okay. I've had the TIF upgrade." His lips trailed to her neck, forcing her to struggle to comprehend what he was talking about.

TIF upgrade?

Oh, right.

The TIF upgrade was the most advanced biyearly augmentation that made a male's sperm inactive. Meaning they could sleep together without any fears or repercussions. The very thought of it made it that much harder for Erica to resist.

"No, Cody. That's not what I meant."

Cody pulled away. "I'm sorry, did I hurt you?"

"No. I'm not in any pain, it's just… We can't do this because I created you. It would just be wrong."

Cody chuckled as he sat up. "You didn't create me, Erica. I get that you and Seth believe you did... But I don't. In fact, I feel in my gut that *this* is right, and that feeling is far stronger than anything I ever felt with Megan."

"You can't be serious."

"I'm very serious. You and Megan are nothing alike... I mean, sure you're alike in *some* subtle ways. But after coming to know you these past few days. It's like... Like Megan was a poor substitute for you."

It was a weirdly worded compliment, but it still made her laugh.

"I've never heard that pickup line before."

"That wasn't a line. It was my way of trying to tell you that... Maybe Jynx is right. I feel like we *have* met before. In another life, perhaps... In countless lives, maybe."

"Like reincarnation?"

"What's reincarnation?"

An adorable reaction. But not the time for her to have those thoughts. "Never mind. The only reason you and Jynx feel like you know me is because, I've been with you all for nine books. You're all underdogs battling to survive in a world that…"

"…Tell me, honestly, how do you feel about me?"

Dangerous question.

"Cody. I can't answer that."

"Please, Erica. Because every time I look at you, I feel… No… I know that there's something between us."

Erica bit down on her lip so hard she could feel her tears emerge, again. "How can you ask me that?"

"Just answer the damn question."

She couldn't.

Of course, she felt something for him. The guy was perfectly imperfect. Though, as much as she wanted to throw caution to the wind and make love to him, this wasn't her world. No matter how much her body had been altered. Knowing Cody, if he was harbouring these feelings, he would either want her to stay in

Maranthina with him, or choose to return to Adelaide with her. But Erica couldn't stay. And she couldn't bring Cody home, either.

She still had a life.

She still had Nick.

Oops!

And she had just kissed Cody.

Double Oops!

Cody crawled past her to get to his feet, snapped his fingers and the apartment lights switched on. "It's an easy question, Erica. Do you have feelings for me?"

"Do you have any idea how impossible it is for me to answer that?"

"Please, just try. Whatever you decide, we can make it work. I know it."

Erica attempted to stand, but the pins and needles sensation had returned, so she remained seated on the side of the bed. "Of course, I feel something for you, Cody. But whether you believe in me creating your world or not, isn't the point. When I was writing about

you, you became real. And from that moment, I felt...
I felt *something*. But it was just some crazy infatuation
because I designed you to be the ultimate love interest.
And you were perfect because you weren't real."

On those words, Cody knelt beside her and placed
his hands on her knees. "But I'm not fictional. When
you kissed me, it was *real*. Maranthina is real. What do
I need to do to make you see that?"

Good question.

Erica took his hands in hers and went to answer.
Though just as she did, her eyes caught sight of the scar
that ran along his heartline of his left hand. She had
never worked that scar into his story, and as an author
she prided herself on knowing every scar her characters
had ever acquired. Furthermore, she had a scar in the
exact same spot.

Noting her silence, Cody continued. "...And
another thing, even if you did create me... which I'm
not saying you did... But have you any idea how many

doctors have built their own partners? I've got free will and I have no issues being your…"

"…Where did you get that scar?"

He stared at his palm. "Huh. That scar should have disappeared by now. Wait, don't change the subject."

"I'm serious. Where did you get it?"

"When I was thirteen my parents accepted a payout for me to be a MIOT test subject. When I came back wrong…"

"…They put you in the orphanage, I know. But *how* did you get the scar?"

Cody shrugged. "I couldn't bear the emotional pain, so I cut my heart wire… and then every time things got bad, I did it again. But it always healed over… Until now. Why is that important?"

Erica showed him the faint scar that ran along the palm of her own left hand. "Because I have the exact same scar, right here."

He trailed his finger across her scar, sending shivers through her wrist.

"How did you get yours?" he asked.

"I... I... don't remember."

It was the truth.

Was it possible that Cody was right, and she hadn't in fact created Maranthina, but was tied to it in some other way?

But MIOT had only just discovered multidimensional travel and there was no way she could have stumbled across it as a child. And the technology of her world was barely on par with that of Maranthina two thousand years ago. So that couldn't have been the case, either. Erica sat in silent contemplation considering Cody's theory. But the more she thought about it, the less any of it made any sense.

###

ADELAIDE, SA – DEETS

Deets paced the loungeroom floor, desperate to come up with a solution to battle the giant spiders that had made it to Erica's world.

"They're everywhere," Adam said, flicking through the channels with the remote control.

"You think I don't know that?" Deets spat. "It's only a matter of time before they find us."

"What do you propose we do?" Seth asked, peering up from his wrist screen with an exhausted look.

"I don't know. But we can't just sit around and do nothing. Look at the guns those officers are using. They're so prim!"

Seth followed her gaze to the television, where police officers had resorted to using firepower on the robotic spiders. The bullets ricocheted in various directions, with one smashing into the camera and disrupting the signal.

Defeated, he turned back to his wrist screen and to his surprise, was met by the successful beeping of a *Message Sent* notification.

"You guys. The message went through!"

Deets felt the sheer relief of his exclamation. Her hope had returned.

"Can you locate Cody's signal?" Adam asked.

Seth pushed a few buttons then gave a disappointed shrug. "Not yet. But I'm going to open a portal to his place. Maybe his home tracker can locate his handprint on any of the Maranthinian networks." Seth input his destination and pushed the button to activate a portal. "Come on, come on, come on!"

Voila!

A portal opened.

"It worked!" He stood in front of the shimmery, silver gateway to home.

"Perfect," Deets said, rubbing her hands together – the same way Megan used to when preparing for action.

"While you search for them, Adam and I will work out a way to stop these spiders."

Seth looked Deets up and down, confused. She knew that look. He didn't think Deets could lead as well as Megan could.

"Are you sure about this?" Adam asked. "I just have a really bad feeling about…"

Deets scoffed. "Cody and Erica could be dead for all we know, and those spiders are from our world. There's no way we can just stand by and do nothing."

Seth and Adam stared at Deets, slightly intimidated. "Who are you and what have you done with Deets?" Seth asked. But she didn't need their patronization. She glared at Seth and motioned her head towards the portal. "Alright, alright. I'm going, Megan 2.0."

Those words cut her, emotionally. But she wouldn't let them see that. Seth turned to the portal just as Adam cupped his head in his hands.

"Just stay safe for me, okay?"

"Always," Seth replied, before kissing Adam and pulling away again. Then, without another word, Seth was gone, and Deets couldn't help but feel a pang of anxiety as she thought back to her vision from last night.

Seth had gone missing.

Where had he gone?

The thought brought static to her sensory system and while it was a mildly uncomfortable feeling, she didn't have time for uncomfortable feelings.

She had a world to save from robotic spiders.

Unfortunately, her expression caught the attention of Adam. "What is it?" he asked.

Damn that emotional sensor of his.

"Nothing."

"That look is not nothing. What's going on?"

Suddenly, there was a knock at the door.

The perfect distraction.

Deets raced to answer it, but Adam wasn't done with his interrogation. "What's wrong Deets? Does it have something to do with Seth?" Deets opened the door to see Chloe standing on the step, holding up her phone, which displayed the current chaos. "There are giant spiders, everywhere!" she said.

"We know," Adam replied. "Deets... Just tell me what's wrong with Seth."

Before Deets could even begin to explain, her eyes turned grey, and she received another vision.

This time, she was sitting at Erica's computer in the home office and on the screen were the words, ...*The core begged for her return, causing a ripple of destruction in its wake... While there was still a part of her deeply ingrained in the very world that she had once called home, her very sacrifice had been lost into the abyss.*

As the vision faded, Deets could've sworn she had heard a whisper, telling her exactly what the vision meant. But what was strange was that the voice sounded eerily like that of Megan.

"Deets? What did you see?" Adam asked.

"Megan wants us to sacrifice Erica." Those words triggered Deets, and not because it meant that Megan was still alive, but because they needed to let Erica die.

###

MARANTHINA – ERICA

"You haven't said anything in a while," Cody said, kneeling beside Erica, as she sat on the bed. She had been stewing through countless theories, thoughts and her feelings for the last few minutes and was now more confused than ever.

She couldn't help but have feelings for Cody.

However, the entire prospect of them having a relationship was just reckless, and damn near impossible. Though despite the complexity of the situation, she was still only human.

And despite Cody's wiring systems, he was too.

...And humans had urges.

Erica pushed the racing thoughts to the back of her mind and focused solely on Cody. The short dark waves which always seemed to look perfectly imperfect. His dark eyes which were actually a combination of black and the darkest brown she had ever seen.

He was truly handsome.

As if he had been built in a lab from scratch, instead of simply augmented on.

She didn't want to hold back any longer, so she kissed him. And he kissed her back.

It was passionate.

Their urgency growing.

The very action made her lightheaded.

Then came the sheer agony, as every inch of her body burned, thanks to the GX572 coursing through her veins. Erica ripped herself away from Cody's lips and fell to the floor in explicable pain. Again, she felt the drizzle of blood running from her nostril. Then, the light of the apartment seemed to grow brighter, almost blinding.

She closed her eyes for an ounce of comfort and thought she could hear Cody calling out to her.

And then, she heard Seth too.

Was Seth there?

The light was too bright to open her eyes, and her ears felt like they were filling up with water.

…Or maybe it was blood.

She couldn't tell.

All she knew was that it felt like she was being held under water and that every orifice was flooding with liquid.

"…Lot of blood," Seth's muffled voice seemed to say.

"…Hold her still… shot of anaesthesia."

Erica was sure that Cody had spoken those words.

But all she saw was darkness.

All she felt was pain.

Until images started to appear before her eyes, and she was standing next to the hospital bed of an unconscious little girl, about seven years of age.

The child was bandaged from head to toe and had clear tubes emerging from her ears and nose.

They were surrounded by peach-coloured hospital curtains, and the scene felt far too real.

While Erica knew that she was sleeping, she couldn't seem to open her eyes. She couldn't force herself to wake up, despite desperately wanting to.

'Wake up!' she told herself. But her voice was but a mere silent thought. 'Come on, wake up!'

Still no luck.

The last thing she remembered was being in Cody's apartment. Kissing him... then excruciating pain.

Wait, that didn't make any sense.

Had she been back at her home in Adelaide?

Was it a dream within a dream?

Why couldn't she remember?

All she could see was that god-awful hospital room and that poor little girl asleep in the bed.

Was this her reality?

No, it couldn't be.

Maybe she was already dead.

She needed to scream herself awake.

"WAKE UP!"

There it was. The voice she had been waiting for.

Only, it hadn't come from her. It came from the mouth of the little girl instead. Erica was still nothing more than a silent bystander, in the hospital room.

To her surprise, the girl opened her eyes. The very action was followed by a gasp from the other side of the curtain. The gasp was accompanied by a familiar, masculine voice, sounding very much relieved.

"By the pit, you're alive." A man, roughly in his forties, with kind green eyes and a lab coat, rushed into the room. On his forearm was a wrist screen with the little girl's vitals. It was a younger Dr Arack.

So, Erica *was* in Maranthina.

Just in another time and acting as nothing more than a fly on the wall.

Maybe it was a spinoff.

Seeing the man, the little girl was overcome with joy. She tried to sit up, but the tubes tugged at her head.

"No, don't try to move," he said, assisting her to lay back down. "You need your rest."

"But I'm not tired, papa. Where's mama?"

Erica saw the pain in the doctor's eyes and felt a pang to her gut, as he scanned his daughter with his wrist screen, then checked her vitals while doing his best to avoid eye contact. "Baby, mama... Mama won't be coming back."

The little girl took a moment to register what he meant, before her face scrunched up and her breathing hastened its pace. An incessant beeping emanated from Dr Arack's wrist screen as tears filled the girl's eyes.

"Did I... Did I kill her?" she asked.

The very question forced Erica's blood to run cold as she thought back to the bathtub memory.

The woman that had tried to drown her in the tub.

The electrical abilities she had used to protect herself.

The screams.

Oh, God!

Those screams!

They echoed distantly in the back of Erica's mind and drowned her with PTSD.

Dr Arack's eyes flashed with grief. "No, baby. How can you think that? It wasn't your fault. You need to calm down. Please."

But the little girl gave into a loud sob as the beeping grew louder and quicker. "Please, baby. It's okay." He hugged her close, careful not to disrupt the tubing.

'Wake up!' Erica pleaded to herself. 'Wake up. Get me out of here, please!'

Then she did wake up.

18

MARANTHINA – ERICA

Erica opened her eyes to find herself lying on Cody's bed absent of blood, pain, and energy. She couldn't remember the last time she had felt so weak. It was almost as if she had just run a marathon. Her synthetic suit had been changed back into the pale blue pyjamas she had been wearing earlier.

Beside her, stood Cody and Seth. Their faces equally filled with surprise and alarm.

...Wait, Seth had returned?

When did that happen?

Surprisingly, the sun shone brightly outside the window.

How long had she been unconscious?

All she could remember was the dream about the young girl. Erica attempted to sit, but Cody was quick to stop her.

"Careful. You've been out for almost a week."

Wait, what?

"A week? But it only feels like…"

"…Shh…" Cody said, stroking her hair from her face. "Don't try to think. Your body's gone through a lot these past few days. Dr Arack said you need your rest."

"I'll mindlink him now," Seth said. "He should know she's awake."

"What's the GX572 doing to me?" Erica asked. "Do we know?"

Cody glanced outside for the briefest of moments before turning to her with a sombre shrug. "We're still not entirely sure. It's like every time we think it's killing you… Something happens. and your body reverses the process by itself. That's what Dr Arack thinks, anyway."

Erica attempted to make sense of it.

Nope, it just wasn't sinking in.

"Do we have any coffee? I think I'm still dreaming and need to wake up."

"I think we can…" His sentence was cut short by Seth opening a portal in the middle of the apartment, allowing in a highly advanced, black wheelchair, followed by Dr Arack.

As Cody assisted Erica to sit against the pillows, Dr Arack stopped the wheelchair via his own wrist screen.

"Hey Dr Arack," Erica said with a strained smile. "Maybe when I get back to writing, I'll upgrade you with your own portal system."

"While that would be a huge advantage. You should know better than anybody that it could potentially interfere with my circuitry systems. And we don't want that now, do we?"

He scanned her, the same way he had his daughter, and the memory brought a knot to her gut.

How he could keep working after all he had been through was a miracle. She was about to bring it up, when he cut her off with a smile and a sudden announcement.

"I might've found a way to help you, Erica."

"Lay it on me… Wait, will it hurt?"

"Why don't you leave your concerns to me?"

He turned his attention to Seth and spoke in such a muffled voice that neither Erica nor Cody could hear.

Though, judging by Seth's expression, it was the last place on Maranthina he had expected.

"Where are we taking her?" Cody asked.

"Have a little faith, would you?" Dr Arack said with a gleeful smile.

"Have a little faith? Are you kidding me? Every single time I put my faith in somebody, something bad happens. So, excuse me if…"

"…Have I ever let you down?"

Cody paused. "That's not the point, Arack..."

As they continued their discussion, Erica diverted her attention to Seth. She thought she saw him wipe away a bead of sweat from his brow, but surely, that couldn't be right.

Maranthinians didn't sweat.

Her focus was interrupted by Dr Arack's raise of voice at Cody. "...Do you really think I'd risk my patient's life if I felt for a moment that my hunch wouldn't work?"

"Alright... I'll trust you. But you better promise me that nothing will happen to her, or I'll drag you straight to the pit myself." At Cody's comment, the doctor's face contorted slightly, and the tension was unmissable.

As if Dr Arack's treatment had something to do with the actual pit of Maranthina.

"What?!" Cody asked.

"Nothing," Dr Arack nodded to Seth, who opened a portal in the middle of the apartment. And again, Erica seemed to be the only person present to notice just how exhausted Seth looked. Yet again, he brushed the exhaustion off smoothly and addressed her with his own concern. "Do you think you'll be able to make it into the wheelchair?"

"I'm fine," she lied. "I can walk by myself."

With all her energy, she pushed her feet to the side of the bed and couldn't remember the last time she had stood up. Nor could she remember how long it had been since she had been to Adelaide. She attempted to stand, but her legs gave out instantly.

"Help me get her in the chair," Dr Arack instructed.

They managed to get her into the wheelchair, which automatically reclined back into a comfortable seating position. As Dr Arack pushed buttons on his wrist screen, Erica turned back to Seth and saw it again.

That simple bead of sweat on his forehead glistening in the light. This time when he wiped it away, he noticed it too and confusion filled his eyes.

Alerted by the action, Erica decided to speak up.

"Seth… He looks…" Her eyes closed, but she fought to keep them open. "Please… He's…"

From Dr Arack's wrist screen, an incessant beeping interrupted her struggle to speak.

"We need to get her there *now*," the doctor said.

The wheelchair turned around clockwise, and Erica could see the portal in its entirety. The shimmery silver circling around a glimpse of what could only be described as the Bucklands forest. It was beautiful.

The chair's relaxing movements increased Erica's exhaustion, but she needed to speak out for Seth.

"…Seth… He's… he's not well… Sweating…"

"…It's okay, Erica." Cody said, taking her hand. "You can relax. We're going to make you better."

As the chair moved forward, the energy vibrated from the portal and the winds of the forest swept through her hair.

And in that moment, she could feel her energy diminishing fast. She couldn't fight it any longer. Erica let herself slip into the void of sleep, wondering who or what she might see in her dreams, this time.

###

UNKNOWN LOCATION – ERICA

Before she could even open her eyes, Erica knew she wasn't alone. But where she was exactly was almost impossible to determine. She felt the soft cotton of the pillow against her cheek and clutched tightly at the blanket that was wrapped around her.

A blanket?

Had Dr Arack taken her home?

In that moment she relished to see her old familiar surroundings. She could die at home, in her bed. Surrounded by... Well, she didn't know who was there.

She could just sense their presence.

"Papa, I think she's waking up." Came a voice from her right, which sounded strangely like Deets.

But if it was Deets, then who was she talking to?

Deets and Megan never knew their parents.

They came to the orphanage at such an early age.

Erica needed to know.

She opened her eyes to find that she was not in her Adelaide bedroom as she had previously thought, but in a pristine clinic. In fact, it looked like Dr Arack's clinic before he had let it go to ruin.

And while it was Deets who had initially spoken, the only other person in the room was…

Dr Arack!

The doctor was standing at a desk on the far side of the room, reading from a large tablet screen.

But why would Deets refer to him as *Papa?*

He wasn't her father.

Not to Erica's knowledge, anyway.

Was this another plot twist in the world of Maranthina?

Erica tried to sit, in a bid to take in her surroundings, only to have Deets attempt to hold her still. "Hold on, sis. That last fall almost killed you. You need to take it easy."

Sis?

Then it all made sense.

Erica was seeing through Megan's eyes. But the very scene was new to Erica. It was not in any of her books.

Erica rubbed at her left wrist, drawing her attention to the intravenous drip sticking out of her arm, through a bandage.

The bandage stopped at her palm just covering her scar.

Wait?

Scar?

Did Megan have a scar there too?

Erica focused on the tube which was feeding a red substance into her veins via IV.

"What's happening to me?" she groaned as she visually followed the tubing to the IV monitor, which was connected to another tube, which led to… Deets's right wrist.

It wasn't medicine.

It was blood.

Deets was giving her a blood transfusion.

At this point, Dr Arack rushed over to Erica's bedside.

"Don't try to move. As Deets said, we almost lost you. Fortunately, she was built for this exact reason."

Built?

Not born and then augmented on like Cody and Seth.

Built.

Like Adam.

"No, no, no," Erica said instinctively. "I'm too weak. It'll... it'll kill her. I can't kill my sister. I know another... I know another way." Those words fell from Erica's lips in a manner she couldn't control. Almost as if she had lived this scene a dozen times before.

Had they been in some of her unpublished pages?

Again, she couldn't remember.

Why couldn't she remember?

"Don't be silly," Dr Arack said. "Deets isn't your sister and if something does happen to her, she can always be rebuilt."

Erica felt a pang of misery as she took in the pain in Deets's eyes. The pain of knowing that it was nothing more than an uncomfortable truth.

"No, she is my…" Erica attempted to remove the IV. "Stop giving me her blood. She could…"

"Hold her still," Dr Arack told Deets. "We can't let her remove it."

On his command, Deets took both Erica's hands in her own, overpowering her with an indescribable strength. "Don't move, Ari. Stop. Let me help you!"

"No. You can't," Erica mumbled. "MIOT can… MIOT can help me."

"MIOT won't step foot in…" Before Dr Arack could continue his sentence, a large beeping emanated from the monitor. "…By the pit, I don't understand!"

But Erica did.

Deets's blood wasn't helping, because Erica was dying. And with that realisation in mind, her breathing staggered.

"Sis, you need to focus on your breathing," Deets said. "Papa? Do you need to set up another line?"

"Yes. Perhaps..." But before Dr Arack could finish his sentence, the door swung open and two white lab-coated scientists stormed in.

"Dr Arack," the first one said. "We're here for your daughter."

But Dr Arack stood in their way. "I already told MIOT. You're not taking her. Get out of my clinic!"

"Stand down, old man," the second scientist said, preparing to use force.

"Deets, send a mindlink to the others. We can't let them take her!"

"Yes, you can, papa," Erica said. "I must... I must go with them. It's the only way to save Maranthina."

"The guys are on their way now," Deets told the doctor before strengthening her grip on Erica.

"Let me go, Deets. I need to go with them!"

"No. They'll kill you. I won't let you go."

Erica stared into Deets's green eyes. Her cheeks were stained with tears. It pained Erica to see her cry, but this was something she had to do. She slipped free from Deets's grip and wiped away the girl's tears.

"You won't be sad forever. I promise."

Before Deets could even comprehend what Erica meant, a large crash caught their attention. They looked up to see Dr Arack land in a heap on the floor.

"Papa!" Deets groaned as the scientists rushed to the bed. She held up her unbandaged hand. "Get back!" she snarled. "If you even think of taking her, I'll electrify you where…"

"…This room was fitted with a proximity dampener right before we entered, miss," one of the scientists said as he removed the IV from Erica's wrist. "So, I suggest you let us do our job or you won't survive this encounter."

But Deets didn't retreat in her threat. She thrusted her hand forward, expecting to see her abilities at work…

But her ability didn't work.

"You need to let them take me," Erica pleaded. "I need to do this. I need to save Maranthina, or we'll all die."

Deets studied her, determined to fight but unable to disobey her sister's wishes.

She wasn't built that way.

"Please," Erica pleaded.

Reluctantly, Deets nodded and lowered her hand.

"And you must not let the others come for me, or they will be killed."

"But Cody... he..."

"...He will understand. Eventually."

As the scientists carried her to the doorway, Erica did her best to hide the earth-shattering heart break of her decision. Her gaze fell from the emotionally battered Deets, to her father lying unconscious on the floor. She'd rather sacrifice herself, than watch her loved ones suffer into extinction.

Maranthina was dying, and she was the key to its salvation.

19

MARANTHINA – ERICA

Ah, sweet darkness…

Silent, painless, and free from chaos.

Until the moment Erica felt herself growing stronger by the minute. But why?

"…Won't lose her…"

Who was that?

The voice was familiar. His concern was almost parental. She needed to think. Needed the sweet darkness to dissipate so she could see.

"…I know this will work… You need to trust me."

Arack! That voice belonged to Dr Arack!

The true father of Deets and Megan... But didn't he have a different daughter? God, what was her name? The Maranthinian connections were so confusing.

"...Idea is stupid!"

Another voice.

Cody's voice, perhaps?

Erica forced her eyes to open. Forced herself to see. And when her eyes finally opened, her view was blinding, thanks to a light brighter than the sun.

Instinctively, she brought her hand to her eyes as she remembered what had happened before her last vision.

Dr Arack had decided to take her somewhere to make her stronger. But where had he brought her? She positioned her hand to block the blinding rays from her eyes. "You guys, she's waking up."

That was Seth's voice.

She peered up at him, standing right beside her. The glowing light illuminating every inch of his face... Including those same beads of sweat on his brow.

Large trees stood all around them. They had to be standing somewhere deep in the Bucklands forest.

At first, Erica didn't understand.

Until she looked to the bright light coming from a large hole in the ground only a short distance away. They were standing at the mouth of an essence port.

A hole which led to the very depths of the Maranthina core, which was lined with the very acid that energised Maranthinians. Standing at a distance could give them the boost they needed... But standing too close or falling in could be deemed beyond hazardous.

A large metal grate sat over the mouth of their current location to reduce the likelihood of accidental deaths. Erica looked to Cody and Dr Arack, who were standing before her, arguing. They hadn't heard Seth telling them that she had awoken.

"Erica has GX572 running through her body," Cody argued. "...And you think exposing her to more would be beneficial to her health? Seriously, Dr Arack... Your mental instability is getting the better of you!"

"...For your information, Cody," Dr Arack shouted back. "I've never been so sure about something in my entire career. The last thing I want is for Erica to die on my watch. I've lost enough to know what that feels like."

Erica adjusted her seating position in the wheelchair and turned back to take in Seth's pale face.

"Are you okay?" she asked. Seth gave a non-committal shrug.

"I was feeling a little uncomfortable earlier, but being here... I think, I feel better. What about you?"

"I don't know. I keep... I keep having these weird dreams. They feel so real."

"Dreams? Do you mean, visions? Like Megan and Deets?"

Erica nodded. "It must be Megan's doing. Maybe she's giving them to me. But I just can't figure out why."

"Megan? But Megan is..."

"...Your daughter died at this exact pit," Cody snarled at the doctor. "I refuse to lose Erica this way, too." Upon realizing what he had just said, something came over Cody and it wasn't just remorse. "I don't... I don't understand why I just said that. It's like..."

"My... My daughter?" Dr Arack stammered as if recollecting an old memory. "That's right... I... I had a daughter. Did you know her? I feel like..."

"...Cody, Dr Arack!" Erica said, slowly staggering to her feet from the chair, but falling into Seth's outstretched arms.

The others turned to her in sincere surprise.

"Erica?" Cody gasped. "You're awake?"

Erica shook free from Seth's assistance and approached them. "I am. And I heard what you said. Thing is. I'm not Megan, nor am I Dr Arack's daughter. But he was right about bringing me here."

Erica bypassed them both and approached the rusted metal grate, several feet in front. Rays of white light beamed through each gap, illuminating the night.

Her eyes adjusted quickly, as the energy filled Erica with an overwhelming warmth and a comfortable sense of belonging, that she couldn't shake.

She turned to the others.

Cody flexed his shoulders, as if he had been sleeping for far too long. Dr Arack flexed his wrists. Seth stretched his arms above his head. Evidently, the energy was affecting them too.

The closer Erica got to the grate, the stronger she felt. "Be careful," she heard Cody call out.

She knelt in the grass and waved her hand through the beams of light, marvelling at the way they reflected against her skin.

That was until a spark ignited at the tip of her left index finger. Erica touched her index finger with her thumb and another spark ignited.

What the…?

All of a sudden, white lightning bolts shot up through the gaps in the metal lid.

She attempted to retreat but was stopped as countless lightning bolts struck through the grate, holding her in place.

Each strike was followed by another… then another. They all connected with a different part of her body, not only shocking her, but also emitting zapping sounds on contact.

As the currents forced her entire body to raise into the air and convulse, Erica witnessed every flash of Maranthina's history within her mind. Millions of lives carried out through countless centuries.

Cody attempted to fight off Seth, who was preventing him from running towards her.

Even Dr Arack looked frightened.

Clearly, none of them had anticipated this turn of events. With each bolt of lightning the pain reduced, almost as if she had become one with the very world itself.

Yet her body continued to convulse at an ever-stronger rhythm. Erica could've sworn she could hear her own heart beating like a deafening drumbeat.

When her seizure finally came to a stop, her body fell to the ground and the bolts disappeared back into the grate, from which they had come.

MARANTHINA – ERICA

This time there were no dreams or visions. When Erica opened her eyes to see Cody, Dr Arack and Seth standing around her, she was still laying on the grass in the middle of the Bucklands Forest.

"I don't understand," Cody stammered. "She was dead."

"What?" Erica sat up, trying to come to terms with the word.

Dead.

"Don't try to move," Dr Arack said scanning her with his wrist screen, then turning it to check the results. "You suffered a severe shock. I need…"

"…A shock?" Cody gasped. "Her heart rate was obsolete. Her Oxygen levels were at zero. How could you call it a shock?"

"Stop talking like I'm not here," Erica broke in. "I'm alive and I feel fine."

It was the honest truth. In fact, she felt better than fine. To prove it, she got to her feet, brushed the dirt off her body and flicked her hair from her face. "I just don't get how I'm fine. That was one hell of an electric shock. How'd you know it would work?"

Dr Arack's eyes trailed from his wrist screen, back to Erica. "It was the only solution. Your body is feeding off the GX572 to survive. While it should be killing you, that chip has altered your DNA in a way that physically makes you a part of Maranthina's life force. I've only ever seen it once before…" the doctor's voice trailed off as the other's considered what he had said.

"You're talking about your daughter, aren't you?" Erica asked. He nodded. She wanted to ask if his daughter was Megan, though that would lead to a conversation about his ill treatment of Deets. So, she decided that now just wasn't the time. Instead, she commented on the other point he had made. "What did you mean by a part of Maranthina's life force? Will I ever be able to go home again?" She noticed Seth tense up at her question, but they all waited for Dr Arack to answer.

"While I can't answer the effects your world will have on your body, I can confirm that Maranthina won't cause you to suffer from extreme temperatures, sickness, or…"

"…Wait," Cody interrupted. "Are you saying that shock gave her a thermo-wiring system?"

"It's not exactly the type of thermo-wiring system you're familiar with… But I have… I do remember seeing it. I think…"

"You think?"

"Yes. Theoretically speaking, the electrical charge mixed with the rooted cables from the chip implanted Erica with an advanced system... It's astonishing. Like..."

"...Woah, hold up!" Erica interjected. "So, I've been turned into a Maranthinian? But Maranthinians depend on essence ports to survive. We don't have essence ports in my world."

"Your point is?"

For an exceptionally bright mind, the doctor wasn't getting it. "My point is that I don't want to die when I go home to my world, and I can't stay here."

Dr Arack bit down on his tongue in thought. "Are you sure your world doesn't have essence ports? Anywhere that GX572 is readily accessible?"

"Positive."

As Dr Arack considered Erica's information, Seth finally spoke up, cautiously. "I know this is a really inconvenient time to bring this up... I was going to say something before, but it also wasn't a good time..."

"...Out with it, Seth," Erica said, not seeing how things could get any worse than the revelation of what MIOT had done to her.

"So, I took Adam and Deets back to your world to escape the spiders... only for the spiders to make it to your world."

Erica laughed. "Yeah, Australia does have some pretty big spiders. The other countries tend to joke about it and..."

"...No, that's not what I meant. MIOT have made it to your world and their robotic spiders are attacking cities everywhere."

Erica's mouth gaped wide open. "Seth, open a portal there, now!"

"Are you sure about this?" Cody asked. "Those spiders are dangerous. They could drag us right back to MIOT."

"Good. I'll make those bastards pay for what they did to me. Seth? Portal, now!"

Seth opened one.

Cody and Erica prepared to leave but Dr Arack tried to stop them. "We don't yet know what your augmentation is capable of. You said yourself your world doesn't have an essence port. What if your system runs flat? What if you have…?"

"…I can't let my world die because I created yours. Even if their governments do suck."

Despite Dr Arack's wishes, Erica, Cody, and Seth disappeared into the portal, closing the gateway behind them.

###

MARANTHINA – DR ARACK

As Erica led Cody and Seth back to her world, they didn't see the vacant expression on Dr Arack's face as he sunk into the abyss of his own memories. A life of love once lived, now lost forever. But as his mind took him back to one of his most treasured memories... the day of his daughter's eighteenth upgrade... he witnessed the missing piece of the Maranthina puzzle. That missing piece was the answer to everything...

His life's work.

His own happiness.

...His daughter's face.

That very revelation was accompanied by the tears of grief which had long since disappeared. Once again, he had been too late to stop the inevitable oncoming destruction of his entire world. The silence of the night was replaced by a sudden voice.

"Arack. Fine night for a walk."

Upon hearing his name, Dr Arack wiped away his tears and turned to see Jynx approach from behind a tree. "I needed… I needed a little air."

Jynx gave a half-assed smirk and turned his gaze to the essence port behind him.

"You're a horrible liar, old man. You could've just said you needed to recharge. I would've believed you… were I not a Reader."

"Alright, you caught me. A client of mine came here and caught a virus. I wanted to do a little research and…"

In one swift motion, Jynx's grip was at Dr Arack's throat, tight enough to control the oxygen flow. "…Cut the crap, Arack. You're lying helps nobody, least of all… your daughter."

"I-I… d-don't… know what…"

"…You don't? Well, let me remind you that it was your lying that had her killed. I loved her and your lies betrayed us… You remember that don't you? How she…"

"...JYNX!" Another familiar voice called out from the distance. This one was feminine. "Put him down."

At the woman's command, Jynx threw Dr Arack to the floor, where he gasped desperately for air, before looking up at the woman who had spoken.

Megan.

She knelt beside him with mock sympathy. "It's been a while, doctor."

"I-I thought you were dead." Dr Arack stammered, dumbfounded.

She chuckled. "Such a fun little plot twist. Don't you think? Not even Erica saw that one coming. You should've seen the look on Cody's face. It was like..."

"Y-You... You did that to her, didn't you?"

"Of course. You of all people should know what this means for all of us. What she can..."

"...You need to leave them alone. Cody, Araca..." Dr Arack's plea was cut short by an instantaneous red spark which shot from Megan's hand, straight to his chest, flinging him backwards.

The beating of his heart was met by a painful rhythm, which radiated through his left arm. His circuits raced into overdrive preventing another heart attack.

That jolt could've killed him.

The doctor stammered to speak with an elevated breath. "P-Please…Megan. L-Leave them… Out…"

"…Why must you always put everybody else before me? Your work… Them… Even Deets, goddammit! I'm right here, Papa! Just look at me!"

Dr Arack clambered to sit with his right hand gripping his left shoulder tight. "You're not… You're not my daughter. You'll never be…"

"…I'm the closest thing you'll have to a daughter when I'm through with her. You should be sure to remind yourself of that. Grab him, Jynx. We'll ensure he never forgets."

On her command, Jynx gripped Dr Arack by the back of the neck, pulling him to his feet and forcing him to follow Megan through the Bucklands forest.

###

ADELAIDE. SA – DEETS

The streets of Adelaide's Central Business District sat in chaos, with pedestrians stampeding through traffic and police officers doing their best to handle an impossible situation.

A fifty-foot robotic spider stood atop the Adelaide Railway Station on North Terrace surveying the crowds below. Despite the destruction, some on-lookers stood in awe of the advanced technological beast.

Amidst the crowd Deets, Adam and Chloe desperately strategized a way to take it down, for there would be no escaping through a portal this time.

"We need to think like Erica," Chloe decided, drawing Adam's attention. Deets, on the other hand, was lost in her own thoughts. She had specifically heard Megan's voice in her head earlier, telling her to sacrifice Erica.

"How would that help?" Adam asked. "These spiders weren't in any of her books... Plus, this isn't Maranthina."

"What I mean," Chloe replied. "Is that every time Erica landed you guys in a tough situation that she couldn't get you out of, she'd take a break from her desk, have a coffee and try to view the situation from a different angle. Normally, she'd use me as a soundboard to determine the adversary's vulnerabilities. These spiders must have a weakness. Or at least whoever is controlling them would have a weakness."

Those words garnered Deets's attention. MIOT controlled the spiders. Megan had been lost to MIOT.

Or so they had thought.

What if…?

A deafening metallic shrill echoed the streets around them, interrupting Deets from her thoughts.

"EVERYBODY, RUN!" Deets yelled, taking off in the direction of the old museum building.

As a Huntress, one of her upgrades included excessive speed. And as she heard the whip of a heavy net hit the ground behind her, she knew her abilities had saved her again… Even if they were weaker due to the lack of GX572 in this world. But then Deets remembered that Adam and Chloe weren't augmented the same way.

Had they made it out in time?

Deets turned back, and to her horror, the large white netting enveloped the crowd, sealing them in.

Amongst them were Chloe and Adam.

"Oh shit!"

Deets wiggled her fingers, igniting minor green sparks to appear from her fingertips. While she knew she was nowhere near as strong as Megan, she could still cause enough damage.

Loud bangs echoed the air, forcing her to notice a swarm of police officers, and what Deets only assumed were armed forces, shooting at the large robotic spiders.

How could they be so stupid?

The spider's exoskeleton had impenetrable plating.

Shooting would only…

Just as she had predicted, the bullets ricocheted off the spider's body and soared through the air in various directions, leading Deets to dodge rogue bullets as if she was on a battlefield. There was no doubt about it, she would need to work solo for this mission.

Then again, that had always been her preferred style.

She rushed over to the nearest light post, in need of a boost. To her delight, the sparks from the pole travelled into her hand, igniting every inch of her body with a euphoric surge.

She had always loved that part.

Deets ripped her hand away and scanned for the best point to make contact with the metallic beast, which had already started to coil the netting into itself.

It was the perfect opportunity.

In a bid to cool down her body temperature, Deets forced her breathing to slow. She needed to remain undetected by the spider's infrared scanners as she made haste towards the large net. Like an insect in a spider's web, it was packed tight.

The screams that came from inside, seemed to die down. A sedative gas, perhaps?

Unfortunately, Deets couldn't make out any faces, just the occasional limb or two as the individuals were packed together tightly.

No doubt, they would be taken back to MIOT.

Deets wouldn't let it happen again.

The net lifted off the ground.

It was now or never.

Deets gripped the white silk threading with her right hand and immediately found herself stuck to the net. She had anticipated that that would happen.

The faster the netting lifted into the air the sooner Deets found her feet parting from the ground. Fears of falling became imminent. But no matter the cost, she refused to hold on with her left hand. She needed to keep it free for what she had planned next.

It wasn't long until she had made it thirty feet above the ground, still holding on from under the net.

The muscles in her shoulder ached, but she merely pleaded with the universe that her plan would work.

Suddenly, something from the ground caught her attention... A silver shimmery portal in the heart of the street. Deets zoomed her focus in to get a closer look just as Erica, Cody and Seth exited the gateway.

A surge of relief flooded through Deets's core, for that meant they had made it out of MIOT alive!

But that relief was merely short-lived as a darkness quickly surrounded her. She had made it into the metallic spider's body.

A floor sealed shut beneath her, rendering her into total darkness... and still unable to remove her hand from the netting. The moment she felt her feet touch the solid ground, she heated her right hand, to break contact with the webbing.

But just as she was about to burn a hole in the silk to break free, her right eye twitched, catching her off guard.

Somebody was watching through her eye.

Using her as a camera.

And in that moment, Deets's intuitive system told her exactly who it was.

Megan!

Which meant that Megan had betrayed them and was using Deets as her own personal spy.

But for Megan to do that to her own sister meant that there was no telling what she had planned for the rest of them.

21

ADELAIDE, SA – ERICA

Words could not express the fear Erica felt as she saw the city of Adelaide falling into despair, thanks to MIOT's robotic spiders.

It felt like a scene from a movie... But those scenes only ever happened in cities like Los Angeles, New York... and sometimes even Sydney.

Never Adelaide.

Hollywood barely knew they existed.

Yet, there she was in the middle of it all.

In fact, she was the very reason it was happening.

And while there was a part of her that felt a pure rush of excitement, there was also a part of her that was absolutely terrified.

Fortunately, the metallic beast nestled on top of the train station was the perfect distraction from the shimmery, silver portal that they had just stepped out of. According to a few onlookers, it had just taken a large group of people.

Seth closed his portal, then pushed a few buttons on his wrist screen. "I can't locate the others. It's like their signals are being blocked."

"Really?" Cody gasped. "Shit!"

"Maybe they were part of the group that got caught," Erica suggested. "The spider's shielding must be what's blocking their signals."

"Any ideas on how to stop this thing would be greatly appreciated," Cody said, under his breath.

Erica noticed a group of army soldiers working alongside police officers, to hold people back. Seth and

Cody were looking to her for a plan, but her brain felt as if it were running a thousand miles a second.

"We'll need to get past the authorities, first. Looks like they're arresting anybody who goes near it."

Her mind went to Megan.

"...I can't believe Megan would do this," she continued. "What was she...?"

"...Wait, Megan?" Seth asked, dumbfounded. "What do you mean?"

For the first time, Erica and Cody became equally aware that Seth had never been filled in on Megan's betrayal. He didn't even know she was still alive.

"Megan betrayed you," Erica explained. "She faked her death and joined MIOT, to reverse our connection and to bring me to your world. Now, she's in control of everything. Including those beasts."

Seth's face drained of colour. Again, Erica thought she could see a bead of sweat on his forehead. She was about to mention it until Cody noticed it too. "Hey man, your face looks..."

Seth wiped the sweat away with the back of his hand. "Ah... This is..."

"...You're sweating, Seth," Erica said. "Maranthinians don't sweat. They..."

Before she could finish her sentence, Seth dropped to his feet. Pale. Weak.

"Seth!" Cody exclaimed. He rushed to assess his friend while Erica focused on piecing together Megan's grand plan.

The visions, Megan's creepy villainess speech and everything that had happened until that point.

Unravelling Megan's plan had to be the key they were looking for, to work out why the spiders were there. And then it dawned on her.

"I was right," Erica finally said. "She's been controlling the narrative for a very long time thanks to our connection. Seth... Did Megan ever help you with any upgrades before she traded in her cape of heroism?"

"Cape of...? Wait. Y-Yes... She did. She took me to some doctor on the outskirts of Datsian. They... It doesn't matter. Point is the doctor did something to my..." As he spoke, he pushed a button on his wrist screen igniting a long beep. Next, he slid the fingers of his right hand under the screen to pry it open. "Erica, I need your help. Help me lift this... owww... off."

The instant Erica caught a sight of the flesh underneath, her stomach churned in grotesque.

"Why can't Cody do it?" she groaned.

Cody turned to her in disbelief.

"I'm a Coder, remember? Me coming into contact with his live wiring system could force Seth's cerebral..."

"...Alright, alright, alright." Erica knew the answer.

If Cody was to even attempt the manoeuvre, he could wipe Seth's entire mind of thinking capabilities.

They had no choice but to let her do it.

Hesitant, she helped Seth lift off his wrist screen, revealing a combination of blood, muscle, metal, bone, and a mixture of red, blue, and white wires. "This is so gross," she groaned. "Doesn't it hurt?"

Of course, it didn't hurt. In fact, Seth's entire forearm was numb to the very wrist screen, altogether.

The most he could feel was an uncomfortable poking and prodding.

"No," Seth said, running his fingers over the wires one by one. There was at least eight spiralled through and around the two long bones in his forearm. Erica could feel herself growing lightheaded with each passing minute, but she needed to maintain her composure.

"Do you see this red cable?" he asked, separating one single red cable from the others. She knew that wire.

It was an important one…

But why would Seth have it?

"Since when did you have a longevity cable?" Cody voiced her concern. "And why in the pit are you removing it now? What have you been hiding, Seth?"

"That's a long story," Seth replied. "But we need to remove it anyway."

"What? Why?" Erica asked.

The longevity cable was exactly what it sounded like. A cable that helped Maranthinians live for a longer period of time. They were normally only added to a Maranthinian's system when the individual was nearing the final stages of their life.

In Seth's case, it must've meant that his body had been battling an untreatable disease. One he had refused to disclose to anybody else.

"Please," Seth begged. "Help me remove it."

Erica looked around. They were still standing in the middle of North Terrace.

The MIOT spider was scurrying after another crowd of people, heading towards King William Street.

If she was to help Seth, she couldn't do it out in the open. "Alright," she finally conceded. "But you both need to follow me."

She led them into the undercover parking lot, of a nearby hotel. Fortunately, it was empty aside from a few abandoned cars. Despite the privacy, they could still hear the commotion and gunfire out in the street, which told them they needed to hurry.

Erica turned back to Seth and readied herself for the most grotesque task she would ever have to do.

"If I do this. What will it do to you?"

Seth looked to Cody, who was also waiting for the same explanation.

"So..." Seth began. "A while ago, Adam and I were discussing the prospect of having kids. When I underwent the testing procedure, I found out that I wasn't very well. Apparently, my body was fighting against one of my newer upgrades and it not only rendered me infertile... but it... it also..."

"...It was killing you," Erica realised.

She knew that part of the story.

In fact, it had haunted her dreams for weeks, but she had refused to write it because the very thought of killing off Seth was too unbearable to consider. She had cared about him far too much to let that happen.

Seth nodded. "Yes. Point is, somehow, Megan knew what I was going through. She took me to see a doctor outside of Datsian who promised he could help. But ever since then… Well, it's like every time I use my screen, I feel weaker. I've never felt like this. I just…"

"…You should've seen Arack," Cody said. "You do understand that if we remove it, we could…"

"…I know the consequences," Seth replied. "So, let's just take down these spiders and focus on the rest later. Okay?"

Erica wiped away a few stray tears from her cheeks.

Seth was right. Now, was not the time to discuss unbearably inevitable consequences. Their objective was to slide the cable slowly out of his body. It was connected to his heart, so she needed to tug lightly without interfering with any other cables.

The very thought terrified her. The stakes were too high. But she needed to do it.

For Seth.

She inched her right hand closer to the red cable, which rested between his thumb and index finger when suddenly, a white spark ignited from her fingers.

Instinctively, she ripped her hand away.

"I-I'm sorry. I can't do it!" she exclaimed.

"It has to be the essence port," Cody assumed, having seen the action too. "Dr Arack did say it changed you. Just... try to keep calm."

"What if I hurt Seth? I don't..."

"...It's fine," Seth said. "You just need to think like a Maranthinian. Breathe and focus on not igniting another spark. That's it."

Though, none of them had any clue as to what the essence port had done to her, exactly. Sure, it had given her electrical abilities. That much was clear. But to what extent?

"Erica, please..." Seth pleaded, wobbling on his feet a little. His face had gone from pale to almost deathly. "...You need to hurry."

Focusing on her breathing, Erica brought herself to a somewhat calm state… despite the external chaos.

Her finger sparked again…

But she continued to breathe and focus. As the spark disappeared, she gripped the red cable between her thumb and index finger and released her breath.

As did the others.

"So, just… pull it out. Right?"

"Do it slowly… carefully…" Seth said.

She gave a light pull with her right hand. At first, the cable refused to give, so she increased her strength, as Seth straightened out his forearm. With her left hand, Erica extracted the wire out of Seth's arm slowly, leaving a smear of blood on his arm and her hands…

After approximately three metres, there was a firm tug of resistance. They had reached the end, at last.

"Just pull a little harder," Seth instructed. She did until they heard a click. After pulling the last of the cable free, Erica allowed it to drop to the floor.

Once he had refastened his wrist screen, Seth set to work on his personal health settings. "I should be okay, for now. But thanks to the time difference we'll have to leave as soon as we deal with these spiders."

While she had heard him, Erica's attention was on the sparks that her hands seemed to be able to ignite by sheer will. There was no doubt about it, her body now possessed the abilities of a Maranthinian. And while that potentially meant she could be in an entire world of danger, it also meant she could potentially be powerful enough to battle the spiders and save her world. "You guys, follow me!" she said, racing out of the parking lot and into the street.

On the corner of North Terrace and King William Street, the large metallic spider had thrust a net over another crowd of bystanders. Erica, Cody, and Seth would need to hurry if they were to make it before the spider could engulf its latest capture into its body.

As Erica neared the robotic arachnid, she noticed the sun rays reflect against its many eyes, all made of glass.

No, not just glass… Camera lenses.

Which meant that somebody had to be monitoring everything the spider was doing.

Controlling it.

It had to be Megan.

She had already admitted to building them in accordance with Erica's arachnophobia.

Why wouldn't she choose to pilot them herself?

According to Seth, the spiders were all over earth, most likely collecting data as well as test subjects.

That meant they had to be running on a network.

Erica stopped running a short distance away from a large mound of people covered in spider silk and turned onto King William Street.

Somehow, she had run from the underground parking lot to the corner, quicker than Cody and Seth could. Was she faster now?

"They think that spider is big," came the voice of a drunk, roughly in his fifties, sitting at the clear-sheltered bus stop to her left. The man was dressed in ragged clothes and had a bottle of vodka in his hands.

Had he seen how fast she had run?

Still, he continued with his slurry conversation. "You should see the one in my kitchen. It's a fucking huge bugger. You'd think it would pay rent, but no. That's the third one I've seen all day."

"Third one?" Erica asked.

Was he referring to the spider in his kitchen or the metallic thing before them?

"Yep. They come here taking insects and eating them. In this case, the insects are people. You know what it really is though, don't ya?"

"No. What's that?"

"Damn government conspiracy. Or a marketing stunt for the electric company. That's why I don't use internet." As the man continued to ramble incoherently, Erica was joined by Seth and Cody.

"There's another one a few blocks away," Cody said.

Erica thought back to what the drunk had said about seeing three of them. The funny thing was that there had also been three when she and Cody had been caught.

"They must be running on a network," Erica told her friends. "Seth, can you run a scan to see if MIOT has any cloaked…"

Before she could finish her sentence, he was already scanning. "…err… They all look like local networks for your… Wait! I found it. M.I.O.T Abroad connection."

"Great! If we can jack into that server just maybe, we can seize control and…"

"…It needs a password." He typed in two separate codes. Both were unsuccessful attempts. "Dammit! One last…"

"…Hold on," Cody said quickly. "Let me try something." He placed his left palm over Seth's wrist screen and his eyes immediately flashed rainbow.

"Shit! I hit a firewall."

Unfortunately, as he had been hacking the network, the white netting of people had already begun lifting into the air. In drunken awe, the man slumped against the bus stop drinking from his vodka bottle.

Erica needed to do something whether the drunkard saw her or not. The question was, what *could* she do?

If this had been one of her stories, Deets or Megan would've channelled the electricity from whatever power source they could and...

She noticed a nearby utility pole. Just maybe she could spark an electrical current to distract the spider, giving Cody enough time to hack the network.

Erica rubbed her hands together, already feeling the static buzzing between her palms. A few small white lightning bolts appeared, and in that moment, Erica remembered the very abilities that Megan had possessed throughout her stories.

Speed, the ability to shoot lightning bolts from her fingertips and limited Reading capabilities.

Perhaps, they were the same abilities that Erica had been given.

Erica flicked her wrist, and white lightning shot from her hand. There was a loud ZZZZZZZ and a beautiful display of electricity, as the bolt struck a red sedan, parked on the side of the road.

"Oh, shit!" she gasped.

"Did you just…?" the drunk stammered.

"Ah, I don't know what you're talking about," Erica said quickly. "Maybe you should go home and get some sleep."

The man looked at the car, then back at Erica, Seth, and Cody. He staggered a little, but then left with his almost empty bottle still in hand.

"Did you actually do that?" Seth asked.

"I think so. How's Cody going with that encryption?"

"I'm not in yet," Cody said. "There's another firewall. Try to get the spider's attention again. This time, please be careful. One time, Megan blew up an entire building. We don't need that."

This time when Erica ignited a spark, she directed it towards the nearby utility pole. The white bolt travelled up the pole, through the wires and made its way to the large metallic spider.

The level of control was exhilarating!

Again, Erica felt the continuous tingling sensation, as if her entire body was experiencing pins and needles.

"What the hell, Erica?"

Uh oh! She knew that voice.

She turned to see a very stunned Nick, approach from the other end of King William Street. His eyes were drawn to the bolts of electricity shooting forth from her hands. Judging by his expression, he had no idea how to logically explain just what he was seeing.

"Ahh… Hi Nick. Don't come too close, you might get electrocuted."

He turned his gaze to Cody who was still working through Seth's wrist screen and then glanced up at the large spider. "You… What… How?" he stammered.

"There's one easy explanation for all of this," Erica said, still focusing on her task. "But for me to give you that explanation, you'll need to… for just once… accept that Maranthina is real. Can you do that?"

Nick stifled a nod.

"Okay, then… Well, that spider is from Maranthina and this… What you're seeing here… is my electrical power."

"Elec… Electrical… Maranthina. Right."

"I'm surprised you're not recording all this on your phone."

Nick pulled out his phone. The screen was blank.

"It's not… It's not working.

"Is your battery flat?"

Nick shook his head. "No. It just died. First the Wi-Fi, then the battery. Every electrical or battery-operated item in the city is out… that's what I've heard, anyway."

While he had managed to speak his first coherent sentence since arriving, his news came as a shock. MIOT had to be siphoning the power supply.

"Seth, did you hear that?" Erica asked.

"Yeah. It's a good thing we're on reserved energy from the essence port. It should last…"

There was a loud crack as Erica's electrical current hit the large spider, illuminating its very exoskeleton in a white glow.

"I'm in!" Cody announced, just as the white glow disappeared.

"Okay. Command it to release the people," Erica instructed, forcing the electrical charge to disappear back into her hands. "Then bring the spider here. I need to speak with Megan!"

"Yes, boss!"

As Cody set to work, Nick turned his attention back to Erica. "Eri, I should really apologise for the way I acted. I didn't believe you when you…"

"…When I told you that Maranthina was real? Trust me, it took almost getting murdered by an automated bathroom and finding out I had a DNA-altering chip in my head for it to really sink in."

"Murdered by an…?"

"…Never mind. Do you realise this is the first real conversation you and I have had in a very long time?"

An honest, though sympathetic, smile spread across Nick's face. "It really is. Huh? And for that, I'm sorry too."

"Who are you, and what did you do to Nick? Wait, you're not working with MIOT, are you?"

"Your *what?*"

"Don't worry."

Nick shrugged off the thought and continued with his apology. "I'm serious. I shouldn't have been so selfish to make you choose between me and your books. Especially now that… well… now that you're probably the only person who can save us. A real sexy heroine. Do you think you can forgive me?"

While Nick had never been one for apologies, Erica had never really been one to hold a grudge.

She shrugged. "Sure. Just… Don't post all this on social media, okay?"

"Deal. I guess that now all is forgiven, you and I should revisit that date... After you stop these spiders, that is."

While Erica should've seen that one coming, it was actually the last thing she had expected to hear.

And while a few weeks ago she would've jumped at the chance, this time the very question forced her to reconsider every little thing in her life.

She glanced at Cody. His rainbow-flickering eyes a clear indication that he was oblivious to the world outside the MIOT server. Her feelings for him felt far more real than anything she had ever felt in her entire life, which included her relationship with Nick.

But Cody wasn't the only reason for her hesitation.

Erica was no longer the same girl she had once been. Not only had her feelings changed, but her physical body had been altered in a way that could potentially complicate the rest of her life.

Just as she attempted to verbalise her thoughts, a loud robotic shrill pierced the air, accompanied by the sound of metal smashing against metal.

Their eyes directed to the fifty-foot spider that was now standing on the road before them. Its legs – the ones they could see – stood impaled into cars.

While Cody had managed to disrupt the spider's hold on the web-covered masses, Deets, Adam and Chloe were still nowhere to be seen.

"What did you do to my toys, Cody?" Megan's shrill voice echoed throughout the streets, coming from the spider's inbuilt speakers.

Cody, whose eyes had gone back to their usual dark, chuckled as he directed his voice towards the metallic beast. "Impressed, Megan? It was Erica's idea. It seems you've been replaced by an absolutely flawless model. Even your spiders heed her command."

"Some things never change. Ah, Erica. I'm so glad you're finally stepping up as the main protagonist. You took your time getting there. Even after I sent you those visions."

"I knew it," Erica declared. "You're trying to be the author and exacting your revenge after everything I put you through, aren't you?"

"Exacting revenge? Wow, so dramatic," Megan laughed. "I'm surprised you haven't figured it out yet. While you'd like to paint me as the hero-turned-villainess, the truth is less so poetic. In fact, unlike you, I'm actually trying to save Maranthina."

"You can't be serious! You betrayed your friends, and now you're trying to destroy my world. That's not something a hero would do."

"Call it what you want. But I guided your adventure, posed as the antagonist to help you build your strength and even gave you…" A short-lived silence cut Megan off mid-sentence, before green lightning bolts appeared from inside the spider, wrapping themselves around the dark metal.

Erica stared down at her hands. The bolts weren't coming from her.

ZZZT! ZZZZT! ZZZZZZ! BANG!

The noise travelled for miles as the metallic spider exploded from the inside out, sending shrapnel flying everywhere.

"Hide!" Erica shouted, leading Cody, Seth, and Nick, to the safety of the bus shelter and out of the direction of raining metal. All around them, debris smashed through the windows of cars, buses, and buildings.

The translucent plastic of the shelter was barely adequate protection, as a shard of glass pierced through, leaving a large crack.

"What was that?" Nick asked. "Was that you, Erica?"

"No, it…"

"…Take that, you evil, lying, traitorous bitch!" The infamous insults of Deets drew their attention to the other side of the bus shelter, to find the augmented Huntress smashing up what looked to be another of the spider's eyes. Her body was covered in scrapes thanks to having blown up the spider from the inside, and her hair hung over what looked to be a bandage across the right side of her face. "An eye for an eye... take that and..."

"...Deets," Erica announced, as she emerged from behind the bus shelter. "Nice work."

Deets turned to Erica and the others, giving visible confirmation that it was a bandage to her right eye.

It looked as if it had been spun from the very silk of the spider and was lined with fresh blood from whatever wound she had sustained to her face.

"Why didn't any of you tell me she was alive?" Deets yelled. "That bitch planted a camera in my eye and has been watching our every move!"

"We... ahh..." Cody stammered, slightly intimidated. "We only just found out when MIOT captured us."

"I take it you removed the camera?" Erica asked.

"Of course, I did. We'll need to stop by Arack's clinic for a replacement eye as soon as we can."

"Where's Adam?" Cody asked, looking around.

"He and Chloe were in one of the nets that the creature lowered before I blew it up. I think it's lined with a sedative or something."

At that point, Erica's mind went to the fact that Deets had mention Chloe by name, which meant that the two had met personally. It was ironic because Chloe had always expressed an admiration for Deets.

Though before she could voice her thoughts, Deets looked to Nick and asked, "Who in the pit is this guy? And where's Seth?"

Wait.

Where *was* Seth?

As Nick introduced himself, Erica and Cody raced back to the bus shelter, where they found Seth passed out on the ground.

"We need to take him to Dr Arack," Cody said. "He'll know what to do."

"Not without Adam," Erica replied. "Besides, do you think his portal will work while he's unconscious?"

"I can try and power it up." Cody turned to Deets who had just joined them, followed by Nick. "Deets, can you free the others? We need to get back to Maranthina. Fast!"

"Yeah, sure. I can fry the silk to tear it open." She left to do that, just as Nick turned to Erica.

"You're not going back with them, are you?"

"I have to, Nick."

"But those spiders are everywhere."

"It's not like she's abandoning you," Cody cut in. "The only way to really stop them is to stop MIOT and to do that, we need to get back to Maranthina and take down Megan. Erica's the only person who can do it."

"But Erica's home is here. What if she can't get back?"

"Cody's right," Erica said. "The only way to stop all this, is to confront Megan once and for all. Besides, you saw what I can do. My body has been altered, and now it relies on the Maranthina core for sustainability. I need to reverse it all so I can come back home."

But was that what she really wanted?

"Erica!" Chloe called out from behind. Erica turned to see Chloe and Adam accompanying Deets, looking sluggish, but otherwise okay. Compelled by emotion, Erica hugged her as Adam crumbled to his feet to hold Seth.

"He's still alive," Cody said. "But his vitals are slow. We're taking him to Arack's clinic." As Cody spoke, he used Seth's screen to open a portal.

"I need to go with them," Erica said, releasing Chloe from her embrace.

"I know," Chloe replied. "I look forward to reading all about your adventure in your next book."

"I hope so. I can't think of a better beta-reader than you." Erica nodded goodbye to Nick, before assisting Cody and Adam with Seth's unconscious body.

Surprisingly, Deets seemed nervous, as she turned to Chloe. "So… ahh… It was nice… meeting you."

"Look after Erica for me. Understood?" Chloe demanded.

"Of course. Erica will come to no harm under my…"

Before Deets could finish her sentence, Chloe kissed her and added, "Thanks for destroying that thing."

Speechless, Deets nodded, and followed the others through the portal, leaving Nick and Chloe in the ruined streets of Adelaide.

Once the portal had sealed shut, Nick asked, "You don't think there's anything going on between Erica and that Cody guy, do you?"

"You never did read a single one of her books, did you, Nick?"

"No. Why?"

Chloe shook her head, amused. "No reason."

MARANTHINA – ERICA

Adam and Cody laid Seth's unconscious body down on the medical bed, the minute they stepped out of the portal and into Dr Arack's medical office.

"Where's Dr Arack?" Erica asked, looking around.

"He should be here," Adam said. "Can you reach him, Cody?"

"He doesn't seem to be responding to my mindlinks," Cody replied.

"Maybe he's in surgery," Deets suggested.

"Well, we need to find somebody," Erica decided. "Deets, and I will go find Miri while you guys wait here with Seth."

It wasn't a request but a command, which Erica was surprised to have delivered so naturally. At the same time, there was a reason she had suggested Deets accompany her, and that was because she needed to relay her earlier visions with the Huntress. Erica had concluded that the only person to help her decipher the visions of Megan's past, was Deets.

As the two strolled down the hallway towards the waiting room, Erica began her interrogation. "Are you sure that you and Megan aren't Dr Arack's children?"

Deets stopped, forcing Erica to do the same. "Where in the pit did you get that from? No way, I don't even think he had kids."

"He did. He had a daughter and… you. I saw it in a vision." She purposely left out the part where Dr Arack had 'built' Deets for spare parts.

"A vision?"

"Yes. Ever since MIOT stuck this chip in my head, I've been seeing... I guess, through Megan's eyes. She even gave me her powers, it seems."

Deets studied Erica for what felt like an eternity with her non-bandaged eye. The stare was so unsettling, Erica could've sworn Deets could see through the bandage too... Even without her eyeball.

Finally, Deets looked away.

"You mind giving me a little more information on this supposed *vision?*"

Erica thought back to the numerous visions she had seen. The young girl in the bed who had killed her own mother, and the vision of Deets with Dr Arack and who Erica assumed was Megan.

"That's what I thought," Deets scoffed at Erica's silence. "There was no vision."

"Yes, there was. Dr Arack's daughter had lightning powers and she killed her own mother to protect herself. The girl was sick, and so Dr Arack built another child to keep her healthy... A sister. That sick girl was Megan, wasn't it? You were built to keep her healthy. Weren't you?"

Deets's stone cold stare was almost unreadable. Either Erica had hit the nail on the head with the answer, or Deets was thoroughly confused.

"No… No. You're trying to screw with my head. She never did any of that. I'm not… I'm not just some… some clone for spare parts!"

"Are you sure? Because your tattoos…"

"…My tattoos are just blatant reminders of what MIOT did to me… What *you* let them do to me! Or have you forgotten?"

A nerve had clearly been struck. But Erica knew she was onto something. She was so close to unravelling the truth. She just needed Deets to listen…

To help her figure it out.

"That must be it!" Erica announced. "The recycling process! Maybe it was in a different…" Erica was struck backwards by a green bolt of lightning coming straight from Deets's right hand.

The girl was pissed off!

"What the hell, Deets?"

"I knew it! Megan sent me a vision telling me that you would screw with our heads. You're not our creator, you're our pit-forsaken destruction. But I won't allow it!" As Deets attempted to fling another lightning bolt with her right hand, Erica gripped her wrist with her left hand to protect herself.

"Stop it! Can't you see she's trying to divide us?"

"Megan is my sister. Whatever her reasons are, I never turn my back on family. So, stop trying to trick me with these weird visions that never happened. Megan is not Dr Arack's daughter, and I am not…"

"…I'm sorry. I didn't mean to get you mad. It's just… I feel that working out what these visions mean is the answer to saving… well, everybody. My world *and* yours."

Deets's glare softened. "Okay, just… Please promise we won't kill her. She's still my sister… Despite everything she's doing."

Erica released Deets's wrist, slowly.

Cautiously.

Deets was a Huntress, and you could never be too careful with their type.

"What's going on in here?" Miri asked from the end of the hallway. "What are you doing?"

As Erica turned to see Miri standing in the doorway, she kept Deets in her peripheral view. The Huntress seemed strangely fascinated by the scar in the palm of her hand. Erica lowered her hand, "We're looking for Dr Arack. He's not in his office and it's an emergency."

"That's because he's been gone for days," Miri replied. "But can I help? Is there something wrong with your chip? I know he was genuinely concerned about…"

"…It's Seth! We don't exactly know what's wrong. He's unconscious."

"Maybe I can be of some assistance," a familiar voice said, joining Miri from the waiting room.

It was Jynx.

"I might not have medical expertise like the good doctor, but my reading capabilities should be able to pick up whatever's wrong with dear old Seth."

As Miri went to gather her equipment, Erica considered the guy's proposal.

"It's so good to see you doing much better, Erica," Jynx continued. "I was really worried about you. In fact, I haven't been able to get you off my…"

"…Alright, you can help," Erica cut him off. "Without Dr Arack here, we'll need all the help we can get. Just don't make me regret it."

"Wouldn't dream of it."

Once Erica led Deets and the others into Dr Arack's clinic, they found Cody pacing the room and Adam sitting at the bedside holding Seth's hand.

The moment Cody saw Jynx, he almost had a heart attack. "What in the pit is he doing here?"

"Dr Arack is missing and he's the only person here with reading capabilities," Erica replied, unapologetic.

As Cody considered her argument, Miri set to work checking Seth's vitals via the use of his wrist screen, alongside Jynx. "Erica was right to let him help us," Miri said. "Jynx, would you mind scanning Seth's cerebral wirings?"

Jynx visually scanned, and his eyes didn't stop moving until he reached Seth's head.

He squinted.

"What?" Adam asked, alarmed. "Will he be okay?"

Jynx exchanged looks with Miri.

"What is it?" Erica asked. Her tone serious.

But Jynx ignored her question and led Miri out of the office.

"I thought he was going to help us," Deets whined.

Refusing to wait around, Erica stormed after Jynx and Miri. "What's wrong with him? I know you saw something, Jynx. Just tell me what it was!"

Jynx looked up and again adopted his overconfident smile. "He just needs his rest."

Her anger merely escalated. She opposed him, standing mere inches from his face. "Quit lying, Jynx. Just tell it to me straight. What did you see?"

Jynx stared into her eyes with an unsettling silence.

Was he scanning her?

His character was the ultimate poker player who always did things for his own best interest. Finally, he sighed. "Seth's problem isn't the wiring or even the multidimensional travel chip in his head..."

"He mentioned something about being sick. Is it cancer or...?

"...Erica, I've heard tales of a virus coming from the very core of Maranthina. Like a toxicity the world is putting off because *it's* dying."

"Dying?"

But Maranthina couldn't die. It was Erica's fictional world for god's sake. She would never let that happen.

Erica looked to Miri for confirmation.

"It's the truth," Miri said. "Dr Arack has seen a few cases like this. Unfortunately, further augmentation only increases the risk of…" Her voice trailed off and Erica knew exactly what the woman wasn't saying. The more augmentations Seth received the more likely death would find him.

"Well, there must be some sort of medicine he can take," Erica pleaded. Miri pulled up her own wrist screen to show Seth's vitals. "Seth's pulse is low, as you can see here. His oxygen levels are also low. There are some significant signs of physical deterioration throughout his lungs and brain…"

She continued with the vitals, but Erica couldn't hear her. It was like a ruthless cancer had taken hold of his body and refused to let him go. "…If you ask me," Miri continued. "I'd say that Seth has known about it for quite some time."

He did know.

That was why he had gone with Megan to see that doctor outside of Datsian City.

So, there was no doubt about it. Seth was dying and Erica had to accept that.

But she was still the author.

She needed to find a way to bring him back.

Somehow.

"What about recycling?" she asked.

This time, it was Jynx who took the reign of the conversation. "Erica, the deterioration of Seth's body has spread to his circuits. That isn't a good sign. Maybe if Dr Arack was…"

"…I'm going to try call him again," Miri cut in. "He needs to know about Seth's condition."

As Miri left, Erica prepared herself to tell the others the news, until Jynx held her still and brought his lips to her ear. She reacted with a violent shove.

"What the hell are you doing? Let go of me."

But he refused to let go. Instead, he spoke in an extremely low whisper. "Megan's watching through your chip. She has Arack."

"What?"

It had to be a trap.

"How do you know that?"

"Shh. She can't hear what we're saying, she can only see through your eyes. But there's so much you don't know. Just promise me, you'll do things differently this time… And don't jump, no matter what happens."

He kissed her cheek then left in the same direction that Miri had gone, leaving Erica silently baffled.

"…Am I intruding?" Cody asked, startling her.

"No. Not intruding."

"He's not gonna make it, is he?"

Words escaped her. How was she supposed to tell Cody that Seth was dying, and there was nothing they could do to change it?

It would've been easier to just write the scene in her book, take a month to grieve and then strategize a way to bring him back.

Unfortunately, The Maranthina Chronicles were no longer *just* stories she had written to entertain the masses. They were her own reality.

The characters weren't just names with bios and quirks that suffered at her hands.

They were her friends.

Reluctantly, Erica shook her head. A simple, non-verbal gesture of the heartbreaking answer that Cody thoroughly understood.

He bit down on his lower lip and nodded.

It was all he could muster.

Erica knew that he was on the verge of emotional collapse, and she wasn't sure how he would react. Would he snip his heartline again? Or would he do something far more drastic?

Unwilling to let that happen, she wrapped her arms around him, as he buried his face into her neck. It wasn't long until she felt the presence of his tears against her skin. And as much as she tried to fight back her own, she slumped her forehead into his shoulder and cried too.

They stood that way for a painfully long moment until Erica finally pulled away.

"We need to tell the others," she said, wiping her face with her hands. "Adam should know."

Cody sniffled and rubbed at his own face. "I think he already does."

As Erica turned into the direction of the clinic, Cody placed his hand on her shoulder and said, "even with Seth gone… I promise, we'll find a way to get you back home, after all this is over."

Home.

Such a funny word.

"Let's just focus on MIOT first, shall we? And we should probably add saving Arack to that list too."

"What do you mean?" Cody asked.

Ignoring his confusion, Erica entered the doctor's office to find Adam and Deets waiting for them.

She took in the sight of Seth still unconscious, and the memories of their very first encounter flashed through her mind. She chuckled reminiscent of how he had bowed before her.

Whatever was going on, she would get to the bottom of it so that her friends could live in peace for the first time in their lives. It was her solemn vow.

"So…" Erica started, but before she could get another word in, Adam stood and embraced her.

"Don't say it," he pleaded. "I already know what's happening, but I really don't want to hear it. His vitals are low. He's been suffering from some serious glitches. Please… don't say it, Erica. Just tell me what to do to stop him from dying."

Ouch!

"But… there's no way to…"

"…No, no. no. You're going to bring him back. "You're the author, Erica! You have to."

Erica's mind went back to what Jynx had said about doing everything differently 'this time.' They already knew that Megan was playing the author.

Yet, how many times had this story been told?

And as she posed the question to herself, the chip told her the answer. In fact, it gave her several answers.

She just wasn't ready to believe them… yet.

"I'm not the author anymore," she said out loud. "Everything that has happened to this point is Megan's doing. She's alive."

As Adam let that information soak in, Cody spoke up. "What did you mean by 'we need to save Arack'? Where is he?" And Erica told them about what Jynx had said out in the hallway.

From there, she told them about her visions. When she was done talking, Deets spoke of her own visions.

Particularly the one where Erica had jumped into the pit. That very vision clawed at Erica in a way she couldn't quite comprehend.

"Why didn't you tell me this sooner" Erica asked, as Deets grabbed an artificial eyeball from the shelf and started unwinding her bandage.

"I don't know, I guess I was little more concerned about you insinuating that Dr Arack was nothing more than a good for nothing papa."

"That settles it," Erica said. "Tonight, we're getting the answers we've been waiting for."

"How?" Cody asked.

As if it would emphasise her point, Erica got to her feet. "Easy. We're bringing down MIOT once and for all."

23

MARANTHINA – ERICA

Erica stared down at the unconscious Seth. Only a few minutes earlier she had declared that they would bring down MIOT. Unfortunately, she hadn't yet formulated a plan as to how, and he and the others were counting on her.

They also needed to rescue Dr Arack and, according to Deets, they needed to carry out the plan in a way that didn't lead to Megan's death. And despite all that Megan had done, Erica couldn't agree more.

But devising a plan was tricky, especially because Megan had cameras everywhere, which according to Jynx, included Erica's head. That very notion meant that whatever plan they came up with, would render Megan two steps in front.

"Erica? A word?"

It took a moment for Erica to realise that Jynx had summoned her from the doorway. She thought he had already left, and judging by the look on Cody's face, he did too. Nonetheless, she left the room with him.

"Did you think on what I said?" Jynx asked, pressing his back against the wall.

She nodded, unsure how to be strategic about their conversation without Megan catching on. "I...err..."

"It's okay, she can't hear us, remember?"

"How do you know? And how do you know she has Dr Arack? Are you working together?" Jynx's expression hardened, forcing her to probe deeper. "You are, aren't you? Seriously Jynx? How could you...?"

He brought his finger to her lips.

"Are you done? We need to keep our noise down. You need to understand that there's so much more going on, and you can't trust anybody."

He pulled his finger away so she could respond.

"No. It's you I can't trust. You think I don't get what's going on? Well, newsflash, I'm actually the author of this world. I created you. Which is why I know you're the most unpredictable character I've ever... I guess, I can say, met."

Jynx's mouth twitched. Then that twitch turned into a chuckle. Was he mocking her? As his chuckle escalated, he forced himself to maintain his own composure. "That's a new one. I guess it also explains the haircut."

"You don't believe me?"

"On the contrary. That's precisely *why* you need to come with me to MIOT."

"...But Seth is..."

"...We don't have time. Now, while the others are all distracted in there, let's go."

"Erica's not going anywhere with you," Cody called from the doorway.

"You don't understand," Jynx replied.

"What don't I understand? That Megan isn't dead, and everybody's convinced she's trying to take author control from Erica? Or that MIOT discovered multidimensional travel and needs to be stopped before they destroy Erica's world, too?" As Cody approached, his words stopped Jynx in his tracks.

"You're not convinced of Erica's supposed author identity?"

"Not exactly."

"Well, according to Megan, Erica needs to die in order for the rest of us to live."

That revelation led to a serious bout of silence between Cody and Erica, and after neither spoke a word, Jynx continued. "I still don't understand it entirely, but apparently, it's related to Seth's virus and the fact that we're all in some weird time loop. The GX572 compound is running out, and if it does that…"

"…Our wiring systems will have nothing to fall back on," Cody finished.

"What's wrong with that?" Erica asked. "Civilizations have lived without advanced technology for centuries. You can always resort to solar…"

"…Are you forgetting that our bodies have become so acclimatised to that compound that we wouldn't survive without it?" Jynx asked.

"It's like the oxygen on your world, Erica," Cody explained. "It's mixed into our DNA."

"Correct," Jynx replied. "According to MIOT, the pit needs a sacrifice and apparently that sacrifice must be Erica."

Erica thought back to the vision of her dying in the bed beside Deets and Dr Arack. She could've sworn that she had been seeing through the eyes of Megan.

Then her mind went to the vision that Deets had recalled. It had been Erica that had jumped into the pit and not Megan, instead.

Now Jynx was coming up with some nonsense about a time loop?

Was that what Megan was doing?

Reversing the connection, so that it would be Erica to jump this time. Self-preservation had always been one of her most dominant traits.

"Why me?" she voiced out loud. "Is it because I'm the author?"

Jynx shook his head, adamant. "You're still not getting it, Erica. You're *not* the author. You just think you are because of how many lives you've lived here."

"That just doesn't make sense."

"When I met you, I knew I had seen you before. And even though MIOT are pure evil, I worked with them because I needed them to unlock my recycled memories. I..."

"...You worked with them? After knowing what they did to us?"

"That's not what's important here."

"It's not?!"

"No, my point is you and I have been together numerous times throughout your lives in Maranthina. Just like you and Cody. Other times, you weren't with either of us. I just know you've played so many different roles. Unfortunately, your life always plays out the same way. You jump into that damn pit, and everything resets, forcing us to live the same events all over again, only differently."

Erica took in his words.

It hurt her head to even consider that he might be right. It didn't seem logical, in the slightest. But at the same time, the notion sounded more feasible than her creating a world, like some almighty being.

Besides, her having already jumped into the pit could potentially explain why the GX572 compound wasn't killing her, like it should've been.

Then, there was that chip again. Compelling her to believe in the sheer nonsense of it all.

Erica peered up at Cody, who was reaching the same conclusion. "I think, I believe you," he told Jynx. "It's hard to comprehend, but all this… It feels like we've relived it before. Like, we've known Erica before."

But Erica didn't want to believe that she was a recycled Maranthinian.

She was from earth.

Born of blood, flesh, and bone.

The only thing either of them were feeling was the author-character connection that she had with them.

But if it was true, then that meant, that Erica and Deets were related, as they had been in her vision.

It also meant that Dr Arack was her…

No!

It couldn't be true.

"You're a real son-of-a-bitch," Erica shot at Jynx. "You would literally say just about anything to hand me over to Megan, wouldn't you? How much is she offering you? Five hundred credits? Six? Tell me, how much am I worth?"

"I'm not a damn sell-out, Erica! Well, not this time, anyway. She has Dr Arack. And if anybody has a chance at saving him and the rest of us, it's you."

In her huff of frustration, Erica noticed Deets leaning against the wall by the doorway, listening into their discussion.

"Okay, say I believe you," Erica said, ignoring the girl. "Where does Megan fit into this? Who was she in the other lives?"

"I don't know. She never told me."

"And you never saw her in these supposed memories, that MIOT unlocked for you?"

"No. Never."

It wasn't a good enough answer for Erica.

However, whether Jynx was looking to betray them or not, wasn't the point. The point was that this was the only viable option to break into MIOT.

"Alright," Erica sighed. "I guess I have no choice. Just give me a few minutes to say goodbye to Seth."

"I'm going with you," Cody decided. "I just know Jynx is waiting for a chance to betray us."

"Were that the case, Cody, I never would've told Erica Megan's plan."

"You would, to save your own…"

"ENOUGH!" Erica demanded. "I couldn't care less if Jynx is with us or not. Let's just do this, so I'll actually have a home to return to, once Maranthina has been saved. Clear?" She shouldered them both in a bid to head back to the clinic.

"I take it you have a plan?" Cody asked, as he followed, leaving Jynx behind in the hallway.

"Not exactly," Erica answered.

As they reached Deets by the door, the Huntress stopped Erica, in her tracks.

"What is it, Deets?"

"That scar on you hand. Where did you get it?"

"I don't know. It's just always been there."

Without a further explanation, Erica stepped into the medical room where she could hear Seth speaking softly to Adam. The sight of him awake brought about an ounce of hope, which quickly diminished the moment she saw him smile weakly in her direction.

"Hey, Erica. If you like, I can transport you home right now. I know you don't…"

"…Don't worry about it. I'll focus on returning home later… After I find a way to stop MIOT. I just wish there was something I could do to help you." She took the seat beside him, as Seth took her hand.

"I've had a long time to process this. I'm sick. That's all there is to it. I'm just glad I got to meet the creator before I passed."

His words made her flinch with an overwhelmingly uncomfortable sense of imposter syndrome. To Seth, she was his creator. Something to believe in.

Religion had never made more sense to her than it did in that moment.

"What's with the silence?" Seth asked.

"Nothing," she lied.

It felt better than the truth.

"You're going to save us all, Erica. I can just feel it."

She bit down on her lip, but it didn't stop the tears.

She wasn't a hero.

She didn't even believe herself to be the author, anymore. Seth pulled her into a warm embrace.

"Thank you, Seth," she sobbed. "Thank you for bringing me here. Thank you for everything. You've changed my life."

It wasn't a lie. The very world of Maranthina had changed her from the very first moment she poured her visions onto the page.

The adventures, love, and hope that her characters provided, gave her a sense of belonging. It got her through the therapy of growing up in the foster system.

But what ached more was the thought that it was no longer just a collection of stories she had written. But a world she was a part of. And for that reason, she vowed, that she would do whatever it took to save it.

Even if it meant sacrificing herself.

MARANTHINA – ERICA

The stars shone brightly over the large, white MIOT facility. The very thought of being back, sent a chill down Erica's spine.

Would this be the last time she'd see her friends?

Or would her plan reset the time loop, as Jynx so desperately believed?

She stood at the facility's seven-foot-tall gate with Cody, Jynx and Deets mentally preparing for whatever might happen.

"Cody, can you jack that console?" she asked, gesturing to the scanner to the right of the gate.

"The minute I do, security will be on our asses like…"

"…Do it."

So, he did.

There was a beep, and then a holographic image of a security guard popped up.

"You have to the count of three to…"

"…No, wait!" Erica interrupted. "I'm here to speak with Megan. I'm the one she wants. I'm Erica."

The hologram disappeared, leaving the four of them in confused silence.

"Plan B, anybody?" Cody asked.

"What's…?" before Erica could finish her sentence, the large gate opened, and several AIA security guards approached, marching in an orderly fashion.

"Did they really need to send out the AIA?" Deets asked. A slight pang of PTSD arose in the pit of Erica's stomach, as she remembered the soldiers who had knocked her out, the last time she was there. She doubted they stood a chance against the six of them that were currently present.

"We need to ask your companions to remain here," the tanned female, who looked to be the leader of the AIA said. "Or we'll have no choice but to shoot to kill."

Deets and Cody exchanged glances.

Concerned.

"What about me?" Jynx asked.

The lead AIA soldier looked Jynx up and down, her eyes flickering a white laser over his entire body. "You're free to enter, Reader unit No# 52321.5."

"It's Jynx!" he corrected. "My name's Jynx."

Not that she seemed to have an ounce of care in her entire body.

"They're letting him through?" Cody scoffed.

"Just stay here. Please," Erica said, looking to both Cody and Deets.

After a brief hesitation, he nodded, yet Deets kicked at the dirt and cursed.

While two AIA soldiers remained at the gate to keep a close watch on them, Erica and Jynx were escorted through the fields.

After what felt like ten minutes, they arrived at the large, brightly lit glass building which offered a full view of the marble interior.

Averting her attention from the interior, Jynx placed his hand on her lower back and whispered, "Follow my lead." A click of a rifle forced Erica to flinch, and the female soldier in front, turned to face them.

"Do not speak!" she demanded.

"My bad," Jynx replied. "I was simply curious as to why we need an escort when Megan and I kinda have this thing going on. You see, she uses me as her Reading Victor and in return, I get full unescorted access to MIOT."

"Reading Victor?" Erica asked. He winked, and she felt the urge to vomit. "Oh, God! That's so gross!"

"Don't be like that, it was you and me in another life. In fact, if my recycled memories serve me correctly, you thoroughly enjoyed it."

"First off, eww! I'd never stoop so low. Second, in another life? How can you be so sure that MIOT wasn't just manipulating you to believe it?"

"Have you ever heard of a life print helmet? Let's just say…" His response was cut short by a violent jolt to his neck, caused by what looked like a taser. His body convulsed momentarily on the floor before coming to an abrupt stop. "What in the pit was that for? You almost fried my fucking senses!"

"It was a request from Megan," the lead AIA said. "If you speak out of line, you get a shock. Now stand and follow, silently."

Erica assisted Jynx to his feet and shifted her focus to the large glass doors before them. If either of them had any hope in surviving, they would need to play it safe.

They entered the building and her focus lingered on every clean wall and grey door that they passed.

While she wanted to assume it was her author imagination that gave her the powerful sense of de ja vu, she couldn't help but start to believe that Jynx and Cody were right with their suspicions.

It was like the more she thought about it, the less she could determine the difference between pure fictional imagination and ingrained recycled memory.

Her train of thought took her to the chip in her head, which seemed to be feeding her memories of the lives she had lived yet had long since forgotten.

Or maybe they just hadn't been imagined yet.

A sudden brush of Jynx's hand against her hair, interrupted her from her thoughts.

"What are you doing?" she whispered, as he lightly held onto a lock of her hair. His eyes were that of surprise and he showed her the reason why.

Her hair was turning white.

###

MARANTHINA – CODY

The squeak of cloth brushing against metal continued as Cody slithered through the air vents, with Deets not too far behind.

"Trust you to choose the primmest way of getting us past security," Deets groaned. "You should've let me obliterate the guards instead of jacking into the air purification sys..."

"...Shh!" Cody whispered, stopping mid-movement, to stare through the vent below into a small laboratory, where two scientists were working with beakers and a strange blue chemical.

Cody's plan was simple. Find the security room, jack into the systems, and save Dr Arack.

If he was still alive.

As much as Cody wanted to ensure that Erica survived her encounter with Megan, him going in blind would be risky for everybody. Cody waited for the scientists to move away from the vent, before continuing with no idea where he was headed. He couldn't help but imagine how much easier it would be if Seth was there to help with directions.

But Seth was…

Nope!

Cody refused to give into depressing thoughts. Regardless of how everything looked to everybody else.

They had always been the best of friends and had gotten each other through the worst of their lives.

Surely, Seth would've told him earlier were he truly dying. But instead, Seth had chosen to keep it a secret.

And it was for that very reason Cody hadn't been ready to say goodbye, back at the clinic.

"What's the plan?" Deets whispered, knocking him from his thoughts. "Because I really hope you have one."

"Of course, I do. We need to get to the security room. From there, I need you to take out the security guards while I jack into the consoles. That way, we can find out where they're keeping Dr Arack. Chances are, Megan's leading them to the pit. Once we have Arack, maybe we can help them then."

"And how do you propose we do that? Help Erica, I mean."

"I don't know. Maybe send a virus through the servers to render the AIA powerless. Or we could manipulate them to work for us? Anything that will give Erica an edge."

"So, no plan. That's great."

"Excuse me if I'm just making shit up as I go along. I don't exactly see you offering up anything."

"I prefer to work solo. You know that. I only ever joined up with you guys for Megan's happiness."

"And your excuse for this mission is?"

He turned back to see Deets quietly ponder his question and wondered if he had just crossed the line with that one.

Finally, she sighed. "Because Megan is my sister."

He could tell by her tone that she doubted her own statement. "I don't buy it, Deets. Megan stopped being one of us, the minute she sided with MIOT. They manipulated you to find that chip for Seth, so he would find Erica. Now, it's our job to stop her plan and…"

"…But what if Megan's right?"

"What? What do you mean?"

"I mean, what if Erica jumping into that pit will save us all? Megan always said, 'a real leader is somebody who will stop at nothing for the better of others.' She might've had a harsh way of doing things, but she was an admirable leader. We all knew that. So, I'm just saying, if she's right, do we really want to stand in her way just because we disagree with her methods?"

Compelled by silence, Cody considered her question. She had ultimately just dropped a conversational bomb and they both knew it.

If Erica jumped into the pit, time would supposedly reset, and they would be forced to relive everything, all over again, only differently, somehow.

But if she didn't sacrifice herself for Maranthina, their very bodies could shut down, and they would be forced to die slowly, without the GX572 compound.

Or so the theory went.

They all knew what was at stake.

But there were still so many questions and doubts alluding either outcome. Not to mention, that nobody really knew just what would happen.

They were all going on faith, which was the one concept Cody had always struggled with.

If Megan was right and they opposed her, the ramifications could be catastrophic.

Yet, if she was wrong... What then?

To answer Deets's question, Cody needed to be honest with himself. He needed to believe in his actions, and the reason why he was taking them.

"Yes," he finally said. "For once, I agree with Jynx. I don't believe Erica should jump into the pit. Don't ask me how I know, but I feel that there is another way."

With nothing further to discuss, Cody continued shuffling through the cramped vents.

"I'm not sure if I agree," Deets said. "Ultimately, I feel like we're going to need to make a choice. Megan or Erica. I just…"

"…I get it. But I guess only time will tell."

Cody stopped just above the vent to the large security room, where there were currently two AIA soldiers watching the twelve security screens on the wall. He turned back to Deets and brought his finger to his lips. It was the same vent that he, Adam, and Seth had used last time. In fact, the screws were still missing.

He lifted the grate slowly and pushed it to the side as quietly as he could. The distance to the floor was roughly ten feet and had caused him to twist his ankle the last time they had come.

Cody shifted out the way for Deets to squeeze past and watched, as she slid effortlessly through the opened vent, into the room below. She crept up behind the first AIA soldier – a man with light coloured hair and a rifle under his arm.

There was a crack as she snapped his neck, without hesitation. She took the rifle from him and turned to face the other AIA soldier – a female with long blonde hair and a mole just under her right eye.

"Hurry up, Cody," Deets grumbled, turning the rifle onto the soldier. Cody dropped into the room and rolled his ankle... Again. "Oww."

BANG!

The sound of a gun firing ripped his thoughts from his ankle and back to Deets who had just landed a bullet into the forehead of the soldier.

"What the...? You shot them?"

"Just get to work, Cody!"

Another AIA soldier raced into the room with his rifle raised. He was a dark-skinned male with half his head shaved to make way for the two shiny streams of wiring that ran from his temple to the back of his neck.

As Deets attempted to fight him off, Cody slammed his palm against the biometric scanner and immediately his mind's eye met a concrete wall.

A firewall.

Sheer concentration forced his head to ache, as his circuits went into hyperdrive thanks to his increased focus. "This firewall…" he stammered. "It's hard to get through."

"Just keep at it," Deets argued from somewhere in the room. But then, the more he focused, the sooner the wall started to fade and was replaced by a virtual maze of darkness and beams of green light.

Cody mentally raced through until he was stopped by another invisible wall. He felt around at the space to the left of him. Another invisible wall.

He felt to the right… A clear path ahead.

The green beams of light straightened. A possible straight road. Though he needed to be careful of traps.

Picking up his pace, he followed the dark pathway straight with his hands held out in front of him. Up ahead, it looked as if there were steps made of green beams of light. At the very top of those steps, there appeared to be a green door. He had almost made it to the end of the maze.

As he picked up his pace, his excitement rose. But before he could make it to those steps, his feet sunk into the darkness below, as if he was falling forever into the invisible abyss. Within his mind, Cody screamed out until he finally hit the ground.

It was so dark; he couldn't even see his hands in front of his face. For the first time ever, he was in pitch darkness. Physically, he tried to pull his hand away from the control panel. But he had no control over his physical self. "Deets, can you hear me?"

But there was no answer.

Not good.

MARANTHINA – CODY

Cody awoke in a rusty old bed with a thin white blanket covering him. What was strange, was that he felt cold. And while that was odd, what shook his core was that there were eleven other beds in the room with him. All rusted and covered in white bedding.

He knew this place.

He *hated* this place.

It was the orphanage where he had grown up after being discarded by his parents, for not becoming the prime synthetic that they had paid for him to be.

After countless surgeries, Cody's body hadn't handled the upgrades well. He couldn't code. His body couldn't handle the thermo-wiring and worst of all, he frequently suffered from involuntary shocks due to his faulty wiring system.

After his parents had received their money back, they discarded him and sent him to the only place that would take a rejected kid like him.

With a glance around at his surroundings, he brought his feet to the grey concrete floor. His bare feet looked smaller than usual. In fact, his entire body was that of an adolescent.

Shit!

He wasn't just seeing his past. He was living and breathing in the body of his past self.

He stood up. Just maybe if he could figure out where in time he was, he could determine how to get back and save the others.

He made his way into the old hallway, listening closely for voices. This was the very place he had met Seth all those years ago.

Two boys passed Cody in the corridor, talking amongst themselves about some new girl and her creepy sister starting fights in the cafeteria.

New girl?

Creepy sister?

He knew exactly what day it was.

Why did Megan have to send him back to the day they had first met? What was so important about it?

Could it be just another one of her vindictive games?

He rushed out of the old building and towards a large brick cabin at the other end of the grounds.

It was the very place he knew he would find Seth.

The medical clinic.

When Cody entered the makeshift hospital ward, filled with mostly empty beds, he found a younger Seth in high spirits, conversing with somebody in the bed opposite him. At least, Seth *thought* he was conversing with somebody. There was nobody in the other bed.

"Hey man, who were you talking to?" Cody asked, staring at the empty bed.

"I'd like to introduce you to our new friend, Megan."

But it wasn't Megan.

It wasn't anybody.

However, in the history they had lived, Megan had been sitting right there, covered in bandages and speaking with Seth. She had been in a cafeteria fight after Deets had been the victim of a serious bullying incident, over the scars that lined her body.

It had been at that moment, that Cody had first fallen in love with Megan.

This had to be the clue he was searching for.

"Ah, Seth?" Cody said. "There's nobody there."

Seth blinked in confusion at Cody, then turned back to the empty bed. This time, he saw what Cody was seeing. "Wait. But there was…"

"…I know," Cody interjected. "MIOT's playing with our minds. What's the last thing you remember?"

Seth thought for a moment and then looked down at his wrist screen, where an *ERROR* message was being displayed. "I was… I was in the library downloading a story when my wrist screen… Well, it crashed."

It was the same story it had always been. Only, this time, for the first time ever, the 'story' part caught Cody's attention. So, this time he asked the question he had never asked before. "What was the story?"

Seth stared. Puzzled. "You actually *want* to know? You hate stories… Besides, I doubt it was the story that did it to me. Maybe it was the con…"

"…Just tell me what it was, Seth."

Humiliation flushed over his friend's face.

Sheer vulnerability.

"Don't tease me, okay? But I was doing a little research. There's this tale about a woman creating Maranthina. Some say she's the very essence of our core. Mother nature or something. There are also theories that one day she will return and put an end to all the chaos. If you ask me, I think she could potentially destroy MIOT for good."

Before Cody could even begin to comprehend Seth's revelation, they were interrupted by a series of voices.

One, was the bitter old Nurse Lakes.

"I'm so glad you could come in, doctor. Getting anybody from MIOT to check on these kids is a hopeless endeavour," she said.

"I understand, Nurse Lakes," came the other voice that instantly forced Cody and Seth to turn around. Dr Arack had arrived. "I've had some trouble dealing with MIOT myself. But as a favour to my daughter, I promised to help as many sick kids, as I could."

Cody's mouth dropped. This had never happened before. Why was Dr Arack here, now?

"Oh, here are some of the students now," Nurse Lakes replied, noticing Cody and Seth for the first time.

As the doctor's attention was directed onto him, Cody nodded dumbfounded. "Dr Arack? Do you... Do you remember me? It's me... Cody!"

"I'm sorry, young man. I don't. Are you a friend of my daughter, perhaps?" The doctor turned his head to peer over his shoulder, at another person that Cody had not yet seen. "Baby, do you know this boy?" the doctor asked. The girl stepped forward, forcing Cody to understand exactly what was going on.

The girl was Erica at around thirteen annual upgrades of age, and she was wearing a one-eyed visor over her right eye. There was a thin line of metal running from her left temple, down her face and neck, and disappearing under the collar of her white blouse.

Her brown hair was kept short, stopping just under her chin. And she had vibrant blue streaks throughout her side fringe which hung over her visor.

But it was the energy about her that ignited the room. That amount of energy could only mean one thing. That she was an immensely powerful synthetic.

Beyond Prime status, even.

Quite possibly an Ultimate Synthetic with the ability to do anything. But to Cody, his emotions were very conflicted. On one hand he knew her as a woman. The supposed creator of Maranthina.

But on the other hand, he was smitten.

No.

It went beyond smitten. This was the girl he was destined to love. And because of that, he couldn't even think of the right words to say.

Erica directed her eyes from her wrist screen to her father with an unshakable excitement. "Sorry, papa. I was mindlinking my sister. She…"

"Your sis…?" Dr Arack rubbed his hand through his peppered hair. Clearly, Erica's supposed *sister* was a secret he did not wish to be revealed. Regardless, he continued as if nothing had happened. "Very well, *Araca*. But I was asking if you knew these boys."

Erica's eyes flashed to Cody and a soft smile crinkled up into her right cheek, accompanied with a slight shade of crimson. That smile forced Cody's very heart to stop beating altogether.

A distant voice in the back of his head, told him that this wasn't a vindictive prank, but a recycled memory. Maybe even a collection of memories rolled into one.

Erica turned her gaze onto Seth and shrugged. "No, I don't. But look. That one has the 1HT model wrist screen. It's gotta be causing him some serious glitches. Let me fix it!"

Before anybody could stop her, she jumped onto the bed and grabbed Seth's hand in hers, to evaluate the error message. "Yikes! What did you do?" she asked.

"I was reading a story on the..." Seth stopped talking, as she held her wrist screen over his, and her eyes went from a greyish green, to white.

"Wow," Seth and Cody said, in unison.

'White eyes,' Cody thought to himself.

She wasn't just *an* Ultimate Synthetic.

She was *the* Ultimate Synthetic.

And she was just so young.

If MIOT were ever to get their hands on such a child… it wouldn't end well.

When her eyes flashed back to their original shade, her smile lit up the room. "All better! I upgraded you to the Zeta 2.3 patch. It has a self-repair system, a navigational system and…"

Seth's eyes were wide. "…Weathering system to better control my thermo-wiring system? But that's state-of-the-art tech! I can't afford that. My family… They…"

"…Relax. It's free. Oh, I also added one of my favourite games. It's this program that allows you to virtually create worlds and people in your mind. It's totally electrifying. Whatever you imagine in your mind, your wrist screen will send data to your eyes, ears and touch receptors and you'll feel like you're actually there."

"That's incredible," Seth gasped. "Thank you, so much."

"You're very welcome!" Erica got to her feet and turned back to Cody, who was in a state of total awe.

He desperately needed to say something.

Anything.

"What do you normally imagine?" he asked.

"The Diamond Stream. It's where my mother is right now." As she said those words, there was a moment of sadness in her eyes. But she shrugged off the sentimentality and focused on Cody.

He was about to say something further, but the transition of her eyes going from green, to white again, caused him to hold his tongue. When her eyes turned back to their original colour, she gave her diagnosis. "You're really faulty. Whoever worked on you... What did they do?"

Her words threw him off.

She had literally just used her reading capabilities to run a thorough scan of his entire electrical system.

Cody merely prayed she didn't read his mind while she was at it. He shrugged.

"Cody, is it?"

He nodded.

"If I help you…" she started. "It will hurt. But it will help, I promise. Do you trust me?"

Stupid question.

"Yes."

She took his left hand with her left, and to Cody's surprise, neither of them had scars running across their palms. Her touch was soft.

Cautious.

Until the moment her eyes turned white again, and he experienced a sheer pain, cutting into the space where his scar once was. As a reaction, he tried to rip his hand away, but it was like he was frozen in place.

Small bolts of white lightning flickered between their hands, and judging by Erica's clenched jaw, she was suffering immensely, too.

"Okay, that's… That's enough," Cody groaned.

Dr Arack looked as if he wanted to pull his daughter away but was frozen by an invisible force.

"Is she alright? Should I…?" Nurse Lakes stammered, noticing the blood trickling from Erica's nose.

"It's fine," Dr Arack replied. "It's what she does. Stopping her would be our biggest mistake."

Finally, the pain reduced, just as the white lighting disappeared, and Erica's eyes went back to their original shade. She wiped away the blood from her nose, and smiled, as if nothing had happened.

"All better!"

Cody stared down at the raw gash of blood, that ran across his heartline and was rendered speechless.

But he felt… He felt powerful. Like she had just gifted him with some of her own abilities.

Then he saw the same scar lined across her hand.

And as she saw it too, there was a mixture of confusion and surprise, written across her face. "Papa, look. I got a scar."

Dr Arack stared down at his daughter's hand.

Horrified. The ultimate synthetic truly did have a weakness. And judging by the look on the doctor's face, that weakness was Cody.

26

MARANTHINA – ERICA

As Erica and Jynx were escorted out of the elevator by the AIA soldiers, the blinding view of BG12 drew them in. BG12, also known as the lowest floor of MIOT, was exactly what you would expect, of the very location that fuelled the facility's entire electrical supply.

The walls and floors were made of concrete, and the entire room was roughly the size of an underground parking lot. Though instead of housing vehicles, a large, uncovered essence port sat in the centre of the room, beaming a bright white glow all around.

Numerous bolts of white lightning struck the air violently, providing a remarkable display. The very sight compelled Erica's feet to drift her closer, until she felt the tug of a hand against hers.

"Don't jump," Jynx whispered.

While she heard him, her very instincts told her to do the exact opposite. They told her that she needed to dive right into the essence port, as if she *had* done it countless times before.

She felt compelled to do it for Seth.

And for Dr Arack.

And for Cody.

And for every single soul on Maranthina.

The closer she came to the essence port, the more the chip in her head fed her memories of times long since passed. She noticed Megan positioned at the mouth of the port, and took her place opposite the woman, peering deep into the abyss.

"Erica, it's so good to see you in person again."

"How is this good? We both know why you convinced Jynx to bring me here. You want me to jump into the pit."

"And why do you think that is?"

"Because the author essence is needed as a sacrifice, so that her fictional world can continue living."

Despite knowing deep within her core that those words were a blatant lie, Erica was beyond desperate to believe them.

"For a smart woman, you really aren't all that bright. I let you believe you were the author, so all this would be far easier for you to comprehend. You didn't create Maranthina. You were..."

"...Born here," Erica finished, knowing it to be true.

"That's right. You were a sick child... So, your father built a clone for spare parts and harnessed the very compound of Maranthina's core, to make you healthier... stronger... and the first ultimate synthetic. But of course, nothing comes for free, and Maranthina's core desired something in return. A sacrifice for..."

"...That's impossible. The core can't demand anything. It's not a living..."

"...Oh, but it is. You of all people should know. Every time you gave up your life, you gave Maranthina a part of your life essence. Thanks to your father..."

Father?

Erica let that news process, and immediately remembered that Megan had captured him. "Where is he? Where's Dr Arack?"

"I'm sorry, but you can't see him. Nor would you want to. You see what's happening to him, and to Seth... Well, they can all be reversed if you do what you're destined to do. Jump into that pit and reset time. MIOT will take care of the rest. I promise."

An overwhelming spell of silence fell over Erica as she considered Megan's words. As impossible as it all sounded, it all made sense. And thanks to that damn chip in her head feeding her memory after memory, there was no doubt that it was all true. Erica was the only person who could save them.

But just what did MIOT have planned?

And how could they prevent another time loop when they had failed countless times before?

"What is MIOT going to do? If you want me to jump, I need reassurance that it won't be for nothing."

Megan turned her attention to the AIA soldiers. "Leave," she ordered. So, they did.

Erica's gaze landed on Jynx's hard to read stare. He didn't want her to jump. That much was certain. But it wasn't his choice.

After the AIA soldiers had left the floor, Megan shifted her gaze back to Erica. "During your last life, MIOT planted a device at the very core of Maranthina. That device was designed to ensure your sacrifice stopped the time loop, and enable Maranthina to withstand another millennium. But that very device spat your soul out into your world, where you were born, this time."

Megan's words possessed a level of sincerity. She had always been a brutally honest character, and Erica just knew that this was one of those times.

So, she continued to listen.

"After they discovered what had happened, they made their repairs. This time, when you do what needs to be done, your very essence will be filtered through the device, and course through the veins of every Maranthinian present, prolonging their lifespans for years to come. Our bodies will be far more resilient against sickness and old age. If all goes to plan, we could live forever."

Erica's mouth dropped. If what Megan was saying was the truth, she was the very key to immortal life.

She understood it all.

She *could* save them all.

Erica peered back into the pit of glowing acid. She was ready to do it.

She was ready to jump.

To *hell* with Jynx's recommendations.

Until her selfish sense of humanity washed over her. She didn't want to die. "There must be another way. Why me? Why not you? You're practically another version of me, aren't you?"

Her words sounded as if she was begging for a way out. Which she was.

For Erica wasn't a hero.

She wasn't even the author anymore.

Sure, she was willing to admit that she had been an Ultimate Synthetic. But that was in another life.

It wasn't who she was now.

"You don't think I pondered that myself? I'm nothing more than a poor substitute for you. Something the core created by your will. A promise you left for those you loved."

"Huh?"

"You didn't know?"

No, Erica didn't. How could she?

With an expressionless gaze, Megan continued. "It's the truth. You are the living embodiment of

Maranthina. By you, everything is possible. I am merely an imprint that you left for Deets and Cody. A vessel to fill their void. It's why you saw Maranthina through my eyes."

And Erica did know it.

And somehow her fears were gone.

"Don't do this!" Jynx demanded, grabbing her arm. "We'll find another way!" Upon contact, he was thrown back approximately a foot away, by a bolt of white lightning.

"Jynx!" Erica cried. "I'm sorry. I didn't…"

"…He'll be fine," Megan said, drawing Erica's focus from his motionless body. "I trust that you will make it all better. You know what you need to do." Megan gestured for Erica to turn back to the pit – which she did. "You truly are the Ultimate Synthetic. Your very essence knows what you need to do. So, just take the last step. Do it for Seth. Do it for your father and for… *Deets?*"

The slight change in Megan's tone, forced Erica to turn her head, in time to see Deets forced into the room by a team of AIA soldiers.

Of course, it would take an entire team to hold the girl down. "Let go of me, you pit-scraping drones before I rip out your faulty motherboards!" Deets demanded, leading Erica to smile deeply to herself.

She had seen Deets blow up a giant robotic spider from the inside, only to land flat on her feet.

So surely a small team of the AIA couldn't hold her down. However, for the soldiers to have Deets apprehended, the very notion meant that something had happened to Cody. The question was, what?

###

MARANTHINA – CODY

For a moment there was nothing more than darkness. Until a new image flashed in front of Cody's eyes, forcing him to comprehend the predicament he was in. There was a headframe with a special set of goggles pinned to his head, blocking his view of all that surrounded him. It was fitted with coverings over his ears, to muffle any noises from the room he was in.

Cody assumed he was sitting in a memory chair, fitted with a Life Print helmet.

The helmet was a device that revealed locked memories to the individual. According to the vids, they could even uncover memories from past lives.

The helmet's frame was fitted with a series of needles, which penetrated Cody's skull, travelling deep enough to pierce his brain. While it wasn't painful, one wrong move could cost him his life, or at least render him brain damaged.

To prevent Cody from moving, he could feel straps at his chin, arms, wrists, legs, and feet, all binding him to the steel and leather chair.

The memory he had just seen must've been of his own lost recollection. Perhaps even a combination of memories if what Jynx had said about a time loop was correct.

As a new memory appeared and the familiar voices spoke within his mind, Cody was met by another strange recognition of the scene.

He and *Araca* were sitting in Dr Arack's clinic, where she was upgrading his hacking abilities.

They couldn't have been any older than seventeen annual upgrades of age. Just like before, the process was unbearable and left another raw incision in his hand.

"If it's so painful, maybe you should just get my dad to do it instead," Araca suggested, while reading the stats on her wrist screen.

"I guess, I just like the challenge of overcoming the pain," Cody replied, watching the scar on his palm heal over. He looked back up at her. "Besides, your dad was busy. I heard he's been helping MIOT with some upgrades to the *Adam* and *Eve* project. I don't see why he'd bother after the way they treated him, last time."

Araca shrugged and looked back up at him with an annoyed expression that he had come to know all too well. "Did you really come here for your annual upgrades? Or are you just here to talk about my father again? Because I really do have other people to see, Cody."

Ouch!

"For the upgrades. Of course."

Erica went back to her wrist screen and ran through the details. "So, your coding capabilities have been upgraded to 10.3, your thermo-wiring system to 2.1... and after all that mess with your home security system, I've made it so you can now disrupt electrical systems for 5.3 seconds... Just please, don't do it anywhere that'll get you arrested... and if you do, don't bring me into it. Okay?"

She sounded cold.

Unapproachable.

Memory Cody had never seen her this way.

He hesitated, disappointed with himself. He had clearly come to ask her to go out to dinner and had failed miserably. Cody placed his hands in his pockets and attempted to leave.

"Wait!" she called after him.

He turned back, hopeful. "Yeah?"

"That'll be eighty-seven credits."

She got to her feet, holding out her wrist screen for him to transfer the money.

"But you've never charged me before. Why now?"

"Well, that was because I thought you were attracted to me. But after waiting all these years for you to make a move, I realised you only ever wanted free upgrades and I'm not just some cheap…"

"…What? No! I did like you… Do like you. I really *do* like you. But your father said…"

"…Twitch what my father said, Cody! The old man refuses to believe that Deets even exists. So, if you like me, just ask me out already."

Cody processed her words. "Wait, why don't *you* ask me out?"

"Get out!"

"What? It's a valid point. You're strong and so much more confident than I am. If you liked me, why didn't you ask me out?"

This time she pointed to the door. "OUT!"

But he refused to go.

Instead, he saw the vulnerability on her face. She hadn't asked him because she had been too scared to do so. Despite how powerful she was, he must've lost sight of the fact that she was still human.

"I won't say it again, Cody."

But he enjoyed frustrating her.

He folded his arms across his chest and cocked his head to the side, refusing to budge.

"Fine!" she said. "You've left me with no choice!" She brought her hands to his shoulders and pushed him towards the door. And he thoroughly enjoyed it more than he should have. He broke into a laugh, forcing her to do the same.

"Don't laugh. I'm seriously mad at you!"

"I know," he said, stopping in the doorway. "Will this cheer you up?" He kissed her and just as he was considering that he might've made the biggest mistake of his life, she kissed him back. And it was as if her armour of fury had just been knocked down.

The kiss was perfect.

Not that Cody was surprised.

For in his eyes, *she* was perfect.

As she pulled away, Cody was glad to see her irritation had been replaced by that same vulnerable smile. "You should... you should probably go," she said. "I still have a few hours left until I finish here. And remember. Don't get arrested for the..."

"…For disrupting electrical systems. I remember… So, are you coming to mine for dinner tonight or what? I'll even cook."

"You cook? You're such a prim! Why don't you just zap…"

"…Hey, you wanted me to ask you out. If you don't like my terms, I can always rescind the…"

"…Alright, fine. But the food better be good."

Her answer forced Memory Cody to smile wider and say, "Only the best for my girl," before leaving her standing in the doorway of the clinic.

Once again, the scene faded to black and as it did, Cody heard another voice. One who wasn't a part of that specific memory.

"…No baby. You didn't kill her."

That voice belonged to Dr Arack.

Present day Dr Arack.

Despite being restrained to a memory chair, Cody had found the doctor. But now, to Cody, the doctor was no longer just the doctor that Cody saw when he needed an upgrade.

Now he was the father of Erica.

…And of Deets.

Which meant that Deets was Erica's sister – and not Megan's. And in that moment, Cody remembered that Megan had Erica and Deets, and was probably torturing them relentlessly.

While keeping his head perfectly still, Cody wrestled with the straps at his wrists and feet, but it was of no use. He was desperate for a plan, though none sprung to mind.

Gradually, numerous memories flashed across Cody's view. And through every memory, another side of he and Erica was revealed.

They had known each other in so many different lives. Yet, they had loved each other in half of them.

Evidently, these memories were a series of data logs which had been archived within his recycled memory core, each time Maranthina reset itself.

This, in itself, left Cody with theories.

His first theory was that the tech must have been built from the blueprints of Erica's true Ultimate Synthetic potential.

If it was, why would MIOT allow him to see these memories? Were they hoping he would piece together the puzzle, in preparation for something big headed their way? If so, what was that *something big*?

Sure, he had seen Erica read the very internal wiring systems of Maranthinians and upgrade them beyond all capability. He had also heard of tales where she had been forced to defend herself, killing others in the process.

In a nutshell, Erica was potentially extremely dangerous. But it was her heart and her need for justice that kept her from losing sight of who she was.

"I'm sorry baby. I should've protected you," Dr Arack cried out, from somewhere not related to his memory. "You didn't mean to hurt her. It was an accident. You're not a killer."

The voice forced Cody to remember that he needed to break free. But how could he, when he was strapped to a chair, forced to watch his own memories?

Just as he was strategizing a plan of escape, the next scene took him by surprise. Again, the Ultimate Synthetic version of Erica was in it. They were roughly twenty upgrades of age and laying naked in a bed without blankets.

Clearly, thermo-wiring had finally become a success.

Erica had been fitted with another line of metal, running from her right temple, down to her right wrist and right ankle.

She was staring up at the roof in deep contemplation with Cody lying beside her, tracing the metal from her temple to her breast, and listening to the soft hum that her wiring made.

"Did you know you think too loud?" he asked. A smile crept into her left cheek as she faced him.

"That's because my mind waves run on a higher…"

"…Shh. I know the reason. I just find it so electrifying."

"You do, huh?"

He nodded. It was a moment where his life was perfect. Observing that memory, Cody couldn't remember ever feeling so happy.

"I do," Memory Cody replied. "So, what were you thinking about? Eradicating the need for recycled parts? The possibility of eternal life?"

She shrugged.

"Please, don't tell my dad. But I think MIOT is right."

Pure anger built up in the heart of memory Cody.

"No. You can't do it."

"Please understand, Cody. I feel like it was what I was made for. What I'm destined to do."

"How am I supposed to understand? You're trying to convince me to let you die. And I'm sorry but I just can't accept that!"

Her response forced them to argue in front of Cody's eyes, as if he was there, physically. And as they argued, the uncomfortable feeling made Cody desperate to tune out. So again, he focused on a means of escape.

And in doing so, he reminded himself that all the memories he was seeing had been made from his own programmed data.

And that memories were a series of data processed in the brain's chip – the motherboard. Cody's coding chip was also located in his brain and while he normally used his palm to connect with panels, the processing was still done in his mind.

That very concept made Cody wonder if he focused hard enough, just maybe, he could use the connection with the Life Print helmet to jack into the MIOT's servers. And as it was the only idea he had, he decided to focus with every bit of concentration to give it a shot.

At first, he was met by a black firewall and an excruciating headache as the needles dug deeper into his brain. He screamed out in agony, but continued, nonetheless.

He was desperate to succeed, so he focused harder until he felt the warm flow of blood run from his right nostril. And then finally…

The firewall was replaced by the black virtual world of the chair's electrical system, filled with neon-coloured lines, highlighting the maze he had been hoping for.

Cody grinned.

He had mentally travelled into the MIOT servers without using his left palm. And to his amazement, he felt less restricted over the network than ever before.

27

MARANTHINA – DEETS

Amidst her struggle with the AIA soldiers, Deets flung a bolt of green lightning at Megan. "You traitorous bitch! How could you screw us over and join MIOT? Have you any idea what you put us through?"

Megan darted out the way and immediately struck back with her own red lightning bolt. "I did it to save you, you naïve huntress. To bring the one person that can save us all, to Maranthina."

If it hadn't been for those pit-forsaken AIA soldiers holding her still, Deets would've been able to avoid that painful strike. Unfortunately, the red current hit her in the left arm, forcing her entire body to seize, before her nerves fought back with resilience.

"OWW!"

From her peripheral view, Deets could see Erica standing at the edge of the pit, clearly contemplating whether to jump or not. Though what struck Deets harder than that bolt had, was that Erica seemed different. Much calmer than usual.

Taller even.

And were they white streaks in her hair?

"I thought you would've been pleased to see your long, lost sister," Megan said, keeping her left palm raised at Deets.

"Well, it just so happens I'm seeing things differently these days. How could you set us up then use us for MIOT's benefit? You saw what they did to us. You experienced just as much as I did… if not, more!"

Megan hesitated but remained silent.

Had Deets gotten through to her?

Or was she waiting for something to happen?

Regardless, Deets raised her guard and studied Megan's left palm as she continued. "They're using you. Can't you see that? They don't care if we live or die, they just want power. All they do is recycle us for better parts and newer generations."

The absence of a scar on Megan's left hand drew Deets's focus. Megan never had a scar, but in so many memories, Deets could've sworn she did.

Like as if one had always just been there, when really it never had.

But Erica had a scar.

The same scar from every one of Deets's memories of their childhood.

But it wasn't just the scar that Deets remembered.

It was the face too.

And with every memory of Megan, it was almost as if they were changing to involve Erica instead.

But Megan was Deets's sister. They were twins.

Even if they didn't look alike.

Even if Deets looked more like Erica than Megan did.

She had known from the very first moment that this would happen. Deets thought back to her conversation with Cody, in the air vents. He was not one to go on belief without proof.

He wasn't Seth.

And neither was she.

She needed to decide for herself. But when the lines of logic and belief blur, it muddles shit up and makes you guess your entire identity. Yet, Deets had sworn an oath a long time ago to protect her sister.

It was now or never – even if it killed her.

Logic or faith.

Megan or Erica.

"Please, Megan. Don't do this. Don't listen to MIOT. They're manipulating you to betray us. And even if they're telling the truth… than I lose my sister and I really can't go through that again."

Upon hearing those words, Megan's stoic demeanour broke. Her eyes closed and she bit down on her lower lip. "Deets… I'm doing this so I don't need to die. MIOT has a plan. With Erica's sacrifice, the core will be stronger. Multidimensional travel will prove a stable endeavour and *I* will take Erica's place, indefinitely. I'll be the first Maranthinian capable of living in two different worlds. It'll be an incredible…"

ZZZZZZZ. ZZZZZZZZZZ. ZZZZZZZZZZZZ.

Megan's villainess monologue was just the distraction needed, for Deets to deliver a high-powered jolt of electricity to the AIA soldiers, in the same fashion she had the robotic spider.

The only problem was that while the AIA soldiers were made up of ninety-five percent wiring, their five percent flesh still possessed the ability to withstand high doses of electricity.

However, her attack temporarily short-circuited their wiring systems long enough for Deets to free herself and shoot another green bolt at Megan.

"I was talking about Erica! You're nothing but an imposter. I might've lost her countless times before, but I will not lose her again. I was born to protect her."

"Built!" Megan retorted recomposing her stance with an outstretched hand. "You weren't born, Deets. That's why Arack never saw you as his daughter. You were nothing more than a box of spare parts."

Like bullets, Megan's words pierced Deets's emotional armour.

She jolted, if only for a moment.

But the moment was long enough for her to remember her vision.

Erica had told Deets goodbye.

And Deets hadn't wanted to let her go.

For the very fact that they *were* sisters, no matter how it had come about.

Sure, the memories told her that she had been built in a lab to sustain Araca... No, *Erica*. But their sisterhood had been a bond, forged strong enough to battle anything.

Erica had even died for Deets.

Countless times.

It was a bond far stronger than what she had built with Megan.

Megan, who had only been created so that Deets and Cody wouldn't be alone. The same Megan who had betrayed them and had made Seth's deteriorating condition far worse.

For a moment – just a *moment* – Deets turned to Erica, whose eyes had turned white. Her once brown hair glistened with frequent white locks. Though what frightened Deets the most, was the look of menacing cold that had taken over her face, entirely.

Before Deets could determine just what had happened, Megan shot her to the ground with an overwhelming blast of red electricity.

Deets seized and crumbled to the floor.

Lights out.

MIOT SERVERS – CODY

Lines of multi-coloured neon lights swarmed the dark abyss that invaded Cody's mind. Everywhere he looked, everywhere he stepped, he was met by it.

He had never jacked into a system so big, nor as complex as the one he was in now. The only comparison would be like being jacked into an entire city at once. And of course, the sharp pounding to the top and front of his head was a constant reminder of that fact.

Despite the agony, he marvelled at the notion of being connected to the entire MIOT server and wondered if anybody had ever achieved such a feat.

Maybe he was the first.

Technically, the process of doing so should have killed him… or at the very least, rendered him brain damaged. Unless it had… and he wasn't yet aware of it.

Regardless, he had a mission to carry out and he would not fail in that endeavour.

Not again.

Turning his head to the right, he saw the neon beams of Dr Arack sitting in a memory chair with the Life Print helmet still over his eyes.

"Dr Arack?" Cody called on approach.

"Cody? Is that you? Where are you? Why can't I see you?"

"Because I'm in the server and you're in a memory chair. I'm going to try to shut this thing down to get you out of..."

"...Memory chair? But that means MIOT... No. It can't be true."

"I'll explain later. First, we need to get you out of here. Then we need to free Erica. Megan has her at the pit and..."

"...Erica? Wait, my Araca? She's still alive?"

"Dr Arack. I need you to promise me that when I free you, you'll wait in the room you and I are both in until I return."

"Wait? Are you kidding me? Megan will make her jump... I – I can't lose my daughter again. I need to..."

"…You need to leave it up to me. You're in no state to save her. Please, promise me that you'll stay where you are. Don't even try to free me."

Dr Arack took in Cody's words before muttering his response. "Alright, Cody. I promise. Just please… Please save her. Before the core's essence takes hold of her."

"The core's essence?"

"Yes. Maranthina is alive. It's the very reason I was able to make Araca what she is. The very reason she's the key to sustaining life. The core needed a vessel, and I needed a cure. But if Maranthina takes hold she might never let go."

Eerie thought.

"O-Okay. I promise."

With no idea how to keep that promise, Cody focused his attention on the flashing gold letters and numbers above the chair. There were about twenty-seven in total, and he could feel in his gut that he only needed six…

Maybe seven?

Shit! He wasn't sure.

But he needed to be certain.

"Umm... F, 3, J, H..." He felt a sudden jolt strike his left temple amidst the headache he was already experiencing. It sent him to the floor. "Owww!"

"Cody, are you alright?"

"I... I'm fine," he lied, before straining to focus on the right combination. "H, G, 8... Owwww!"

Another jolt.

This time harder.

He could feel the blood trickling from his nose. He wasn't strong enough. "Eri... Erica! I know this is a long shot..." he cried, thinking back to the time he heard her voice assisting him with the sequence during his first mission at MIOT. "...I know you're not the author and this isn't just some story you cooked up... But I know you heard me, last time. So, if you can hear me now... Somehow... I need you to help me again. Please."

They were the pleads of a desperate madman.

To his dismay, he didn't hear her voice in return. He even waited a few more seconds. "Please, Erica. I'm trying to save your father. You need to just... just tell me the sequence. Please!"

Still, there was nothing.

"I don't think she can hear you," Dr Arack said.

"Yeah." Cody's voice was small, and he knew he only had one more shot to get the sequence correct.

He needed to make his third attempt count.

Again, Cody focused on the letters and numbers. He tried to envision the correct sequence revealing itself. Maybe shining brighter than the rest, before dulling again. "W... X..." The X seemed to dull then shine brighter again. "...X..." At first, he thought he had gotten it correct, until the jolt struck him again, crippling him to his knees.

He couldn't bear it.

And to make matters worse, the doctor was also punished for Cody's failure.

Of course, Cody failed.

He would never be the hero, no matter how hard he tried. It just wasn't his role.

He was just a boy who had been augmented on with cheap parts… A boy whose very parents discarded him in an orphanage throughout every life he had ever lived.

A boy who had always lost the girl.

No matter how much he wanted it, he would never be the hero. Tears of agony and disappointment poured from his eyes as he attempted to block out the painful screams of the doctor. The headset was clearly frying the man's brains and there was nothing Cody could do about it.

"STOP IT!" Cody yelled. "JUST STOP BEING SO IGNORANT AND HELP ME!"

He didn't know who he was yelling to, nor was he expecting a response to come.

…Until it did.

"Cody. You need to save my father."

He couldn't tell if the words were in his head or all around him. But the voice was so calm and so - unmistakably Erica's – that he figured the pain in his head had rendered him insane.

Even the accent was correct.

"I'm sorry I failed you, Erica," he sobbed. "I can't save him. I'm not the hero."

"You're far more than you think you are. You just need to believe it. Just as I asked you to believe in me. And let's face it, right now you believe in me more than yourself. Perception is power, Cody. So, use it."

"W-What? What does that even mean?"

"You managed to breach MIOT's system using only your mind. That has only ever been done once. In this state, your powers are almost limitless."

"Limitless? That... That's impossible."

"As impossible as believing in world creators, Cody?" That second voice sounded almost identical to Seth's...

But how could Cody be hearing Seth's voice in the MIOT's servers?

Unless...

No!

Cody wouldn't allow himself to think like that.

He went back to the previous point made... Thanks to his mental link, his powers were almost limitless. Which meant, he could potentially help Dr Arack another way.

He opened his eyes to see Dr Arack's body still convulsing. Still struggling to bear the pain.

Just as Cody was with the electrical energy coursing through his mind.

Like liquid fire burning his brain.

"ARRGGHHH!" Cody grimaced. "L-Let... Let Arack go. Sh-Shut down the power... Shut it..." Beads of sweat dripped down his face. His body temperature ran hot as if his thermo-wiring system was struggling to do its job. "SHUT IT DOWN NOWWWWW!"

And then, it happened.

Dr Arack's body stopped convulsing and faded from view, while the green lights of the memory chair switched back to red. Seemingly, the power to the Life Print helmet had been switched off.

"Dr Arack?" Cody called. "Can you hear me?"

The lack of response was all Cody needed in order to believe that his plan had worked, which left him with one more task. And that was to use MIOT's electrical system to find Erica.

###

MARANTHINA – ERICA

Something… Something was happening to her. She was… *Transitioning.*

Erica's eyes, while opened, could see countless scenes right before her, like hundreds – maybe even thousands – of television screens, all displaying different programs, at once. Logic told her that processing so much stimuli, could render her mind unstable, but like an advanced AI, she analysed, processed, and reacted at lightning speed.

There was no other way to explain it, she was the living embodiment of Maranthina, and Maranthina was her. She could see through every camera on the planet and hear through every listening device too. Every memory of MIOT technology built had been stored into her brain.

There was no doubt about it, but she was an Ultimate Synthetic with the world's very core fuelling through her veins.

And it was simply the eighth-hundred time she had stood at the edge of the pit, ready to give up her physical body to sustain Maranthinian's everywhere.

Erica fixed her freshly woken eyes to the screen, which displayed Megan shooting red blasts at the unconscious Deets.

Her eyes were fuelled with anger.

Pain too.

With a subtle flick of Erica's wrist, the other screens faded away, and the scene of Megan zoomed into full view, enveloping Erica into it.

Erica raised her white glowing hand. It was as if something else had taken over her body entirely.

A possessive demon, void of emotion.

And while her eyes were white... she could see beyond that of a merely augmented Maranthinian.

She saw the internal wiring system which ran beneath Megan's skin. The cables which lit up as her body performed usual Maranthinian bodily functions.

501

Erica could even see the lights flickering in Megan's fleshy brain. "Why so much anger, Megan?"

At Erica's voice, Megan transferred her focus with delight. "I-I did it! You're the Ultimate Synthetic."

"Yes, you did. And while I'd normally agree to sacrificing this vessel for the greater good, this time, I will not."

"You...? Why not?"

Erica looked around and focused her hearing on the sounds of numerous beating hearts – all beating at various rhythms.

Her eyes travelled to Jynx, where she could see the glow of an internal wiring systems against his flesh. She looked to the AIA soldiers, who were nothing more than rotting flesh controlled by cables and motherboards...

And then she looked to Deets, where the rhythm of the heartbeats stopped, and the cable lights had darkened.

With another subtle hand gesture, Erica's view of Deets magnified, but there was still nothing more than darkened silence. Removing her focus, Erica turned back to Megan.

"You killed our sister. Why?"

"She's not... She's not dead. She... she can't be dead."

"Tell me, Megan. You wish for me to sacrifice my physical form to sustain life, yet you only wish to end life. Why is that?"

Megan turned her attention from Deets and took in Erica's full demeanour. Instead of sorrow, her face resembled admiration.

"Wow, you can sense a beating heart from a mile away. You really are incredible. When I saw those memories... Your memories... I just couldn't believe it. You're the Ultimate Synthetic. The very reason I exist. It kinda feels like a waste to make you jump into that pit again."

"I will not jump. Maranthina seeks balance. Power. Control. Instead, I suggest we merge."

"Merge? What do you mean?"

"Simple. I will consume your life essence leaving your physical body to return to the dust from which you were built."

"But that'll kill me. Why don't you take Deets?"

"She's already dead. I could bring her back, but it would be a waste of my energy." Erica raised her right palm towards Megan and focused, as Megan readied her defensive stance.

But as Megan conjured a red bolt of light into her palm, her entire red energy that coursed throughout her veins illuminated her very body, from the inside out.

"What are you doing to me?"

Erica drew the red energy into the palm of her hand. But Megan wouldn't go down without a fight. She shot a bolt of red lightning at Erica from her other hand, only for Erica to raise her left palm, and catch that strike too.

Megan's legs buckled under her weight. "You're... You're taking my abilities? How can you do this to me?"

"Looks like you pissed off the wrong Synthetic, Megan," came Jynx's voice. His body had recharged.

In Erica's mind, she pulled up a peripheral camera, where she could see him, assisting somebody who had just entered the floor.

…Dr Arack.

"Jynx, help me," Megan groaned.

"Sorry. You should know better than to trust a Reader. Why do you think she's not jumping this time?"

Hurt surprise, was written all over Megan's face. It had been Jynx who had told Maranthina to rebel against MIOT.

"You traitor. How could you turn against me? We had a deal."

"Arack and I go way back. I promised him a long time ago that I'd help get his daughter back. Whether he can remember it or not."

"His daughter is lost," Erica said, still siphoning Megan's electrical force.

"I refuse to believe that. Araca is still in there," Dr Arack said, approaching to oppose the Ultimate Synthetic. "I know she is. Araca, if you can hear me, I just want to tell you I'm sorry for failing you. I'm sorry for…"

With a subtle shift in movement, Erica moved her left palm to face the doctor, and instantly illuminated the white energy of his body.

"ARACK!" Jynx cried, knocking the man out of her path. The Reader's reaction caused himself to be struck by Erica's siphoning ability instead.

"ERICA, YOU NEED TO STOP!" The voice was unmistakably Cody.

Was his voice coming through the speakers?

She couldn't be sure.

While she did halt her siphoning, Erica neither lowered nor raised her hands. Even with both Megan and Jynx crippled on the floor.

Erica glanced around as Dr Arack assisted Jynx to his feet and Megan did her best to avoid their eye.

Nobody else seemed to be hearing Cody, except Erica. Was it a mindlink?

"Cody? Are you... Are you in my head?" They were the first words that belonged to Erica, and not from the AI of Maranthina.

"That's not important right now. What is important is that I can see what you're doing, and I know it isn't you. It's Maranthina. But you can beat it, Erica. I know you can."

"No. I can't, Cody. You said it yourself, I'm powerless. I'm not the author. I'm just a vessel... A vessel for Maranthina."

"Perception is power, Erica. You told me that. You just don't know it, yet. You need to focus on Deets. Please!"

Deets?

Erica focused her attention on Deets, listening for her heartbeat, but still heard nothing.

"Oh no! Deets!"

She wanted to run to Deets's side and find a way to help, but she couldn't. It was as if she was frozen in place. "Cody, I can't... I can't do anything about it. Maranthina needs me to act. Needs me to fulfill..."

"...No! Because Maranthina is just an AI and AIs don't have emotions. But you do. There was a reason the core sent you to your world. You needed to learn to be human for a little while. You needed to be powerless to learn just how powerful you really are. Maranthina is what's killing us. Not Megan. And you're the only one who can control it."

"How can you say that? It sounds like something Seth would say."

Cody's voice hesitated. "I believe in it because I believe in you. Sure, Maranthina has made you stronger. But it's not because you're the Ultimate Synthetic. It's because it killed you, and you came back stronger. But now you need to harness those abilities to save us. To save Seth... And to bring back Deets. Because this... This is only the beginning."

As she stared down at her palms, Erica considered his words. He was right. She needed to take back control. Maranthina had always been a part of her.

It even haunted her dreams when she was living in an entirely different world. That was why she could tell her stories so vividly.

She was more than just an author.

Erica *was* Maranthina.

And it was time to take back control. Against the emotionless energy's will, Erica raced over to Deets.

"Deets, you can't be dead. You're my sister. We promised we'd protect each other. I should've..." Erica sniffled back tears. Tears at having not realised their relation a long time ago. She felt an arm around her shoulder and remembered the tight embrace easily. "Papa..." she sobbed. "I'm so sorry. I should've realised who I was. I should've..."

"...No, I'm sorry. I should've stopped MIOT from taking you... I should've..."

Again, the words of Cody rung through her mind. He said Erica could bring Deets back.

Was that even possible?

That being said, she had created Megan from dust. Well, she hadn't. But Maranthina had. And while she needed to be cautious of overusing Maranthina's abilities, just maybe she could use them to help her friends. "...I think I can bring her back," Erica said.

"No," Dr Arack replied. "It's too risky. You could..."

"...Papa, I need to. When Maranthina was siphoning Megan, she was using my body to do it. That just shouldn't be possible."

"Ara... *Erica*, the very notion of using those abilities to bring somebody back from the dead could exhaust you to the point of..."

"...I won't just let Deets die. It's not who I am."

The doctor stared at her in contemplation, before sighing in defeat. "No, I know it's not. Okay. Help her. Help your *sister*."

With those final words, Erica closed her eyes and brought her hand to Deets's forehead. Instantly, she was mentally transported to a medical room where she was laying on her back, in a bed with a blue sheet draped over her.

Judging by the petiteness of her body, she couldn't have been any older than seven years of age.

Erica turned her head to the left to see a shelf filled with medical supplies. To her right was another bed, with another young girl sleeping.

"Deets!" Erica called out. "Deets, wake up!"

And Deets did wake up.

There was a violent gasp for air, as her head flung up and her eyes opened. "W-What happened? Is that you Erica? Why are we in the body of kids? I remember Megan. And Jynx... Erica, something happened to Cody. We need to help him."

Erica tried to analyse just what was happening in that moment. For Deets to be able to recall the moments before her death meant that Erica had succeeded in mentally travelling to the void of life and death. While Erica wanted more than anything to climb off the bed, she felt that strange sensation of being locked in place. Bound by invisible straps.

"It's okay, Deets. Cody's fine. So is Jynx and… our father."

"Our… *father?*"

"Dr Arack. They're all okay. But right now, I need you to do something. I need you to reach for my hand."

Erica stretched out her hand, while the girl just studied it. "Please, just reach for it."

Cautiously, Deets took hold. The minute she made contact, white electricity sparked from Erica and into Deets…

Right before everything went black.

"Erica?"

###

MARANTHINA – CODY

The moment Cody entered the large floor that was BG12, he knew that something was wrong. He raced to the centre of the room right beside the pit, were Deets took in the sight of him, Jynx and Dr Arack.

It was great that she was alive. But beside her, lay Erica's unconscious body.

"Erica?" Cody gasped.

"Her vitals are low," Dr Arack said, scanning her with his wrist screen. "But it's like she's in a deep sleep."

"But she... she saved me," Deets added, clearly still stunned about what had happened.

"She brought you back from the dead," Cody clarified.

"I, err... I'd hate to really add onto the problem we have going on," Jynx said. "But Megan just jumped into the pit."

"She *what*?" Cody exclaimed. He, Jynx and Deets raced to peer over the edge, where they were just in time to see Megan's body disappear into the glowing white energy. Within seconds, the entire facility began to quake. "Oh, shit!" Jynx exclaimed. "That shouldn't be happening. Megan isn't Erica."

"Or maybe it's because of Erica?" Cody wondered.

"Either way, now's not the time to debate," Dr Arack said. "Cody, Jynx, retrieve Erica's body. We need to get out of here. Now!"

"We can use the transport hub," Cody decided, as he and Jynx lifted Erica into their arms. "There's one on every second level… so by my recollection the floor above us." He didn't go into detail of how he knew, for he was still trying to figure that part out.

With Deets in tow, they raced towards the elevator, just as it opened before them – as Cody had mentally predicted it would.

Again, he couldn't determine how he knew.

"Get in," he said.

They did, and once Dr Arack pushed the button to close the doors, the elevator soared upwards, with the entire facility shaking all around them.

"What in the pit happened down there?" Cody asked.

"Twitch what happened," Deets shot back. "I'm a little more interested in what's going to happen next!"

Dr Arack gave a subtle shrug. "Theoretically speaking, there are three possible outcomes that spring to mind. The first being another time loop. The second... the core could shut down, entirely."

"Shut down?" Cody asked.

"Yes, which means we could die slowly or very quickly."

With a look that meant absolute fear, Jynx scratched his chin with his free hand. "What was the third outcome?"

This time, Dr Arack shook his head softly. "The third... with multidimensional travel being possible... both our world... and Erica's world could collide in a cataclysmic explosion... It's hard to say how many other worlds could be destroyed in the process."

"Are you saying that by Megan taking Erica's place, we might've just brought about the end of the world?" Jynx asked.

"Quite possibly."

"By the pit," Deets exclaimed. "Quite literally."

"*The beginning of the end,*" Cody mumbled, remembering those words spoken earlier before forcing a brave smile. "Megan sure did have a habit of making an entrance… And going out with a bang."

28

DR ARACK'S CLINIC – CODY

While the MIOT Transport Hub had been in chaos, thanks to employees evacuating the facility amid the Maranthina-shattering quakes, Cody and the others were fortunate enough to find a portal that brought them back to Arack's Medical Clinic.

They exited the portal directly into an empty surgical office where the doctor worked tirelessly on Erica, while the ground continued to rumble all around them.

"She's going into cardiac arrest!" he cried as Erica's body, again began to convulse. "Get Miri in here, NOW!"

Jynx flew out of the medical office, while Cody could only sit and watch, dumbfounded.

He wanted to help but didn't know how. And all he could think of was that it was his fault for convincing Erica to save Deets.

To save them all.

"What can I do?" Deets asked.

And Cody hated her in that moment.

Why hadn't his own mouth asked that question?

Why could he only sit frozen in place, watching as Erica's body reacted to the overpowering energy, coursing through her veins?

Deep down he knew the reason. He had seen it in those memories. She had told him so herself. It was the exact same reason she had given her life in exchange for Maranthina.

Because no living creature could tolerate that much power without short-circuiting. The heart would beat so fast that the rest of the body would not be able to keep up. It was physically impossible and had been something Dr Arack should've known when he made it so.

But Arack had been blinded by the love for his daughter and desperate to keep her heart beating.

One operation was never enough, for she would always get sick.

And Araca had known that.

"...Some space," Dr Arack's voice broke into his thoughts, forcing him to snap back into reality.

"What?" Cody asked.

"Give Miri some space."

To Cody's surprise, Miri had entered, and she was trying to squeeze past him at Erica's bedside.

This time, Cody obeyed. He shifted aside and watched as Dr Arack debriefed Miri, and the two worked to stabilize Erica.

Finally, her body stopped flailing about, and the doctor went over her vitals, via his wrist screen. "She's stable."

Those two words were a relief, but Cody knew they were a long way off from Erica being okay.

"I'm sorry I asked you to help us," he told her.

"Don't blame yourself," Dr Arack said. "She's capable of so much more than that. She's..."

"...How can you say that! She was... *is* your daughter. No matter what you do, you're just prolonging the inevitable. She was always going to die, and this time, you..."

"...CODY, SHUT UP!" Deets interjected, pointing to Erica. "She's waking up."

And true to those words, Erica did wake up.

"What's... Where am I?"

Cody breathed a huge sigh of relief. But that satisfaction was merely to be short-lived. "It's okay. You're safe. We're back at Arack's office. Megan is gone and..."

"…I'm sorry, what did you just say?" Erica asked.

"Just as I said. Everything's going to be…"

"…That's not what she means," Dr Arack said, staring down at his wrist screen with concern. "Maranthina's energy wiped sections of her memory core. Erica appears to be suffering from…"

"…She doesn't even know we're in Maranthina," Deets said. "She thinks she's still in her world. I can read her thoughts. It's absolutely insane."

Deets's revelation hit them like a ton of bricks. Most of all, it threw Erica into an absolute state of shock. "Ahh… What? You've gotta be kidding me. There's no way in hell I got suckered into my own book series. I must be dreaming. God, how much did I drink, last night?"

"Let me get this straight," Jynx said with his back against the wall. "We managed to stop the time reset, only to bring on the end of the world, and have Cody break the mind of the only Ultimate Synthetic who can save us?"

Erica stared at him, utterly confused. "Such an amazing plot. I really hope I remember this one when I wake up."

While Cody was utterly tempted to say something… Anything to that remark, he changed his mind the moment he saw the look on Adam's heartbroken face, as he stood in the entrance.

Silence filled the room as they all understood the gut-wrenching notion. Seth was dead.

###

ADELAIDE, SA – MEGAN

With a smirk in her left cheek, Megan stared up at the words on Erica's laptop screen. *'The warmth of the Maranthinian sun cut through a crack in the boarded-up window. A true Maranthina Summer. Cody would've loved to stay in the shelter of their temporary base, but he couldn't fight the gut-feeling that something wasn't...'* Megan deleted the paragraph and immediately got to typing.

'It had been a year since the explosion at MIOT which had resulted in Megan's death. Cody was determined to survive the robotic spiders that continued to track he, Seth, and Adam down at every turn. Little did he know, that it was only the beginning of the end.'

An incessant beeping from beside the computer drew Megan's attention to Erica's phone on the desk.

NICK CALLING.

She answered it, and before she could even get a word in, Nick instantly got to talking. "Oh, Erica. Finally, you answer! Are you back from your book world yet? I've been to your place five times this week.

Have you even been following the news? We need you. Turn on the news right now. The world's in chaos. It turns out those spiders work for some company called MIOT… and to make matters worse, they have Chloe. Did you hear me? They have her!"

With a one shoulder shrug, Megan gave her unphased response. "Thanks for the update. I'll be sure to keep that in mind."

"Wait, you're not Erica. Who…?" Megan didn't wait for him to end his sentence.

She simply ended the call.

End.

Driven on her quest for female-empowerment, Reign is an Australian author and screenwriter with a passion for telling action, fantasy, comedy, and Sci-Fi stories to a worldwide audience.

In her spare time, Reign loves spending time with her family, playing video games and bingeing television. Her guilty pleasure shows are telenovelas.

For more information or to find other titles by
Reign Atkins, scan the QR below.

www.ingramcontent.com/pod-product-compliance
Lightning Source LLC
Chambersburg PA
CBHW020239120726
47904CB00001B/26